The House Ate Souls

The House Ate Souls

Cithara Susan Patra

First Edition

Library of Congress Control Number: 2025948859

Casebound ISBN: 978-1-62720-650-1
Paperback ISBN: 978-1-62720-651-8
Ebook ISBN: 978-1-62720-652-5

Design by Amiyah Cobb
Promotional Development by Emily Gott
Editorial Development by Abby Hill

Published by Apprentice House Press

Loyola University Maryland
4501 N. Charles Street, Baltimore, MD 21210
410.617.5265
www.ApprenticeHouse.com
info@ApprenticeHouse.com

For AZ Louise who put up with my ups and downs in writing this book as well as many others. Thank you so much for you patience and support.

Chapter 1

Radha swirled the red wine around in her glass, one eye focused on it and the other focused on the fresh crack on the ground. Her toe brushed over it, hiding it from view as the guests around her burst into laughter. Not that this was surprising: she kept missing all the jokes thanks to the house. Twice, they nudged her and both times, she nearly spilled the drink on herself.

"I'm sorry, I'm sorry! I missed that one!" She apologized to their guests, eight men who they invited for dinner. "Please excuse me. I'm...I need a little breather."

If these men cared about her words, they showed no sign of it. All of them hung around the back of the wall, enjoying themselves and soaking in the night. She narrowed her eyes at the wall, waiting for one of them to lean into it. She sent them those telepathic messages for them to lean for support. *Come on, I know you are tired. Just lean in once. Just for a little bit.*

These eight men arrived at their house only two hours ago, excited to share a dinner with all of them. They didn't question who Radha was, or why they were invited. Men like this lot didn't care to ask questions. Peering over her glass, she marked each one as she remembered their details. Two men got away with sexually assaulting someone, one of them committed manslaughter and survived the trial, one killed someone during a robbery, and the four others were nothing more than creeps who preyed on the young and elderly. They escaped the law once. Not tonight. Radha and her family would make sure of it.

Any second now…the house will feed at any second. As the guests continued to talk, her gaze fell on the statues in the corners, their empty eyes locked on the people in this room. Amid all the artwork and woodwork, her cousin Veena put up several of these statues to add a little softness. Normally, they appeared all cherubic and sweet, but they scowled around the room. Like Radha, they craved some action. She held her breath as one man, the thief, brushed past an angel statue and missed brushing his arm against the wall. So close.

Dammit. Nothing's happening. Her pulse raced as the walls formed new cracks. If the rest of the guests saw them, they never commented on them. All eight of them remained happy, healthy, and very much alive. Annoyed with how slow things were going, she grabbed another vegetable spring roll from the table. As she poured herself some of the sweet sauce, a bony finger jabbed her in the shoulder, and she dropped one. "Don't take any more of those."

"I don't intend to, Ma." She pulled away with her plate. Her mother, Swati, eyed the four rolls on her plate. "These four are all I will take."

"Four rolls are four too many." Swati wagged a finger. "I made this for everyone to enjoy. This shouldn't be your second meal of the night."

Radha's forehead throbbed over those words. No one else went for the food. Her mother didn't like these simply because they were storebought, not homemade. They were frozen rolls warmed up in a small oven. Once her mother got into how bad frozen foods were, she'd launch into a lecture on all the sodium they contained. Anxious over things moving slowly, Radha dipped a roll in sauce. "They're spring rolls, Ma. They're too small to make a meal out of."

All the same, keep away from them. And go easy on that duck sauce there. Do you know how sweet that is?"

"Of course not, Ma. I only took this because I thought it had no flavor in it." Radha rolled the entire roll in the duck sauce. "Let's not talk about this, okay? We've got more important things to worry about than what I'm eating."

"Is that so?" A baritone voice cut in an arm wrapped around her shoulder to pull her in. There he was. Terry. This man didn't belong here. He ended up with them thanks to his friend driving him over. He was their extra guest. She shivered as she clutched the plate, duck sauce dripping down her fingers. "Why are you so worried, Swati? Your food was great, don't get me wrong. It's the reason I can't take another bite!"

"See, Ma? That's a good sign."Radha wiped her fingers clean before she leaned into that giant arm. Terry, a former classmate, ended up at this party even though she never invited him. Years later, he still smelled like fresh-cut grass and clean linen. "I must admit my mother does cook everything wonderfully. Still, these spring rolls called me out. Are you sure you don't want anything else?"

"Oh, no! I'm good for the night!" Terry held up his glass. "If I get any more of these, I might have to stay for the night."

Please don't. Radha's gaze fell on the flower vase in the corner. Once filled with bright pink and red roses, turned brown and wilted. That was the house's way of sending a message. Let him go. He's not wanted here. To distract herself, she counted the guests around them. Seven including Terry. In the craziness, she missed some action and bit down on her tongue. "Ow!"

"Are you all right?!" Terry went to her sidealmost missing the floor opening below him. She thanked everything above that he didn't get swallowed, but now he tried to check her out."Do you need anything?"

"I'm fine, I'm fine." She swallowed the food down. "I accidentally bit my tongue. Stupid move." She chugged down some more wine to cool that pain in her mouth, then pretended to stretch. "My, it's getting late. I should probably turn in."
"Already? We barely got a moment together." He lowered his voice. "Are you not having a good time?"

"I'm sorry. I'm just a little tired." Radha shook her head, wishing she could tell him the reason. Terry had always been a good guy when they were younger. He kept secrets, didn't hurt anyone, and stayed true to himself. Even now, she saw the glimmers of that young man she liked years ago. She couldn't reveal that this party was the last night for the remaining guests. He most likely didn't research them the way she and her family did. He didn't know the dark secrets they harbored. As she relaxed, she smirked at the sight of a guest getting swallowed by the hole in the floor. He never got a second to scream.

"Well, let me get you some coffee." Terry got up, avoiding yet another hole in the ground. "Sit tight, Radha. I'll be back."

"I'm sitting." She turned to the wall, narrowing her gaze at it. In a few minutes, the plan would go right into motion. There were all the statues, ready with their hands clasped in prayer. Only one of them held their arms out, reaching into the air and grasping it. If anyone walked by that statue, they'd get snagged on the fingers. Maybe even caught in that grasp. She noticed two people getting close to it while she held her breath. In the last second, they turned away and avoided the statue's grasp.

"Damn." She cursed into her wine bottle. "So close."

The statue held out its arms, though she sensed the disappointment. As the guests moved away from it, they stood next to the plants, and she held her breath. Any second now. If one of them could inch one foot closer or lean into the wall, everything would end. Still holding her breath, the couple moved off the wall. She huffed as the statues stared at her. They wanted to grab the guests, pull them in, draw them into a world unlike any other. She didn't know where they'd go, but they'd get there one way or another. All the guests went there.

In the corner, her cousin Veena tapped her glass and called out to them. "Excuse me, everyone! Can I have your attention?" Everyone stopped talking as soon as that fork hit the glass. Radha checked on the two guests standing in front of the wall. There they were, chatting and leaning into it. She turned for a second as her cousin crossed the front of the room, facing everyone sitting and standing around. "Thank you. I just wanted you all to know that in a few minutes, I'll be starting our tour of the house. I know it's a big place. You probably want to know where we got all this stuff. How did this house come to be? It's been in our family for years. It's got its share of secrets. And tonight, you're going to learn all of them. So, go ahead and finish your last drink. We'll start soon."

Last drink. She clearly meant it as a pun, though no one laughed. Once Veena finished, Radha checked the two guests who'd been standing in the back. She didn't find them. Gazing around the rest of the room, she didn't see them in the other corners. They didn't go to other rooms. They didn't leave the house. They were gone. From eight people, they were down to five. The house shivered at that moment, satisfied with its newest meal.

That's three down, four to go. Terry's off limits. With the walls vibrating, she bounced on the sofa cushion in celebration of getting rid of three guests. The other four would follow. The house took its time with everything. It didn't care about the crime these people committed. All that mattered was that they got away with it. Either they paid off a jury, a weak judge let them go, or someone else pulled strings for them. In the end, the house passed the final judgment on everyone. They all got the same fate: ceasing to exist.

A rose petal wilted off and another crack formed on the ground, she sat still. It started. The house tried to eat the others while Veena prepared for the tour. Yet, anytime it tried to devour someone, its food escaped its clutches. None of the guests got wise about the happenings in the house.. She patted the wall for a little comfort. No worries. I'll feed you soon enough. It's not time to eat, but it will be here soon. You won't starve tonight.

"Jesus, you're that bored?! Get off your butt and help them out!" Radha groaned as her mother pushed her off the couch, pointing in the other direction. "They're waiting for you, your highness."

"I'm going, Ma. I'm going." Radha rubbed her forehead. Go figure they'd call for her when things were about to start. "Why do they need me anyway? Veena does the tour, not me."

"Who am I, the person with all the answers to the universe's questions? Ask them!"

Radha shot a glare at her mother as she followed her cousins into the kitchen. As she walked, she brushed Terry's arm as he tried to speak to her. She held up her hand to keep him from getting a word out. He handed her the cup of coffee, swimming in cream and sugar. Taking a quick sip, it jolted through her body. She wasn't getting sleep after this. "Thank you. I have to take care of something for the tour."

"Right! Go ahead and do that. I'll wait for you." He glanced around the room. "That's strange. This place seemed to have more people in it."

"It did?" Radha sipped her coffee, pretending it wasn't shaking her up inside. "I haven't been paying attention. They might have left early. Anyway, let me see what my cousin wants." With that excuse, she went over to where Veena and her other cousin, Lata, waited for her. They pulled her in, motioning her to stay quiet until the door closed behind her. Once away from the group, Radha held onto the cup as they walked.

"Ma said you needed my help. What's going on?"

"We have a little problem with the guest list. Even though I went through it so many times, I must have overlooked this guy." Lata weaved through the long hallway, spotting the gargoyle statues in the corner. "Oh dear, they look so ugly."

"They're gargoyles, darling. They're not supposed to look like beauty queens. Let them do what they need to do: be scary, be ugly, and take care of our company. In fact…" Veena checked the next couple of rooms before signaling the others to follow. In the distance, she caught sight of one guest leaning into the wall before falling in, barely able to get a scream out. She didn't blink as the guest vanished into the house, filling the room with more light. "Come on. We still have about an hour before the feeding. The house got its appetizers, now it wants the main course."

"Well, who's the wrong one?" Radha asked, though she was aware of the answer. Terry wasn't involved in anything shady; he wasn't on their lists. "More importantly, how do we get rid of them?"

"That's where you come in." Veena led them inside of

the kitchen, covered in dead rose petals. She handed the dustpan and broom to Lata as she closed the door. "Let's clean this up. The poor thing is demanding its meal. Well, it's coming. It's taking its sweet time, but it's coming." She went to the windowsill to close the blinds. Lighting flashed through, illuminating the ornate decorations in the backyard. More gargoyles and angels lined up the garden they put up in the summer, protecting flowers and the few crops they grew. "Oh goodness, a storm! They'll all want to stay longer."

"What's the big deal? We need them to stay." Lata pointed out. "In case you don't remember, these are evil people. They'll be enough food to last a lifetime."

"Everyone but Terry." Radha confirmed her fears as Lata stiffened up. "He's it, isn't he? He's not wanted by the house. I didn't see anything suspicious about him in any article or list that I read. I even went to some TikToks for information. Nothing."

"You got that right. That's why the house hasn't devoured him." Veena touched the walls. "Oh yes, I know. You want the rest of them, don't you? Sit tight. I'm starting the tour after I finish here."

"And I have to get Terry out even if it is raining right now." The thunder boomed, shaking the pictures on the walls. Her phone buzzed on the counter, reminding her of a flash flood warning. That grating warning rang throughout the room. No one could leave unless they absolutely had to. Driving in the rain was a risk most people didn't need to take. "Great. What am I going to do?"

"You must get him out. We already got rid of three people. He's going to get suspicious of us." Veena dumped the rose petals in the trash. "Look at this place. My garden is wilting! My house is coming undone! The house I lived in with my husband for several years, the house of our family, lasting for generations…it's dying, and I can't find enough worthless souls to feed it! Can you imagine that?"

Radha could imagine though she couldn't get as overdramatic about it. The average person could tell the house was dying without knowing the truth. Their home nestled right into the darkness, far from the rest of the world. Her great-grandparents, the very first owners, never wanted to move into a house filled with people. For years, different relatives came and went, doing their part to keep the home alive. They never bothered changing anything until Veena opted to move in. When she got married, she decided to add some life to the black, gray, and white walls. In parts of the home, there were splashes of color and plants that brought about life. These were the rooms people loved staying in. Three seconds around all that color cheered them up. Veena referred to it as the life room. Everything came alive in there.

Life and death, both thrived behind these walls. The house rarely made mistakes with its choice. She normally stuck to the information she found on legitimate websites. Terry though? He threw all their plans off. "You want me to remove Terry from this place."

"Remove him as quickly as you can. Force him out of here if you can.." Veena rubbed the cracked wall on the side. These cracks formed on the door frame, ready to fall apart. "Push him out, break up with him, throw him out the window. Just make sure he's not here when I start the tour. Speaking of which…" She straightened out her clothes, taking a deep breath. "It's time. Help me out here, Lata. Radha, you know what to do."

Radha gulped, peering at the deep cracks in the door frame. She hated being the one to take care of Terry. He liked her. He wanted to see more of her. Yet when he mentioned seeing fewer people, she couldn't let him stay. He noticed that guests weren't around. What would happen after the tour when very few people were left?

As she entered the room, Veena launched into the big history of the house, the story of their great-grandparents and all they endured to get to America. Every single person listened intensely as Radha took her place by a statue. Veena walked around, guiding them from room to room. With each stop, a guest disappeared. Gone. They were gone for good, and no one knew where they went. If Terry noticed something, he didn't react. He locked eyes with her, silently asking her to sit next to him. Patting the spot by side, she almost went towards him, but Veena blocked her view. Good. Her cousin kept her from getting too close too soon.

With other guests going away, she struggled with getting rid of Terry. No man ever spent more than an hour with her. She still couldn't get over to him as Veena interrupted her thoughts. "Well, that concludes the tour! Now there's one more room to show you. I hope you all stay very quiet because this is a special place. It's the room where my grandparents...well, you can guess what they did there." A few chuckles arose from the crowd. "It's always the last thing people see."

Everyone followed Veena out while Radha stood right behind Terry, blocking him from any statues, walls, or gaps in the floor. He admired the faded cracks around them, unaware they were all that remained of last time's guests. Radha rubbed her arms to stay warm. Death was coming, which meant a cool down period in the house. It would end.

Be patient. She stroked the wall behind her. You know the drill. She's gonna take those that stay into the last room soon.

She didn't need to know the story behind the final room. That's where the darkest part lay. Her family always claimed the house held both good and evil within it, hence all the demon and angel statues. Nothing else suited this place. When things went well, everything brightened up. No cracks forming on walls, no rose petals wilting, no angry angel eyes locking in on their guests. With its hunger almost satisfied, the house would warm up again. It would only take a little time.

Stamping her feet into the ground, Terry finally caught notice of her. He sauntered over, swishing his glass around. "Is it just me or did there seem to be more people here?"

"More people?" She smiled tight enough to stretch from ear to ear. The caffeine still rushed through her body as she led him away. "I, um…I didn't notice. So much is going on over here."

"Really? I thought I heard someone scream." He listened closely before shaking his head. "It could have just been in my head, though. It is getting late, so maybe I'm seeing and hearing things cause I'm tired. Anyway, where did you go?"

"Oh, just the kitchen. It turns out my mother did leave the stove on." She nodded at Swati who waved at her to move on. Death was on the way. "You know what? I don't feel like going to that last room. I've done it so many times. Would you…"

"I thought you'd never ask." Terry chuckled as she took him towards her bedroom. Along the way, her feet trampled over a few dead rose petals. Terrific. The house grew impatient and wilted the plants within it. "You gotta do something about those flowers though. They're falling apart."

Tell me something I don't know. With her foot, she brushed away the dead petals leading to her bedroom door. This house, the room…she still couldn't understand how she got roped into feeding it. Her family claimed it was something they all had to do. They owed everything to the house. The very least it deserved was some food. There was no better food than some creep on America's Most Wanted List. The house loved those the most. Police couldn't catch them, but they always found their way to one of the parties. These creeps kept the house alive.

And it's still standing. Her hand fell on the wall as it shivered. Her home. In a way, it was a child who always needed attention. Treat it like a child. Care for it. If anyone knew about this, they'd never believe it. Not until they saw the house swallow someone alive. As she pushed the door open, Terry bounded inside and took a place on her bed.

"It's about time!" He took his place, putting his glass on her nightstand. Outside, the wind picked up, drowning the sounds in the house. The thunder boomed as the lights flickered. That had to be the power going out for a second. For a magical house, it still suffered with the usual things such as leakages and power outages. Not even eating humans could fix that. Terry stretched out on her bed, crossing his feet on top. "I don't know about you, but I'm all partied out."

"I feel the same way." Terry showed no sign of leaving as he got comfortable over her floral-printed covers. She tried to push him off as he got situated. "Um…if you don't mind, please keep your feet off my bed. I sleep in there."

"Oh, right. Sorry about that." He patted the spot next to him. "Come on. We're finally alone to talk and…well, do anything you want to do. You don't have to pretend to be a good hostess anymore. Relax a little bit."

"I don't think I can." Her eyes focused on the paintings in her room. None of them were real artwork by masters like Monet, Da Vinci, and Picasso. Only replicas made perfect for a home. She cleaned them up every week, letting them shine in their frames. Not once did the house's cracks move to the pictures. "I think…I'm sorry. This is too hard to say. It's been so hard to explain anything to you. We've known each other for a long time, and you've always been so nice to me. I wish I could be the same to you."

"Oh, don't sweat over it. Don't apologize. I'll listen to anything you have to say." Terry nudged her side. "I don't know about you, but I want to see what makes this house so special. It's so dull when you first step inside."

"Dull?" Radha blinked. "You don't like the artwork?"

"Oh no, that's not what I mean! The art is beautiful. The ones in this room…remarkable." He stepped back to admire a small statue of the goddess Venus rising out of the sea. It contrasted against the statue right next to it, one of the Hydra being slain. "I'm curious about the decision for all the art based on Greek mythology. Aren't you Hindu?"

"I am. That doesn't mean Hindu people can't like Greek myths." Chewing on her bottom lip, she tapped her toes on the creaking floors. It started. The house waited for something. Her friends hadn't fed it yet. If they didn't move quicker, it would cave in. "Listen, I like you a lot but, I think you need to go."

"So soon? We just got together!" He laughed as he took her arm. Behind her, she caught another crack slowly forming in the wall. The house was crying for her, but she couldn't give Terry away to it. He hadn't done anything wrong. "Come on. I get that you're nervous. I'll go slow if you want. I don't want you to be uncomfortable."

She leaned into the wall, the crack growing behind her. The house threw out its warning. The way it shook gave away the message. Not him. I'm not hungry for him. Let him go. He's not the one for me. Let him go. He deserves to live another day.

Radha pushed away. "I'm sorry. This is just…"

"No, I'm sorry. I guess I'm still moving too fast for you." Terry moved back for a second. Radha pushed the cracks out of her mind. The house wanted something that could hold it together for a long time, not a few minutes. Terry wasn't it. "Do you want to go somewhere else?"

"On another day!" She jumped to her feet. "I would like to see you on a completely different day. I'm pretty much free next week. We can meet anytime then. Is that fine?"

"Why wait till next week? What's wrong with now? I can take you out of here, and we can go…"

"No!" She cut him off. He leaned back as she watched the wall crack behind him. "I mean…look, this is complicated. I haven't been with a man since my husband left me. I don't know how to have fun anymore. I know you said we'd take it slow, but…I'm not sure what that is. I've never taken it slow before."

"Then we'll just…"

BOOM!

Lightning crashed across the sky, lighting up everything outside. Then followed the booming thunder along with the lights flickering in the house. Radha pressed her hands against the walls, her fingers grazing a brand-new crack in them. Not now. She turned her head slowly to face one of the angel statues in the corner. There it was, a plump cherub with its hands clasped together. Carved in marble, it faced downward despite its eyes locked on her. Though the statue had no pupils, it gazed away at nothing.

God, I hate those things sometimes. Radha moved away from the wall and motioned Terry to follow her into the hallway. She couldn't keep him in the bedroom. He wasn't getting it. He didn't get that the people who came with him were never coming back out. The thunder rumbled outside while the lights dimmed. "I'm sorry about the weather. I didn't think it would get so bad."

"Ah, don't worry about it. I can hang around here a little longer." Terry admired all the statues around them, all cherubs staring at them. "I must say that your friend has impeccable taste in art. She's also the only person I've seen who keeps both statues of angels and gargoyles around."

Radha stifled laughter as they turned the corner and faced rows of gargoyles ahead of them. Unlike the cherubs, these demons stared at them straight on. Their eyes blazed in fury with their claws clinging to their stands. At any second, these creatures could take flight and terrorize anyone in their way. They'd been carved in black stone, all bumpy and rough. No one dared to touch them. Some guests asked to touch the cherubs but never the demons. They all sensed the evil within that carved stone.

Right now, those demons sent those subliminal messages to her to stop this guy. Send him home. Keep him from the house. He wasn't worthy of being a meal, which saved his life. Her heart broke as she didn't want him to go. He liked her. For the first time in ages, someone found her attractive enough to keep talking. He inched closer, his breath fanning the nape of her neck. His hands pressed against the small of her back, bringing her towards him. His cologne swallowed her, a mix of pine needles and ocean water.

Radha pushed him away, facing the wall. "I can't do it."

"What do you mean? We were having a great time!" Terry exclaimed. "I haven't gotten this close to anyone since my wife passed away. I haven't enjoyed anything in life. Not until you came. Why the sudden change? Did I do something wrong?"

Radha's eyes focused on the cracks along the wall. Not here. Not right now. They couldn't remind her about the house falling apart. Next to her nightstand, a few rose petals fell out of the flower vase. The house warned her not to get too close. It needed her. It needed to thrive, or else those would widen. Bit by bit, it would crumble till nothing remained. The walls vibrated before her, calling out. Feed me. Nourish me. I'm famished. The tour's still going on.

"Are we moving too fast?" Terry took her hand. "If you want, I can slow down. I understand that this is a rough time for both of us. We don't have to rush into anything right now. I'm fine with taking it easy."

"It's not that." Radha's head pounded. The house called for her again. Feed me. "You are…You're a wonderful person, Terry. You are truly great, and that's why…I wish you'd leave right now. It's for your own good."

"Leave? My own good?" Terry blinked. Above him, the ceiling cracked and sent dust flying down. It settled on the bed as he pulled himself up. "What's going on here? You're acting strange. Between that and people suddenly disappearing, I'm not sure what to think."

"It isn't anything you did! Or maybe it is…" Radha turned around, brushing the dust off the sheets. He knew. The people who came into this house weren't leaving with him. "I'm sorry. I don't want to do this to you! That's why I want you to go now! Go before the moon comes out."

"The moon?" Terry stared out the window as dark clouds rolled across the sky. The tree branches grazed against the glass while checking out the scene around him. Bright red and white flowers lined the sides, with thick, green grass sticking out. He couldn't get it. The moment the moon came out, it all ended. "I don't know what you're talking about. I don't know what's going on. I thought you liked me."

"I do! That's why I'm saying these things and…"

BANG! BANG!

The thumping at her door nearly knocked her over. Lata

burst into the room, ignoring Terry's confused self on the side. She pulled Radha up to her feet and set her down on the sheets. "Oh, Radha! Thank goodness I caught you!"

"I'm fine! Terry was…he was just leaving." Radha nodded at a hurt Terry. She hated this part. She wanted him to get out of the house before the moon came out. There was still time. "You can call me later, okay?"

Feed me. I'm famished. These guys weren't enough.

Terry slowly pulled himself off the bed. "Are you sure about that, Radha? We can go somewhere else if you'd like. If this is the wrong place…"

"It is!" Lata cut in before Radha opened her mouth. Around them, the walls cracked again. "You can see this house needs a lot of repairs. You might be better off seeing us another time."

"She's right!" Radha threw in. "We can meet up somewhere. This isn't the right time and place." Her mind sent him messages to get out. Leave this house! Leave this house! The moon isn't out yet, so go while you can!

"…All right then…" He started to follow Lata out the door. "I'll call you later, okay?"

"That would be nice." Radha clutched her chest. Those heartbeats were slowing down. The final guests disappeared. The house showed no more cracks as she waved at him. The three of them walked down the long, dark hallway lit with small candles hanging on the walls. With all the curves and corners, anyone could get lost here. They always led the guests towards the front door, showing them the right way. In case they came back, they could get out on their own.

Radha swallowed as the angel statues around them stared at her. They were angry. She let a guest go tonight, but she knew it wasn't time. Terry wasn't the one. He was lucky that they had another chance to see each other. She caught up with him and Lata as they reached the front door. Lata handed him his coat while he turned to Radha, hands out. She took them and interlaced her fingers through his. It hurt to let him go. Her first date in a long time, and they were calling it an end to the night. He's going to see me again...if that's what he wants. She stood in the doorway with Lata looking over her shoulder. Terry stepped on the gravel towards his car. Around him, rose petals scattered as a gust blew through. She gripped the sides of the door frame, unable to speak. Her mouth opened and closed like a fish, though no sounds came out. A part of her wanted to pull him back. She wanted to get through the night together. The other louder part reminded her to stand back. Not yet. Their time was coming.

"I'm sorry things didn't work out tonight." He waved at her. "I hope you feel better."

She lowered her gaze and scraped her toe against the dusty stone ground. Tiny cracks appeared as sweat dripped down her forehead. It wasn't hot out, but the moon started to peak out of the clouds. He wasn't close to the house anymore. "I'm…I'm…oh, I don't know what to say."

"I do." Lata cut in, motioning Radha to go back inside. "I'm sorry, Terry…"

"Oh, it's okay. I understand she's a little shy and isn't ready for a romance. We can always try it…oh!" A tree branch snapped off and fell inches away from him. It lay there with its smaller branches all stretched out with tiny buds and leaves sticking up. "That was a close one!"

"Very close." Lata slowly started to close the door on him. "I'm sorry, Terry. I'm sorry, but we can't let you stay. You probably heard Radha say this, but it's true. This is for your own good."

She slammed the door as several rose petals shook off

their stems and blew away. Off in the corner, screams filled the air as Radha dragged herself back to her room. Veena got them in the room, the final resting place. The cracks around her healed up, closing in and filling their gaps. She pressed against the wall, now smooth and clean. Next to her, the flower of roses bloomed again, bright red petals decorating the vase they sat in. Her heart ached over the screams leading to silence. Every night they had guests, they got the screams in the end.

The pain grew unbearable. She ran towards the window and pulled up the blinds to find Terry's car gone. He left as asked, yet her soul crumbled at the dark sky. No matter what he said, he wasn't coming back for another date.

Lata squeezed her shoulder. "You did the right thing. We don't want him to suffer."

"I know." Terry survived this, but her heart shattered. She couldn't keep him. She couldn't let him stay the night. Once again, she let another man go to protect him and keep the house standing. The screams died around her along with any hope of falling in love. If the house approved of them, they'd get swallowed. If it didn't, they left for good. She was alone, no matter how the night went.

Closing the blinds, the final scream died out behind her. Another night, another healing session for their home. Everyone else would go back to their normal lives, ignoring the cars in their driveway. Those, too, vanished in the morning. The house took them along with everything belonging to their owners. She never knew where they went, just that they were gone. These people left the face of the planet once the house got its food. Everyone got what they wanted in the end.

Not her. Another night went by, and she ended it like she ended the other nights. Alone.

CHAPTER 2

One week later…

Black metal gates swung open as Radha drove the car down the long rocky path ahead. The drive up to the garage was her least favorite part; the sound of rocks crushed under the tires gave her a migraine. For years, she wanted to smooth out this driveway, but Veena refused to go through with it. The gravel was part of their home. Driving down it led people to the giant stone house waiting ahead with its sharp gray features and intricate vine-like designs around it. Tall like a castle and filled with art, no one came here until they were invited.

Another week, another interview down the tube. She gazed down at the folder and pile of papers on the passenger seat. The community center opened a part-time position for a pottery instructor. Although her specialty was painting, she studied ceramics in college and had experience to lead a class. The interview itself went well, but she didn't hold her breath. These days, it took months for them to fill a position. She still waited to hear back from three other jobs, losing faith each day. It hurt her, she was qualified, yet not good enough to work.

I really hope they move the process along. She went through her resume, checking every little detail. No one ever complained about her skills. Even when they tested her or asked for a portfolio, she was ready. They always praised her art ability and creativity, but they never called her again. She wished she could spend days creating art, but without work, she couldn't focus on her hobby alone. They all needed the money to get through the day.

"I guess I'll file this away with the other jobs I'm not getting." She grabbed the folder and stepped out of the car, locking the doors behind her. Time after time, rejection got easier to endure. She reminded herself that not hearing anything meant good news would come later. It had to come for her. There were only so many days of silence she could take. *My personal life is suffering. My professional life is non-existent. What else could go wrong?*

She didn't need an answer to that question. Nothing went right since moving back in the house with her family. Veena tried for years to get her to come back. She always wanted help with the house, but Radha wanted something more than staying with her relatives. In a perfect life, she'd be far from them, taking care of herself. She wouldn't be a burden to her siblings or their families. She didn't dare ask her ex or her children for their help. She wanted to endure the problems alone, get through her issues by herself. They all sounded like a good idea at the time. Of course, she was more confident in her skills and hopeful in the economy.

Somehow, she ended up back where she started, back where they all started. The magical and eternally hungry home. She never learned how it came to life, except for a story her mother told her years ago. Back in the day when her great-grandparents came to America, they didn't have very much to go on: very little money, no one hiring immigrants for work, and no place to stay. After wandering for a week, they came across the house with an unlocked door. Somehow, the house was letting them in. It wanted them to come in. Since then, her family claimed their family's fortune in the food industry, opening several restaurants bakeries, and cafes and the luck grew. Her great-grandfather found construction work which added to their wealth. Since then, no one in the family struggled. If the house stood standing, they were safe. Of course, it came with that tiny price of feeding the house every now and then. If it didn't get food, it ate whoever it wanted, swallowing them up in the walls. To keep their family and friends safe, her great-grandparents decided to start searching for lawbreakers for the house's dinner/appetite. The disguise of a party worked well for years. Veena found no reason to change it.

"This is how it started. Why fix something that isn't broken?" She'd always pointed out. "It's how it's gone for years. This is our home. You belong to it too."

Radha believed that bit, which was the main reason she opted to marry and move away. The house didn't hook itself into her immediately. Her eyes wandered down every hallway, checking every room, and assuring herself that things were fine. The house welcomed her anytime she went through the doors. Every statue held out its arms to let her in. Yet while she lived here now, she didn't want to be here forever. No matter what secrets the family held, she couldn't bring herself to love it the way the others did.

Her mother insisted that she stay there even after finding work. "You don't have to pay rent. You get your own space. It's beautiful and I do most of the cooking and cleaning. Not to mention, we don't have to worry about people breaking in. The house will get a little snack in the process. What's so bad about that?"

She couldn't complain about that bit. Her mother did do most of the chores, with everyone else helping here and there. She did get her privacy when she needed it. She didn't waste money on anything, saving it for groceries, gas, and paying her phone bill. She has a few credit card bills to pay. Outside of that, she didn't have many financial burdens. She couldn't complain about any of this. Many people her age struggled to make ends meet while she had all the necessities plus more.

On the other hand, she didn't like the parties as much as the others, only agreeing to them for the sake of getting rid of lawbreakers. For days, all of them spent time researching their guests. She hated picking them out when she read their rap sheets. So many crimes, so little time in jail. Going through various lists, checking out articles, even searching social media for them. She wanted to spend her time on some other hobby. Doing something with someone else. The luring of these awful people, letting the house swallow them, standing at the back and watching it all happen...she grew tired of it now and then.

"I hope you're happy." She wiped her feet on the rug before opening the door. "They were hard to find, and we almost didn't get away with it. You were a little too loud with your chewing."

If the house heard, it didn't respond. Out of everyone, she found some comfort in speaking to the house. It reacted when it wanted something to prove that it heard her words. At the same time, she didn't worry about it giving sarcastic remarks or fighting back like the rest of her family. She could tell it anything she wanted without getting judgment in return. Pressing her hand on the wall, she ran her fingers down it. Something bumped on the other side, as quick as a pulse. A spirit lived here, keeping them together for years.

"Thanks for looking after my family as always." Raindrops sprinkled on her shoulders as she went towards the coat rack. She shook the few droplets out of her dark hair as she untied the red plaid scarf around her neck. Peering down the hall, she listened for someone to do something. Walk. Talk. Anything to show her they were there. She braced herself against the cold stone walls and called out. "Hello? Is anyone home?!"

From a distance, her mother replied. "I'm in the kitchen! Can you come here?!"

What else is new? She cooks something even when we have enough food. She put on her slippers. "I'll be there in a second, Ma!"

She took two quick peeks into the bedrooms on the right. Veena and Lata's bedrooms. They were lucky to have their rooms close to each other. If they needed support, they went to each other for comfort and help. Her room was much farther down, hidden all the way down the hall in the back of the house. She got a good view of it, of course. It overlooked the vast garden in front of her, full of blooming flowers and lush trees. Every season, something new grew out of it, adding some brightness to an otherwise dull life. That garden was the only thing that stood out in the castle. It didn't have that drab look. It bloomed every single time.

At least it was supposed to bloom every time. When she went through the gnarled black gates, she discovered several dead plants in the driveway. Leaves, and flowers dead, and pine needles browned. The house needed more food. The last few guests provided enough nourishment for the past week, but it grew tired of eating people with bad records. They hadn't found new guests for it to feed on. No one appeared to be a worthy meal for their house. She stopped in front of the wall, rubbing it for some comfort. They'd feed again. Once she found a decent meal for it, the house would get its energy and life back.

Radha strolled down the long hallway with only a few lights guiding her path. For the lower level with few rooms, it held far too many pathways. She remembered Terry, so confused and hurt, walking away from her. He hadn't called her despite texting her before the party. Maybe he truly believed she didn't like him. Maybe he heard the screams in the distance of the other guests. Whatever the reason, he drove off and never looked back. He wasn't going to seek her out again. He'd forget all about her. Everyone who came to this house forgot about it, whether they survived the night or not. If she saw him on the streets, he wouldn't know her.

I shouldn't dwell on this. The less he remembers us, the better his life will be. Those words repeated in her head. They kept her sanity intact. Terry wasn't the right man for her. The perfect man was out there for her too. He'd be someone allowed to live in the house. Someone who'd last longer than the night. Someone who'd grow old with her. She deserved that much after the rest of the hell she went through.

She paused to sniff the fresh-cut roses sitting in the corner. Bright red and pink, they added a splash of color to the dull gray walls surrounding her. They were little reminders that there was life inside this place. Granted, most of that life was old and withering away, but it existed. Radha left the house for hours at a time to mingle with others. Being out there gave her something the house didn't.Even if it was for a job interview, it reminded her of life outside the stone walls.

Another smell spiked the air as she licked her lips. Instead of floral scents, she gathered spicy aromas from her mother's cooking. Though she couldn't figure out what it was, she still wanted to get a taste. Only eight in the morning, and she craved whatever her mother cooked up. Picking up the pace, she burst into the kitchen where her mother stood over the stove. Despite the fan whirring around, the entire room burst with warmth and aroma. She went over to the stove, rubbing her hands.

"Good morning, Ma! What are you making?" She gazed into the pot. Despite the vegetables and simmering red sauce, it remained a mystery. "It's not Indian food, that's for sure!"

"It's cold in my room so I figured I'd make myself some soup." Her mother sipped a little bit of the soup. Waving her hand over her mouth, she checked the side of a can. "Bring to boil…yeah, it's boiling all right! I have no more taste buds!"

Radha stifled her laughter. Leave it to her mother to taste something while piping hot. She never failed to burn some part of her mouth whenever she brewed something. "I tell you all the time, Ma. Wait until it's cooled down a little bit."

"Then it becomes lukewarm. Lukewarm soup warms nothing up. However, this soup could use a little more onion." She tossed several chopped onion pieces into the pot. "There! I'll finally have some flavor in this!"

"What are you talking about? You've put a lot of different flavors in it."

"I know but I need some flavors that warm me up. Your cousin over here decided to turn down the thermostat. I'm shivering down to my bones."

Radha checked the thermostat on the side. "I can't see

why you're so cold. The thermostat is high. If you need more heat, there is a heater in your room."

"Am I allowed to turn on the heater or will I freeze to death here?" Her mother dumped several spices into the pot. "I woke up to icicles forming above my head!"

"Oh, Ma! Give it up! It's not that cold!" Radha waved it off. "The heater was on last night!"

"At the lowest degree possible. An ice cube wouldn't melt in this place." She stirred everything. "That's why I'm cooking dinner so early. I want something warm to eat before I go to bed tonight."

Radha sniffed the stew. "Well, it's morning, but I'm ready to eat this now!"

"Good. I left the recipe on my dresser. When you're ready, just grab the ingredients and get to work." She poured herself a bowl and switched off the stove. "Now if you'll excuse me, I'm taking this to my room and hiding under multiple sheets. I gotta do some research too. The last couple of lists gave me nothing but a bunch of pickpockets and people writing bad checks. Not exactly mastermind criminals."

Radha gave up arguing with her mother, though she agreed with the lack of decent guests. She did her own research and found very few people to invite. Most of the criminals were petty crooks. The house didn't like those at all, especially since most did their time and never caused problems again. They didn't make decent meals at all. If that petty crook stayed clean, they didn't invite them over.

Unfortunately, it left them with more things to tend to, namely the garden. No one went out there this morning to water the plants. With the cold weather coming in, they needed some tending. Maybe she'd throw a tarp over them to keep them warm.They deserved to survive cold winds even when they didn't have enough guests. She didn't want to lose any more flowers. After finding trash bags of wilted petals that Veena cleaned up, she couldn't let the garden suffer with the rest of house.

Let's go check them out. Pulling on her coat, she wove her way out of the kitchen and into the garden. There they were between all the greenery, those bright flowers glistening with morning dew. If Lata had come here earlier, she showed no signs of it. No trimming hedges, no digging in the dirt, no watering. Granted, none of them bothered doing much to the garden these days. No one came around to see it.Their last few guests admired the garden in full bloom, remarking on how bright the petals turned out. Bursts of red and pink led them around, reminding them that spring would return. They just wouldn't be around to see it.

Not that people who deserved to live would see much either. Winter mornings grew bleak and darker as they moved deeper into the stone house. The only lights came from the lamps on the sides and ceilings. The walls cracked along the sides, though Veena assured them they didn't need fixing. The cracks gave them character, along with the vines curling upwards weren't going anywhere. They were a part of the house. She leaned against the wall, recalling many moments where they took guests around before the feedings. Her heels clicked on the ground as she rocked back and forth. Memories. Every hall, every day, every second inside held memories.

"My husband planted so many of these trees and flowers when we moved into the house. Some of them are old, but others are brand new and thriving." Veena always told people who came by, be it neighbors who stopped to chat or guests they were planning to kill off. "I can't bear to lose any of them. They're like children to me."

Much like a child, the house was a part of all their lives

now. The cracks, the low lights, the angel statues littered around the garden were all children of the house. As more people visited, the house flourished, and the garden grew. Her heart burst with excitement whenever their house healed itself. Happy. The housewas happy after a meal, nothing else. Those last few guests were the perfect food. If only Radha as could find more like them. That would keep the house standing for a few more years.

"Radha?" Radha jumped as Veena's cold hand landed on her shoulder. "I'm sorry! I was wondering if I could talk to you."

Radha clutched her chest. "Sure. Let me make sure my heart's beating normally first. What are you doing home so early anyway? I thought you were spending the night with Norman."

At that remark, Veena rolled her eyes. "You are so cruel sometimes. I'm home only because Norman decided to make me pay for half the meal. At that point, it wasn't worth taking him anywhere else. Not even to the dump."

"That bad, huh?"

"On a scale of one to ten, it's about a four." Veena shrugged. "I hate this. Every time I think I find the right person; he turns out to be a complete dud. I think my charms are fading away."

"Oh, I'm sorry. Maybe your standards are a little too high."

Veena dropped her keys in her purse. "Since when is the 2 for $20 special at Morty's Crab Shack a high standard? The best thing about that place is the shrimp cocktail and the chairs you sit on. If you don't get food poisoning, you're the luckiest person alive...if you make it out alive."

Radha smirked. Go figure Veena would head out to Morty's Crab Shack for companionship. The last few months, she wasn't so lucky with meeting people. She got far enough for a conversation, but that was it. None of her old tricks worked. It was always dinner and a goodbye. She was convinced that she withered with the house. Her charms faded away whenever the house got hungry.

Veena sniffed the air. "Mmm, that smells good. Who's cooking stew at nine in the morning?" "It's soup. Ma claims the house is too cold." Radha rubbed her arms. "Although now that I say it out loud, maybe she's right. The thermostat's up, yet it's freezing here. Is something wrong with the heater?"

"There shouldn't be." Veena jogged towards her bedroom and flung the door open, letting cold gusts of air rush in. "Oh, goodness! What is all this?! It's not supposed to go cold!"

"Well, it's cold outside. It can't..."

Her gaze followed Veena's as her sentence's died on her lips. The garden. While Radha's bedroom got the better view, Veena's room was where all the best flowers were. Bright red and white roses lined the sides, petals dropping on the ground. They were always opened and taking in sunlight. Right now, all that remained of them were pieces of red and white. Her flowers were dying. They died alongside the brownish blades of glass and crunchy fallen leaves. Veena shuddered as she drew the curtains closed.

It's dying. This house, this garden...it's dying.That's why we have dead plants. We didn't tend to them after the last party.

"I knew it." Veena shuddered. "I knew those guests weren't enough. I found another crack in the bathtub today. Do you know what that means?"

"That...you have a crack in your bathtub that can easily be covered?"

"Don't make fun of me! You know what I mean!" Veena

closed the other windows of her room. "I knew my looks were fading! I can't attract anything except…the men at Morty's Crab Shack! No, we need to do something! I'm looking in the wrong places for love. Maybe…Maybe I need to bring them here first!"

"Oh, really?!" Radha threw her hands in the air. "You think men are going to waltz into this home without a reason? You live in the oldest building in town. They'll run away the moment they see the gargoyles."

"Gargoyles?" Veena scrunched her face up. "…I wasn't planning on bringing the men around when you're giving yourself a facial."

"Not me! I mean…" Radha rubbed her temples. "No, you're not doing this. We're not dragging guests in without good reason. There's got to be a better plan than this. We're searching for everything in the wrong places. Guests, your dates, everything…"

"Oh, I'm trying to do that too. I can't convince the men to aim higher. No one wants to go to nice restaurants anymore. No one's got a membership to any country clubs. No one even wants to stroll down the park with me. I'm at a loss." Veena sat down on her bed. "How do we fix this, Radha?"

"I'm not sure. All we can do is more research. Something's bound to pop up." Radha held up her hand. "Don't fret about the guests or your looks. We'll get them both."

Her worries mounted over those red and white petals in the garden. Like drops of blood, they sat there, taunting them. The house creaked with each step they took. No, this couldn't be. This home needed them. It needed someone to bring life back into it. They haven't invited anyone in recent years. Maybe now was the time to break out the nice China and glassware.

As they pondered over possibilities, Lata burst into the room and put down the bags she carried. She slipped out of her coat, folding it over her arms. "Hey, you're not going to believe what I saw!"

"I know. The garden is dying." Radha motioned her to sit down. "You saw all those petals around, huh?"

"Well, I was going to say that I saw Pikachu outside the grocery store. He was selling those Vienna sausages on a tray. But yes, the garden is dying!" Lata gulped. "I've never seen so many dead leaves around here. Even in the winter, we always managed to have some greenery. What happened now?"

"It's the house. We didn't give it what it needed." Veena glanced at her reflection in the mirror, poking away at her cheeks. "And I know why. Look at me! I used to be gorgeous! Irresistible. I could attract men from far away distances! When I see myself now, do you know what I see?"

Lata blinked. "Yourself?"

"No! I see an old hag. My skin's sagging, my eyes have bags, my lips are puffy…no wonder no one wants to come home with me." Veena grabbed the makeup remover from her vanity and started to rub everything off. "I don't know how else I can attract anyone. My looks were all I had. Well, that and…what's under the sheets."

"What's under your sheets?"

"The pot she makes her rotisin. What the hell do you think she's talking about?!" Radha pulled Veena away from the mirror. "Come on. Forget about your appearance for a second and focus on the house. It's falling apart because we haven't gone after anyone. We're not doing enough research. There's only so many lists that Ma alone can look at. Her eyesight's not the best, so we must pitch in. There are scumbags all over the world. They think they got away with their crimes. We're here to remind them that they'll get caught.

The police can't get them, but we can."

"But my…" Veena went over to a flower vase in the corner. She reached it, another bright red petal floated off. "Oh God! Now it's affecting the plants inside the house! Next thing you know, my jewels…"

"Will draw in the people we want." Radha lowered her gaze. "Think about it. They'll come in for the wrong reasons. Of course, we will still have to invite some people that we know. Decent people. We'll make them a nice dinner and talk for a while. We're not celebrating anything major, just a night with friends. We'll have to figure out howto bring them here. Also, who can we invite?"

"How about the man in the Pikachu outfit? He seemed nice." Lata pointed out. "He gave me four of those Vienna sausages. Not that I ate them, but it's the thought that counts."

"Oh, forget it! You have no idea who this person is besides the fact that he gives away samples. We're not inviting someone dressed as a rabbit to this place."

"Pikachu's a mouse, not a rabbit."

"Who cares what that rodent is? He's not coming!" Veena rubbed her forehead. "I don't know if I like the idea of a party for normal people. It's a whole lot of planning. I got to figure out what to make for food. What kind of entertainment we'll have. I must clean the whole place. It's going to take a long time to put together. I'd rather someone come to our door so I can take care of this."

Radha ignored their bickering to turn her gaze at the ceilings. So high and covered in cobwebs, echoes bounced off them whenever a person screamed. The only place that never happened was the feeding room. Her great-grandparents wouldn't be thrilled at their bedroom being a feeding area, but it was the best way to describe it. All those screams changed to muffled cries as the house devoured its food. Any innocent people wandering around would get a small squeak from them. Their screams of help died with them since no one helped them. Innocent guests brushed those squeaks off as someone sneezing or creaking floorboard. No one cared to poke around and discover the dangers below.

Perhaps the change in parties could help. They always planned the same way: a dinner party where they'd eat and talk about anything. Maybe Veena would play some music, and they'd get up to dance. Maybe they'd watch TV or some movies. They were quiet parties among friends until the moment feeding time rolled around. Veena took them around the home and lectured them about the family. During that time, people disappeared into the house until very few remained. Those few went into that feeding room, which appeared to be a bedroom untouched since her great-grandparents were there. No, they needed a little change in this plan. It wouldn't take long for someone to find out about them. The house kept them safe for years. If it crumbled, their protection was gone..

DING-DONG!

The doorbell caught everyone off guard as the walls shook. A visitor. Someone came over here. Someone went through their black, twisted gates and made it to the front door. Lata and Veena nodded at each other. Radha pushed aside all the party plans as another crack formed along the sides. She couldn't read anything between these cracks, couldn't understand why it was coming undone, but it didn't matter now. The only message she got was that the house was hungry. It wanted something, be it a delivery person or a law breaker. It was starving.

Veena's eyes sparkled as a grin spread across her painted cheeks. "Look your best, ladies. We have company."

Chapter 3

The walls closed in on them as shadows cast down, dancing across the floor. Every stone piece, every angel statue gazing down, they waited for the surprise guest. Their home hungry for something new. It wanted a new life breathed into it. Only then would the flowers bloom and their cracks would heal. Radha went ahead of the other, keeping her eye on the angels. So many angels. They symbolized purity and innocence though their faces held no expressions. No softness, no sweet smiles, only blank stares. They scared her more than the gargoyles outside. At least those statues appeared menacing and angry. The angels had nothing except emptiness. A complete contrast to the house itself.

As they turned another corner, a groan erupted down the hall followed by moaning. Hunger pangs. She glanced over her shoulder. "Please tell me we have something to feed it."

"Uh…I bought some meat earlier." Lata said. "Once we figure out who's at the door, I'll go up and feed it."

Go up and feed it. Those words made sense when it came to pets. If they owned a dog or cat or even some endangered species, people wouldn't think twice about it. Instead, they fed their house giant chunks of beef. All they did was run up to the empty room, toss those pieces, and close the door. After a few minutes, they checked the room to find nothing left behind. On a rare occasion when they threw in meat with bones, they'd find a few pieces there, but that was all. The house devoured everything in that room.

When will she ever change these things? Why do we need angels here? We've got plenty statues around the other areas. She paused for a second to glance at more vases with wilting flowers. One by one, petals fell off and littered the ground. Small bits of red, white, and pink surrounded them. She pushed that image aside and picked up speed. Those angel statues kept careful watch as she, Lata, and Veena made their way to the front door.

*Almost there...maybe we'll be lucky now.*Her hand pressed against the wall as the cracks slowly filled up. There it went, the last bit of food. The leftovers from last week fueled the house. It lasted for a while, but now it wanted more. Maybe now they could give it some dessert with this new guest.

As Radha rounded the corner, she found her mother closing the door and bringing a box. "Ma, wait! Who was that? We could use them!"

"No, we can't! It was Agnes dropping off another package." Swati put the box down. "Thanks for making the old lady carry this box. It's not like I have a bad back or brittle bones or anything of that sort."

"Oh, Ma!" Radha picked up the box and shook it. "It's so light! A five-year-old could carry this."

"Sorry I don't have the stamina of a five-year-old anymore." Swati checked the top of the box. "Agnes was asking about you. She wondered why she hadn't seen you in ages. She's also wondering why the hell everything looks so dead in here."

Radha ran her fingers down a crack in the wall. It grew longer the last time she stared at it. In the corner, another vase of flowers dropped wilted petals. The hair on her arms stood up as her mind ticked away over the party idea. "That's why we're here. We're losing the house, Ma. That's why I was telling the others that we should draw people over here. Give them a different kind of party."

"A different kind of party's a terrible idea. I'll be the one cooking while you three mingle away." Swati shook her head. "Why can't you just go on a date like everyone else?"

"We've tried that, Ma. People aren't showing up like before. I don't really want to date these people anyway. You've seen what they've done. Even if I'm pretending to be interested, I'll be sick deep down." She stepped back to admire the arched ceilings with their vine-like designs. "If we make it look a little more presentable, we can get the people we need here. And if you're worried so much about the food, we'll get catering."

"Over my dead body you will! You never know what those people are going to make or how long they took to cook it." Swati warned her."I'll make something, don't worry. Just tell me how many people you want to invite, and I'll get to work."

"I'll know that once I know when we're throwing this party." Radha paced around the hallway, listening to the floorboards squeaking underneath. Their poor house. It stood strong for years and it crumbled before her. The vines outside of the windows now rotted away. No, this couldn't be. Their house deserved more than a few fixes. It deserved to thrive and live in such a dreadful world. Its plants, its vines, its walls...they all deserved to grow. If they had to come up with unorthodox ways to save their home, they'd do it.

"Well, we may have to go through a couple of lists. See if there's anything new." She wondered. "I mean, there are plenty of creeps getting away with crime. Maybe we got to dig a little deeper for them."

"Oh, let me think…" Veena went over to the wall where her calendar was. "Mmm…I had a date last night. I have one tomorrow night. I have one the following night. Then the next five nights, I'll be with Chet. And then…" Her finger ran down the days. "Ah, here we go! In three weeks, I'll be free! I can help you with research then!"

"We don't have three weeks!" Radha went over to the calendar and tapped on the upcoming Saturday. "Our house is coming undone with each passing hour! We need guests! It needs food! Can you come home quickly after lunch to help us out?"

"I don't know. Usually, lunch dates lead to dinner dates which lead to…" Veena blushed. "Well, you can figure out where it leads to."

"Where?" Lata blinked.

"To Comic Con, Lata. What the hell do you think?!" Swati snapped. She blew dust off the table in the corner. "Eh, I see what my daughter is saying. None of us have done a good job of luring people in. It might be time to have a different kind of party."

"I still don't know…" Veena eyed the angel statue right next to her. Every word made sense to her. Her home needed some nourishment, something they could not provide. "The old parties always worked. Why do we need to change it?"

"Well, I think it's a great idea! We help the house, we have fun, and above all else, we keep these guys off the streets!" Lata threw in. "I like having a potluck dinner where everyone makes their own dishes/plates. Maybe to make things a little easier, we can invite some people we know. Some good people. Maybe some former friends and lovers."

"Good people? I'm not sure the house will want them." Radha chuckled. "That, and I'm not sure I want to forgive my former lovers. I don't know if I can bring them here."

"You're not willing to forgive two people?" Swati frowned. "Oh, come on! We don't need a stupid theme for the party. Invite them, feed them, and if they cooperate, they'll go home. If they don't…well, you know the rest. I think Lata has a good idea…for once. Let's mix it up. Some jerks and some good people. The house will leave the good alone. It always does."

Radha leaned against the stone wall before turning to Veena and Lata. They said nothing but both of their expressions read the same thing; this was necessary. "I guess that makes sense. I'll go through my book and see if there's anyone we can invite. Just remember not to bring up what we're really planning. They don't need to know everything. I might try contacting Terry again, see if he's still interested. It'll be like our usual parties. Just a small change."

"Please, Veena?" Lata clasped her hands together. "I promise it'll be a good time! Maybe you'll find the right person here!"

"Well…okay, we can throw a party!" Veena caved in. "You two are gonna help me though. I have no problems doing the tours. We start off after dinner with whoever is left behind. I might add a few stories about what our family did. When they came to the country, how our grandparents found this place, what they vowed to do. I can go on for days with that."

Radha rolled her eyes. "Veena, please, they will only be here for a few hours. Let's not try to have all the fun right away."

"Oh, fine. I'll just tell them all the boring stuff. Most won't last before the feeding room anyway." Veena waved this off, then frowned at the wall. "Oh God, my poor baby. We haven't been keeping you healthy. We'll do our best though."

Radha followed her gaze, swallowing the lump when she saw the damage. The fresh new cracks in the wall gave away the worst fears: the house needed more nourishment. Finding people who got away with crime took a little longer now. They dug around for information, checked up on every guest, and then fed the house. She didn't want another situation like Terry, who wandered into the party uninvited.

Terry. There he was in her memory again. The phone hadn't rung all day, and he never sent a text or email. The poor man never knew how close he came to losing his life. Him and the others that she got close to. Somehow, she found the good ones in the groups, the ones who came in as extra guests. Not that it did her any good. Anytime she found someone decent, they never stayed long enough. They revealed their true colors within seconds. Even if she fed them to the house, it wouldn't keep the walls from cracking. The flowers still wilted whenever it got food that didn't satisfy them. The further Terry stayed from her, the better it was for their home.

But it's not good enough for me. As important as the parties were, she found herself growing more bored during them. The only bit of excitement came from all the alcohol she drank during it. Not that it helped her much on either a professional or personal level. She had no job and didn't get many dates. The alcohol soothed her for one minute. After the drink, she'd spend the rest of the night wallowing behind cracked walls and artwork. It hurt to go through these nights with nothing in the end.

She faced the wall behind her, cracks slowly making their way to the door frames. Their poor house. It never mattered how much food it got. It was never fully satisfied. There were still criminals on the loose, many with blood on their hands. The police were completely useless if they weren't complicit in crimes themselves. The house loved eating them the most; corrupt cops and politicians made the tastiest meals. No one ever missed them. No one came looking for them. They faded out of everyone's memory, and the world turned into a better place. If only it helped her mood in the process. *Cheer yourself up.*She scolded herself as she picked up some wilted petals on the ground. Even if the house fell apart, they still cleaned it.*Terry might have ended up like the others you've dated. Good men that eventually drop you. Maybe it's not meant to be.*

She clapped her hands. "All right, that's enough wallowing over the house. Let's start planning this party. Who wants to find our guests?"

Lata threw her hand in the air. "I have free time tomorrow to do some research. I know there's got to be someone we can pull in. Tell them they are invited because we think they're important."

"And you won't make a mistake like the last time?" Swati warned her. "My daughter's still waiting for a decent date."

"I am not, Ma! I don't need a party to get a date! I'm perfectly capable of getting a date on my own!" Radha brushed aside the rest of the fallen leaves and petals. "You don't need to worry about my love life. I'm fine."

Oh, she hated lying to them, and they saw right through it. She expected nothing exciting at this party either. Not that she wanted to date a scumbag, but the loneliness killed her afterwards. She waved to the others, nodding towards her room. "I'm gonna rest for a little bit and come up with some party ideas. I'll share some stuff a little later."

"Just don't cook anything for the party." Swati warned. "I know you love your imitation foods and pre-cut vegetables. You're too scared to go the extra mile with cooking. I'll do the food. You just do the other stuff."

Radha ignored that bit but it lingered as she went into her room. No dates, unable to cook a decent meal, no job. She didn't get any breaks in any area. Staring down at her phone, she got no messages from the previous interview. Employment got harder to obtain as she stared at her old artwork. Most of the ones on her walls were copies of old masters, but her own paintings sat in a corner, hidden inside of a bag. She never got the will to hang them up since they didn't spark joy in her. They were all basic landscapes, seascapes, and portraits. There wasn't anything unique. Nothing that could create interesting conversations. She could make more art yet didn't know what to make. As a result, she hid it all. They were her greatest shame now, not worth anything. She tried for years to come up with an amazing work of art. She put all her sweat and tears into it, yet no one wanted it. No one garnered any inspiration out of her work. One person called her work 'a piece of tripe' and that stuck. That's all she churned out now: tripe. She preferred a simple 'I don't like it' to an insult like that.

*Maybe one day.*She lay on her back, eyeing the fresh new cracks above. This party would help their house, but not her. She'd find no one there.*Maybe there is someone out there who can bring inspiration and love to me.*

As another crack formed right over her headboard, doubt settled in. Her mother was right: her dating life was dead on arrival. No man out there wanted to spend more than a few minutes with her. Veena held all the charm while Lata amused them. Swati threw out the sarcastic zingers to hold them in. She only talked to them. Nothing grew from their conversations. Perhaps Terry would get tired of her too. If he stayed here, he wouldn't stay for long. That special someone in her life wasn't there.

"I can't help being who I am...even if who I am is boring."

She told herself. "People are just gonna have to get used to that."

Grabbing a handful of petals off the ground, she crumpled all the red and pink in her palms. Love. She lacked it in all stages of her life. The perfect man wasn't going to waltz through that door today. He wasn't coming to see her. She tossed the crumpled petals as the cracks grew around her feet. A broken house, a broken life…nothing healed her right now.

*Crunch!*The house shivered around her as she leaned against the wall. Her parents told her about this situation. Back in the day, her ancestors kept plenty of food around. They brought in the damned souls for the house to chew on. They didn't have phones or computers to search for them, just relied on good old word of mouth. They succeeded in keeping the house alive back then. Why couldn't she? The poor house grew hungrier with each passing day. Once again, they'd get guests in the house to satisfy the house. It healed in time.

If only her heart healed with it. Unlike the house, the cracks in that never sealed up.

Chapter 4

The following morning revealed more cracks in her bedroom wall that led towards her ceiling. Some of the cracks formed a word on top: HELP. Anyone else would have fainted at the sight, but not Radha. The cry for help came up when the house demanded food. She went to bed doing a little research yet wasn't satisfied with what she found. Too many petty crooks were on these lists. The house wanted a disgusting scumbag to feast on. The more she went through the lists, the less interested she grew in them. Ultimately, she gave up and closed her phone down.

*Sorry, house. We're trying. Seriously, we're trying hard.*She rolled over as her feet grazed across the floor. More cracks. They didn't cover the walls anymore. Those cracks went all around the room. This party had to be a hit. No matter what, everything rested on it.As she went from room to room, changing her clothes and getting ready, she caught sight of those gargoyles in the hall. They knew as well. They spotted those same cracks growing along the walls. As she passed them, a few sported new marks on their bodies. Squinting closer, she spotted a few cracks on their polished faces, dirtying them more. Hand clasped over her mouth, she turned away and ran down the halls, ignoring the falling petals on the ground.

It started. It always started with cracks and falling petals, but now the statues faced destruction. First the gargoyles broke, then the angels. Then everything else would come crashing down with them inside. Frantic and mind swimming in fear, she put her party plans into action. Their house craved more food to stay standing. She patted the walls, smoothing over a new crack, with a silent promise to bring something. Staring up at the ceiling, she relaxed to find nothing falling off that. It wouldn't be long before that caved in.

Don't fall yet. I'll feed you.

Right after breakfast, she set her mother straight to work in finding guests. Swati grumbled over not knowing technology that well, despite having worked on a computer and inviting people for decades. She wanted to go out, but with time ticking away, she couldn't leave without a good group of guests. Veena and Lata worked today, though they promised to help in the evening. That didn't stop Swati from griping. She plopped herself in front of the laptop with a cup of coffee in one hand and the mouse in the other. All she had to do was pop things into a search engine.

"Why am I allowed to do work on this, but I can't pirate any dirty movies?" She went through the search engines for any unsolved cases. The same old cases popped up, cold cases with no new leads. Radha's soul hurt on how long some of these cases went unsolved. These victims weren't resting in peace, not until someone got their killers. "At least let me have some background noise while doing all this."

"Ma, background noise is stuff like music or podcasts or watching shows you're familiar with. It's not for watching porn." Radha went to the counter to grab her purse. With each step, the floorboard creaked. It started. After a relatively quiet morning, the house reminded her to bring food. Hands to chest, she slowed down her heartbeat and took the car keys. "Now, I'm going to the supermarket to get a few things. Do you need anything, Ma?"

"I'm eighty. All I need is peace on Earth, quiet time to work on this stuff, and food I can chew on." Swati sipped her coffee. "Remember to get the freshest produce. Check the expiration date on things. Don't forget about the cream!"

"Yes, Ma. I remember all that." Radha slipped on her shoes. "If you remember anything else, just text me. And I better not catch you trying to pirate anything!"

"Sure, sure. I'm only doing my job as a good little worker. I'll have a list of creeps for you when you get home." Swati grimaced as Radha pulled on her coat. "You're wearing that thing to the market? Can't you dress a little nicer?"

A headache throbbed at the front of her forehead. She didn't take a step out that door, yet her mother found something wrong with her outfit. Ignoring the pain, she grabbed the doorknob. "I'm going to the store, Ma. That's it."

"You should still wear something better. You never know who you'll run into." Swati got up to pour herself some more coffee. "I mean…it can happen. People run into each other, and they fall in love. That can happen to you."

"You really think so?"

"Hell no, but I'm your mother! I'm supposed to make you hopeful about the future!" Swati waved her off. "Now go! I got work to do. Get the food and we'll get this party rolling."

The wall on the side revealed more cracks to form a short little sentence: GOOD LUCK. Go figure, the house showed more kindness towards her than her own family. It was the only reason she still took part in all this. She patted it on the wall with the silent promise that she'd get food for it soon.

Radha finally made her way out of the house, got in the car, and revved it up, tires squealing as she backed out. Her mother still held hope that love was around the corner. For all the griping and moaning, she wanted her eldest daughter to fall in love again. Not that her dreams ever came true. Most people wanted someone younger and prettier. Someone who could keep up with, someone they could mold into the perfect lover. Radha refused to let anyone push her to become someone she wasn't. She knew herself very well. No one could change that.

*If only.*She caught bits of gray hair sticking out. A constant reminder that she was no longer in her twenties. Hell, she was no longer in her forties. Veena and Lata still had a great deal of charm to invite others. They could send out invites that brought every scumbag to their front door.

The supermarket filled up with people at an early hour, though she managed to find a spot up close. Easing her car into that spot, she got out and grabbed one of the shopping carts nearby. The items wouldn't take long to find. She came here mostly to calm her headache and watch people wandering around. Before moving back in, she went out a lot to people watch. She envied everyone who walked around without a care. They didn't have to worry about a house crumbling simply because it didn't get the soul it wanted to eat.

*This party better be worth it. I gotta save this house.*Radha pushed her grocery cart down the produce aisle, grabbing vegetables that appealed to her: eggplant, tomatoes, potatoes, squash, and carrots. She eyed the garlic on the side and couldn't decide how many cloves they needed. In the past, she bought diced garlic and onions. It saved her the trouble of doing it herself. With her mother around, she couldn't get away with shortcuts. Swati demanded that everything be fresh and prepared in front of her. No pre-cut veggies or pre-minced garlic was allowed in the house. Anyone cooking with pre-made things shouldn't be allowed near a stove.

Swati stuck with that rule forever.

"As long as you live under a roof with me, you will make it all from scratch." She reminded Radha anytime they cooked together. "Back in my day, we had no such thing as pre-cut veggies. Your grandparents didn't have them. Your great-grandparents didn't either. We cut them ourselves. You can do the same."

"Of course, Ma." Radha answered with those words every time. And every single time, her mother cut in to chide the way Radha cooked anything. "Everything fresh, all the time. If I cut myself and bleed over the food, serve it anyway."

"...I'd rather you not cut yourself. You really can't cut anything with knives. Look at this." Swati would then hold up pieces of mismatched vegetables. "This one's fat, this one's thin...what are you doing to these things?"

Radha never had a good answer for that. She could cut veggies, just not to her mother's standards. These were the times she wished the house didn't keep her mother safe. She loved her , but she didn't love the constant bickering and nit-picking about everything. If the house went into shambles as it currently was, somehow Radha ended up as the scapegoat. She couldn't find anyone worthwhile. She didn't go through the lists with intensity because the people always disgusted her. Killers, rapists, everything in between... she hated reading about them, let alone wanting to contact them. For that reason, Swati took shots at her.

"You fail at finding people. You fail at dating. And when you do get lucky in the dating pool, it's always some dud." Swati complained every five days. "Can't you find a doctor, engineer, or lawyer? Get someone with some stability. God knows you have none of it!"

That memory did it. Radha dumped the minced garlic into her cart before adding some tomatoes, eggplant, and basil. Veena and Lata told her they were fine with cooking anything. When Radha brought up making eggplant parmesan, they let her have free rein over it. She didn't tell her mother about anything. So far, everything moved according to plan. The problems would occur once they needed to use the oven.

*Eh, I'm making this dish. I'll add this when she isn't looking.*She pushed ahead, gazing up at the signs labeling different things in different aisles. Finding the aisle for flour, she moved towards it. No one was keeping her from making this eggplant parmesan. She had the perfect recipe and, outside of her mother, everyone else loved it. Starting at the different types, her mother's griping got into her mind.*Don't get that brand. I've told you anything that's made by the is bad! Get the cheap, good kind! And if it isn't cheap, get it anyway. I want real flour. You can't make anything with fake flour.*

"Oh God! Shut up, Ma!" Radha grabbed some flour from the bottom shelf as well as the breadcrumbs a few shelves down.*Why doesn't the house want her? Taking her will save us all a great deal of trouble.*

She knew the answer for that already. The house didn't eat family members. Swati grew up in it, knew every corner and hole within the walls. Much like Radha, she had a lot of fond memories and love for it. The house would never swallow her since she always fed it the best food: the killers who got away for over a decade. Since the house was happy, Radha dealt with her mother's complaints.

As she neared the corner for the eggs, memories flooded of her mother's first time in the house. She hated it, of course. She didn't like the gargoyle or angel statues, thinking they didn't fit in with the pretty flowers growing around. She despite the hard floors to walk on as well as the gray colored walls. Then there came her complaints about the hallways.

Too long, too ugly, too much trouble to walk around in. Now that the cracks had settled in, she complained about the appearance.

"Fix this damn thing already!" She'd yell at Veena. That boiled Radha's blood more; she didn't take out anything on her daughter alone. Veena and Lata dealt with her cantankerous ways. Unlike Radha, who often had an answer that shut her up, the others fell silent around her. They fumed under their breaths but didn't shoot anything back. They did it out of respect, but Radha wished they'd speak up. Maybe then, her mother would get the message. Don't yell at everyone in the house.

*Goddammit, she's on my mind again!*Radha nearly slammed into the glass doors where the milk was. She grabbed the cart and steered it away, staring at all the plastic bottles and containers behind it. Milk. Did they have any of that? If her mother made dessert for the party, she'd use the entire carton.*Let me get another one to be on the safe side. We'll need milk sooner or later.*

She grabbed a carton and started backing away, fuming over her mother. Why her? Why couldn't she go live with other relatives? Radha's brother and sister lived nearby. They both had much nicer houses that didn't crack. They lived in neighborhoods surrounded by neighbors, not giant trees covering everything. They got that excitement Radha longed for in her life. Her mother would enjoy their homes far more than this one, this giant castle in shadows. More than that, her siblings had steady work. They could provide for their mother.

*Maybe I should give them a call. Send Ma to them for a weekend.*She stared at the eggs, wondering if she needed more than a dozen. At home, they used up eggs as quickly as the house used up their guests.

"Excuse me?" The baritone voice from behind interrupted her thoughts. Hands gripping the shopping cart, she pulled away from the eggs. "I'm sorry. I just need to grab something over there."

Her eyes moved away from that aisle and faced the man right behind her. He couldn't have been older than her with that salt-and-pepper gray hair and warm brown eyes twinkling at her. Well-dressed, smiling, very polite…this was the kind of man she missed being around. She attracted scumbags in the past, the ones who weren't welcomed in the house. This one, whoever he was, didn't reek of scumbag. He reached over and grabbed a carton of egg whites.

"Sorry about that." He apologized again. "I wasn't trying to startle you."

"You didn't." Radha murmured. His voice, oh dear. His voice melted all over her. He was a good one. He belonged in their house, but not as a permanent guest. Just someone who visited now and then. "I shouldn't have been standing here and staring at eggs. Especially since I got the ones I wanted." She held up the carton of brown, cage-free eggs. "It's just one of those days."

"I get what you mean. One of those days." He grabbed a carton of brown eggs. In doing so, he caught sight of her cart. "Making dinner tonight?"

"How did you know?"

"Spaghetti, eggplant, breadcrumbs, eggs, flour, garlic… let me guess, you're making eggplant parmesan." He chuckled. "My wife used to make that too. Though she usually made her own pasta."

"I can make my own pasta!" Radha blurted out. "We just…it's our pasta maker…it's broken. My mother's not too thrilled with eating boxed pasta, but it will do."

The man backed away. "Relax. I wasn't accusing you of

anything. I don't mind boxed pasta cause sometimes, you don't have time to make it fresh. Especially with my busy schedule, I gotta do what I can."

"Don't we all?" Radha started to move away from the aisle. Every bit of her wanted him to follow but a small voice warned her not to attract him. Not this man. He was good. He didn't insult her. He smiled and talked like he knew her. He didn't give her any creeps so she couldn't invite him over. She didn't know him. Yet her stupid mouth opened and continued to talk to him.

"What do you do, if you don't mind me asking?" She grabbed some butter in the following aisle. There was also a chive and onion cream cheese spread, which would work for their snacks. Grabbing that, she added. "I'm a high school art teacher…granted, I'm not teaching at the moment."

"Because of a school break?"

"Because of layoffs." The headache she suffered earlier came back in full force. If it wasn't her dating life or the house eating away at her, her lack of working got under her skin. Layoffs happened all around, and most people weren't hiring at the moment. She applied to schools all around and even offered to give art classes at the local community center. Nothing picked up. The days at home sank her spirits lower; she couldn't escape the house. It reminded her that no good news was on the horizon; people either ghosted her or flat out said no. She wasn't what they wanted.

"That's rough. I'm sorry to hear all that." The man grabbed the same cream cheese spread. "I'm a marine biologist. Right now, though, I'm teaching marine biology at the local university. My current work is extremely slow."

"Sounds interesting." Radha noticed him grabbing butter as well. "Are you throwing a party as well or do you enjoy buying the same things I'm buying?"

"A party? I just picked these up because I need them too." He held out his hand. "Since I've bothered you long enough, I might as well introduce myself: Andrew Geller. I moved here a few weeks ago and am still figuring out where everything is."

"Ah, the slowness at work probably explains why you're here. We have no oceans nearby. Just trees and darkness." She laughed. "Oh, I'm Radha, by the way. I'm picking all this stuff up for a party at the house. If you're new here, maybe you can come by."

*No, Radha! What are you doing?!*Her brain yelled at her. *He's a good one! He doesn't belong in the house! You can't take him there!*

"Well, give me the address and time and I'll see what I can do." He held out his phone. "Just type it in there. Is it this weekend?"

"Yes, actually! Will you be able to come?"

"This weekend?" Andrew's face fell on that. "I'm afraid not. I'm going on a trip to the beach for work. I won't be back till Sunday night."

Her brain quit yelling at that moment. He was safe. He couldn't make it this weekend. The other part of her mind came up with other ideas. "Do you mind having dinner next week? When you get back, that is? We can talk more about this town, our jobs or lack of…anything you want. If it will make you feel better, I'll make you fresh pasta."

He picked up a carton of low-fat yogurt. "I've got one better; let's go out to eat. Do you know any good places? I'm open to anything."

Oh God, he wanted to go to a restaurant. Radha had many in mind, some more expensive than others. Italian, Mexican, Japanese, Chinese, Indian…she had a place for all of them. She could pick any and, if he was honest about being open to anything, he'd accept them. Her stomach grumbled at the hot sauces in one corner. Hot sauce. Wing sauces.

"How about the Upper Deck? They have the best chicken wings around." She cursed herself as soon as those words left her mouth. Chicken wings. Instead of a romantic restaurant where they'd have privacy, she picked a sports bar that blared games over the TV and served people alcohol twenty-four seven. "I'm sorry. You probably want something a little more…well, not a place where the best cuisine is wings and beer and the music is usually drunks screaming at the TV."

"A sports bar? I have no problem with that." Andrew wrote something down on a piece of paper and handed it over. "That's my phone number. You can text me the directions."

"Sounds good. I know you can't come on the weekend, but how about tomorrow for lunch?" Her mouth went on. Her brain short-circuited, yelling at her to stop. This man didn't need to come to the house. Not next week, not the one after, never. "They're usually not as packed during weekdays at lunch. If that's fine, then_"

"Perfect. Text me the address of the place. Is noon okay or do you need to go earlier? I can even do it later than that."

"Noon is fine." She checked his phone number. "I'll text you once I get home, all right? I must get started on some of these dishes. My mother's gonna throw a fit if I don't help her with some of the prep."

"Ah, you take care of your mother?"

She winced. Her mother, Swati, was the one with the big mouth and incredible cooking ability. She never wanted anyone else to help her for anything. Yet whenever she needed help reading directions or grabbing something from the top shelf, she begged Radha for it. "More like she lives with me. She's been in this country too long, and there's no one in India to take care of her. She might as well stay here. My siblings don't have enough room to keep her."

This was a bit sad, but true. Being the oldest, her siblings expected Radha to look after their mother. Her sisters Rupa and Manik traveled the world with their families, trying new things, and posting all their pictures on Instagram. Her nieces and nephews showed off their adventures on TikTok, going on and on about all they saw. She couldn't help cringing at some of the videos. Sure, they danced like idiots as most people danced on TikTok, but her jealousy grew at the very places they danced in. Bangkok. Mumbai. Paris. Vienna. Lima. Somehow, the rest of her family explored more of the world than she did.

Then there were her brothers, all three of them doctors. They saved lives for a living, which her mother reminded her. She rarely spoke to them since they spent ninety percent of their lives in a hospital. As the oldest with no job, the only place her mother could stay was at their house. Swati had no complaints over the house eating souls of terrible people. If anything, she craved every moment they disappeared. She lived for the distant screams going down the long hallways and echoing around the vaulted ceilings. For those reasons, she wasn't leaving. Radha couldn't push her into the streets either, given that she was old. Throwing a senior citizen out of a house left a bad taste in her mouth. For those reasons, Radha let her stay and continued to envy her family.

Not that she minded the time with her mother. After her father passed away, Swati couldn't live in the old house anymore. Being all by herself didn't give her much of a life.

"I think it's nice that you look after her." Andrew said. "And I would love to meet her one day. She sounds like a character."

"Oh, no, you would not." Radha held up her hand. "My mother is quite old and…let's say she has no filter. If she says something awful towards you, I wouldn't know how to explain it. I've learned to let the insults slide off, but…"

"It's okay." He stopped her. "We'll take it slowly, one step at a time. I'll meet you at the restaurant if that'll make you comfortable."

"Yes!" Radha jumped up, nearly knocking her grocery cart over. Grabbing it before it rolled off, she grasped the handles tight enough to whiten her knuckles. "I mean…let's take it slow. We must see how much you enjoy the Upper Deck first."

As soon as those words left her lips, she kicked herself internally. Enjoy the Upper Deck? Everyone who went there enjoyed it. The good food, the music, the various contests they held…it was a dream place for both, the regular person and those who lived well above their means. Of course, he'd love it.

"I can't wait." Andrew glanced around for an open checkout kiosk. Spotting one in the corner, he grabbed his cart and rolled towards it. "I better pay for this stuff. It was nice making your acquaintance, Radha. I hope I see you soon."

*Me too.*Radha stared at his back when he started checking out his things. She moved to the other kiosk, taking glances in between checking out items. Pretending to go down the receipt, she noticed him weighing veggies out before putting them away. He tied the plastic bags up before dropping them back in his cart. Her heart up in her throat, she finished bagging her things and paid for everything. She couldn't think about him right now. Even as he took the cart, waved at her again, and headed towards the exit, her mind went back to the items in the bag. She finished up, grabbed the receipt, and walked out while still checking over the prices. Each step she took, she watched Andrew doing the same. He also wanted to make sure he never overpaid for anything. Once he walked away, she dumped the receipt in her bag and pushed the car towards the parking lot.

Their party. The guests coming over. Their home craved a new meal. That's where her heart needed to be. Make the eggplant parmesan, with or without her mother's complaints, wine and dine the guests, and lead them to their doom. She could worry about Andrew tomorrow. It was a simple lunch, after all. Nothing could come out of this.

And if it did, if he had dark secrets or not, the house couldn't have him.

CHAPTER 5

Radha waltzed down the gravel driveway, ignoring the gargoyles guarding the garden. She noted that the flowers weren't wilting anymore. The petals were swept away in the wind, but all the roses bloomed under the sun. The branches swung with bright green leaves and the roof of their home no longer loomed over them. The house wasn't scary today. With the sun pouring, it was just an ordinary house.

Not that ordinary though. Our family's not ordinary so we didn't get a normal house. She opened the trunk of the car and started pulling out groceries. Her heart started beating rapidly over her lunch date tomorrow. Poor Andrew couldn't come in the evening but that didn't mean they were through. Right before leaving the store, she texted him the address of The Upper Deck and he texted back that he got it. He was real. He wanted to go out with her tomorrow. This was real.

"A date. I have a date." She dropped the bags on the front porch and rang the doorbell. "I have a date with a man from the supermarket. I can't believe it..." When no one opened the door, she fished the keys from her pocket. "Go figure no one can hear me in there."

Once she opened the door and got the groceries inside, she came up with ideas on how to announce the date. Everyone waited for the day for her to find someone new.

She spent more time in the house than the others. She sat around reading books, watching TV, or working in the garden while the rest of them enjoyed life. They griped about her being so boring, sticking around and doing nothing. That was what she was to them: a big, old nothing. Radha was dull. Radha was pathetic. Radha couldn't impress a single soul.

Not tonight though. She found someone. She found a man who appeared intelligent and kind. He wasn't repulsed by the way she stumbled over words or stared at things. He didn't mind that she used boxed pasta or didn't have a job. He wanted to go out with her. He replied to her text with a promise to be there tomorrow. Andrew Gardner. Brand new to town and the only man in years that made her heart jump up. Even now, she clutched her chest to make sure it still beat inside.

Why, though? She pressed down on her chest. There it went, thump thump thump. *This is ridiculous! He's a nice man, but that's all!*

She entered the kitchen with all the grocery bags. No one greeted her as she placed everything on the counters and started to put the groceries/ingredients in their right places. Checking the stove, she found a small saucepan of milk that wasn't even hot. Whoever put this here didn't even check to see if it was boiling. She turned the stove on and grabbed the coffee from the pantry. Since the milk was here, she could use it for something. "Oh Ma, how many times do I have to tell you? Nothing cooks if the gas is off."

"I'm aware of that!" Swati snapped from behind. "I, uh…I made that milk for the cat.

"We don't have a cat, Ma."

"Oh right, I mean…that's my dinner." Swati grabbed a plate and then went for the saucepan. "I can't chew anything, so I'll eat whatever requires less work for my teeth." She glanced at all the grocery bags. "Did you get everything we need for the dinner party?"

"Yup. I managed to get a little more than normal too. This will be enough to feed everyone for at least three days."

"Three days? I only want them here for one night…provided they stay long enough to eat dinner." Swati sniffed the container of coffee. "And what is this crap? I know you're not putting that in my milk!"

Radha held back all the retorts under her breath and got the milk out of the fridge. "Of course not, Ma. I plan to drink this coffee like this, as dust in a cup."

Swati rummaged through the bags and pulled out the minced garlic. "What the hell is this? You're an adult and you need minced garlic?"

"I have a hard time cutting it, Ma. It's fine. A lot of people can't chop garlic for a variety of reasons. That's why this exists: to help people who have trouble cutting things. We went through this before." Radha took the minced garlic. "Besides, it's mine, not yours. I'm sure I can live eating pre-minced garlic. Anyone can."

"Fine, fine. Take the easy way out." Swati moved out of the kitchen. "I'll be weeping in my bedroom over not teaching you how to cook properly."

Once her mother was gone, Radha grabbed her phone and checked the messages. Andrew replied quickly with a message. **Hello, it's me. Andrew Gardner from the store. I'm waiting to see if you're still fine meeting tomorrow afternoon.**

She texted a quick **'yes'**. Putting the phone to her chest, her body hurt over the broken home she was in. The house's beauty faded around her. This party was all they had to save it. Breathe life back into it. Her hands went to the flowerpots by the windowsill. They hadn't wilted yet, though petals dropped into the dirt. It wasn't just the roses and walls anymore. Everything was dying.

Don't worry. We'll fix you. Radha picked up the petals and buried them in the dirt. *You can't have Andrew though. He's innocent. I don't see anything wrong with his soul. Give me time though. Let me have time with him.*

As Radha finished putting everything away, Veena burst in and raced to the fridge. Her face flushed as she bounced on her heels and flung the fridge door open, cold air blasting into the kitchen. "Oh, please tell me you bought something sweet! I have cravings!"

"Cravings? I thought those stopped at menopause."

"Not that kind of a craving. This is an emergency craving!" Veena pushed everything around the fridge and came across some left-over chocolate mint cake. "Oh, thank God! We have cake! Do we have ice cream too?"

"I, um…I bought a carton of rocky road for us." Radha grabbed the handle before she could open the fridge. "Tell me what the emergency is first. This ice cream was for our guests."

"Well, there aren't going to be enough guests. Eight of the men I asked told me they've got something else to do. I don't know. I think I've lost my appeal to them. I can't pull them." Veena put the cake on the counter and grabbed a knife. "Want a slice? This is going to be a long day."

Radha handed her a plate. "Just a small piece please. Look, maybe they are telling the truth. Maybe they truly can't come. You're just going to have to accept that not everyone can drop everything for you."

"Oh, please. One of them is in the hospital with a bad back and another one is recovering from hip surgery. You mean to tell me they can't come?"

Radha pressed her fingers against her temples. "Usually when one is in the hospital, they can't go anywhere. They're healing, Veena. Besides, the ill and injured are usually not welcome in the house. They aren't going to have energy to do anything. If there are enough people to make the flowers bloom and the cracks, we'll be alright."

Veena got to the freezer and took out the rocky road ice cream. "I suppose you're right but…a little ice cream won't hurt. Not as bad as my feelings do."

"Oh, come on. You asked twelve men out, right? That's four guests right there. Lata managed to ask five of them, Ma found one guy, and I…" She bit down on her lip. Andrew wasn't coming to their party tomorrow. He wasn't welcome here. He couldn't come to the house ever. "Never mind."

"…You found no one, huh?"

Radha took a fork and headed to the table with her slice of cake. "No one that the house could use. I can't feed them. They're not welcome."

"Damn." Then Veena's ears perked up. "But you asked someone?"

"The few people I know. Like you, they're busy tomorrow night with other affairs. I couldn't push them to come." Radha dug into the cake as Veena pushed a bowl of ice cream before her. "Oh no, I don't need that either. This cake will be enough."

"You don't have a date, Radha. That's a bad thing."

"I, um…" Radha grabbed the ice cream and started to eat that instead. "I was going to wait until Lata came in, but I guess I can tell you. You are an expert in relationships."

"Guilty as charged." Veena dumped a load of chocolate syrup and whipped cream on top of her ice cream. Licking some of the sauce and cream off her fingers, she swirled her spoon around. "I can help you attract anyone you want,

Radha. Say the magic word and I will do it!"

"Magic word? Please!"

"Okay!" Veena pushed the whipped cream towards Radha. "Who is the lucky man? Is he good enough for the house?"

Radha swallowed. The house couldn't eat Andrew's soul. She couldn't draw him closer. The lunch date was fine. A party in the house would end his life. Her heart ached at the cracks in the table. Now their furniture was coming undone. "Well, he's not coming here. He's busy."

Veena threw her hands in the air. "You got me worked up for nothing! Pass me the chocolate sauce." She grabbed the bottle of syrup and started to pour it down her throat. "We have a crisis and we don't have enough desserts!"

"Relax. Lata's buying a pie and a cheesecake for the guests."

"I'm not talking about the guests! I'm talking about you!" Veena leaned in close. "You found a man and he's not coming to the party? What's so important that he can't be… you know…one of our special guests?"

"He's heading out of town after lunch tomorrow. Which reminds me…" Radha eased into the next part. "We do have a date at noon. I met him at the store and he's new in town. Asked me where the best place to eat was. And…well, I'm seeing him at the Upper Deck tomorrow."

"So, he's staying long enough for lunch but not dinner?" Veena shook her head. "Oh, sweet Radha. That's not how you rope in a man. You don't take them to places like the Upper Deck! That's where all the men hoot and holler and take off their shirts when their teams win! I should know…I found out the hard way that he wasn't getting naked for me. You know how embarrassed I was then?"

"I can imagine. He's excited over something that's not…

you." Radha smirked. She took another bite of ice cream while Veena fumed. "I'm sorry. You're right about one thing; I'm not used to this. I haven't been on a date in ages. I don't want to jump into anything serious right away. That's why I picked the Upper Deck at lunch time. It's not as loud then. He didn't hate the idea of going there tomorrow. The problem is I have no idea what we're going to talk about. How do I make myself appealing?"

"Well...what are you going to wear? What does he like?" Veena dug her spoon into the ice cream. "What does he do for a living?"

"He said he's a marine biologist who's currently teaching at the university."

"There you go!" Veena slammed her hand on the table. "You're teachers! You can talk about teaching and students and how terrible the whole education system is now! And face it, your line of work is going through hell."

Radha nodded. The layoff messed with her brain over the past few months. Not being able to work or teach others added one more awful layer to a crummy life. No one was hiring teachers, no matter where she went. If they were hiring, they didn't want art teachers. English, math, science... those were needed. Not her. People also wanted librarians but, when she applied for those positions, they wanted someone with a library study master's degree. She didn't have time to go back to school nor the energy to put in any effort.

She swirled the spoon in her bowl. This was her shot. A man showed interest in her. She was stepping back into the world of dating again. Above everything else, he kept that date. He promised to come there tomorrow. Her phone stayed silent the whole time she sat here, but they were on. *Maybe it will be better if he ghosts me. Then, I won't have to worry about bringing him to the house.*

Veena appeared to read her mind. "You don't want him ghosting you. Yes, we want to help the house, but you don't want a broken heart either. You've been through that before many times. Many, many times. Can you handle it again?"

Radha stared into the remains of her dessert. Suddenly, that sweet goodness didn't hit the spot like before. Years passed since moving in with her friends. The other three were always so successful in getting souls. They had jobs and social lives. Veena met men within seconds and lured them towards her home. She'd wine and dine them before leaving them to the house. Lata's sweet nature lured in those who loved those personalities. They found her naïve enough to manipulate, which came in handy when she brought them over. Then there was her mother. Somehow, even her old mother attracted people. Maybe they loved her honesty or sense of humor. Whatever the reason, she had more people in the house than Radha did.

"Well?" Veena prompted. "Can you handle it?"

"No, Veena, I can't handle the rejection." Radha dropped her spoon in the bowl. "I don't know if I can do this. This is the first time in ages that a man seems interested in me. What if I bore him?"

Veena rolled her eyes. "Oh, there's no way you can bore him. He got interested the moment he saw you at the supermarket. You were in what, sweatpants and no makeup? If he likes that, you don't have to do much."

"I'm not talking about appearances! I mean…during the date, what will I say?" She shrugged. "I haven't had work in ages so I can't talk about that. I doubt he'd be interested in the life of a former high school teacher anyway. It's not like I have many hobbies outside of it either. I haven't seen any good movies or gone anywhere interesting. I really have no idea what to say to him."

Veena stared at her for a second. "Boy, you're right. You don't have much going on. The good news is that he might have stories to tell you. He's a marine biologist, right? Well, he'll probably talk to you about sharks or squids or…" She wrinkled her face. "Oh God, you're a boring match made in Heaven."

Radha gave up trying to figure anything out. "Thanks, Veena. It's good to know I'm going into a date completely unprepared."

Lata entered the kitchen right then, carrying some small plates. "Who's going on a date unprepared?" She emptied out the plates full of dead petals. "Oh, you won't believe this! Our flowers are wilting!"

Radha frowned. "We already know that. It's why we're throwing another party. I can't stand waking up to dead flowers on my nightstand every morning. Our poor house is coming apart and I can't figure out how to impress a man!"

Lata stood for three seconds, trying to put everything together. "Well, you've never been able to impress a man, but what does that have to do with the house falling apart?"

"She has a date!" Veena cut in, pushing her bowl away. "She ran into the man at the supermarket and asked him out to Upper Deck. Can you believe that?"

Radha held up her hand. "Don't start about the place, Lata. It slipped out of my mouth. I was just getting everything for our party when we bumped into each other. We exchanged numbers and he told me he was new in town. I offered to show him around. It's not much of a big deal." She clasped her hands together, squeezing them tightly. It didn't sound like a big deal, but she sweated bullets on the inside. Neither could understand how important this date was to her. She picked Upper Deck for its familiarity. She trusted the people working there and liked the food, so at least she knew what to order. If she screwed everything up, at least she could enjoy a side of wings and fries while she wallowed in pain.

"Well, I think it's great you made a date!" Lata exclaimed as she joined in on the sweet feast, scooping up some ice cream for herself. "Come on, tell me all about it! Who is what? What does he like? When are you going to see him?"

"I see him tomorrow for lunch at Upper Deck. It's not a dating place, but we love it!" Radha threw her hands in the air. "As for what he likes, I'm not entirely sure. That's why we're meeting each other. To find out what we like."

"Child's play. Finding out what he likes." Veena murmured. "You want to go the distance, take him to the nearest hotel. You'll find that out as well as other important things such as…boxers or briefs. Satin or silk. What whets his appetite after a long night of…" She giggled before she could finish the sentence. "Oh, why spoil the surprise? You gotta find some of this out by yourself."

Radha lost her appetite then. Her mind never went as far as Veena's did. Veena's family lived in this house for generations, feeding it evildoers who never expected punishment. Somehow, Veena always got them to the bedroom first. A simple night of pleasure right before they ended up in a world of pain. Veena claimed it was to ease their minds. Give them one nice thing before they fade into oblivion. It worked most of the time. The men enjoyed themselves until the moment they became food.

Radha stared down at her phone as another text came in from Andrew. **I hope you made it home safe. I can't wait for tomorrow.**

Veena glanced over her shoulder and gasped. "Oh my goodness, he is missing you already!"

Radha pushed her away. "He's being polite! He wants to make sure I got home safely. He's looking forward to tomorrow. What on there made you think he's missing me?"

"No man sends this many texts to a woman he met an hour ago. He can't stop thinking about you, Radha! You have entered the deepest annals of his mind and you're never clawing out of them. He wants you. Your body, your mind, your soul. You're all that he wants. You might be what he needs."

Radha rolled her eyes. Veena now stood up, one foot on the chair, and gazing into the ceiling. "The annals of his mind? He's only telling me how excited he is, he's not painting portraits of me naked!"

"Of course not. That comes well after the first date." Veena winked at her. "Oh, you relax a little bit! It's your first time dating in a long time. Be yourself…but the exciting part of yourself. Not the boring one."

"I have an exciting and a boring part? How do I know the difference between them?"

"Well, the boring part of you enjoys talking about mundane things. Books. Work. Art. The exciting part of you is the sarcastic part. That's the side that shows men you've got a spicier side. They'll know not to make you angry, but they'll do everything you ask. Show your better side. You'll have him in your hands."

Radha frowned over those words. "So, talking about books and art is my bad side?"

"Radha, look around. How many men call you just to talk about books?" Veena waved at the area. "I don't see any around. Face it. You don't get dates that often. Don't let this one go."

The house shook around them as Radha waved it off. "Okay, you made your point too. I intend to keep him if he turns out to be a great person. If not…well, that's why we live in this house." She ran her fingers down the wall. "Let me just see what he's like. Hope he is a good man. We don't have many of those."

Once more, the house shivered while she leaned back. A date and an upcoming party. Things could not get more perfect for her. If all the pieces fell into place, then maybe he'd be the one. No need to rush, of course, but she prayed he was the one. He was her second chance, and she couldn't blow it.

And as long as the house accepts you, you'll be fine. She patted the walls. *It won't eat you until I tell it to…hopefully, that won't ever happen.*

The house shivered in response. Radha's stomach churned with every little shake it made. A shiver. The house shivered for one reason only: hunger. It starved when it shook. The hunger pangs took over.

It was time to feed.

CHAPTER 6

Radha didn't sleep with the tree branches rapping against her windowpane during the night. With no winds in the forecast, they reminded her of arms reaching out to grab her. Long, black arms stretching into the air. The shadows danced around her room, taunting her to bring in more food. As she rolled from one side to another, the cracks revealed a new message. FEED ME. I'M HUNGRY.

"I know." She whispered as her eyes closed. "I'm working on it."

It didn't stop the shadows, but she ignored them all the same. She fell asleep to nightmares of the house and screaming down the halls. She ran down those halls, chased by an unknown entity, and falling through giant cracks. From one crack, she ended up in another room, and then fell through another one. Every single second of the nightmare was falling and screaming. The relief kicked the moment her alarm buzzed, waking her in a giant sweat.

"Oh God!" She slammed the alarm clock shut and stared up at the ceiling. No giant cracks now, at least none that would cave in. She had a new nightmare to endure: her date with Andrew along with the party. Somehow, she'd have to entertain him with her 'exciting side' while entertaining the guests, hoping they enjoyed her eggplant parmesan. Those were only the tip of all her problems. "Another night, another crack, another pain in the ass."

She stared at her nightstand, wishing never to get up. The roses by her bed wilted overnight. She woke up to more petals turned brown and lying all around the nightstand. She grabbed a fistful of the crumpled petals, her heart breaking as they fell apart. The poor house suffered with no souls inside of it. None of the people they brought satisfied that hunger. They weren't worthy enough. She didn't understand it as none of these people stood out from other victims. They were copies of each other, all terrible in their own ways. Why weren't the previous victims enough? They all committed crimes. They all provided enough for the house. What more could it want?

Checking the clock, she rubbed her eyes and got out of bed. She had about five hours before her date with Andrew and even longer before the party. Her eggplant parmesan would take about an hour to prepare, which she'd handle before anyone came. The only worry was her mother trying to butt in and change her recipe. She'd add something extra or complain about how Radha breaded the eggplant before frying. Maybe she'd hate how much sauce or cheese was put in the dish. In any case, she wasn't preparing ahead of time just so her mother could alter everything. Swati's touch wasn't needed here, especially when her touch was throwing in extra peppers and hot sauce. She tolerated all kinds of spice. She just didn't believe everyone else couldn't do the same.

The date scared her more being the first one in years. She shoved her feet into her slippers and went to the bathroom, ignoring the dead petals leading the way. She crunched them under her weight, the floorboards creaking below her. There it was. Another reminder that the house cravedsome souls. Decent souls. She patted the side of the wall, massaging the new cracks in it.Her finger dug into one, picking away the bits of dirt stuck inside.

"Don't worry. Tonight, you'll be fed." She promised. "I know you're anxious. We're trying to get you food."

She stumbled into the bathroom, washing up and turning on the bath water. With everyone else still asleep, she opted to get that shower before her date. She didn't want to show up with stinking armpits or untamed hair. Andrew deserved to see her in a better light. Or at least see her in a place that wasn't the grocery store.

From the store to...Upper Deck. I really made a great choice there. She scrubbed her body, cursing herself for that place. She liked the Upper Deck in general. Every other weekend, the four of them went down there to have some wings and enjoy trivia and bingo nights. She often won trivia contests, getting them free food and the occasional free merchandise. Lata was still the bingo champion for the over-50 group, winning more prizes than all of them combined. Upper Deck was their place to unwind and forget about the world's troubles. It was a place for friends to be friends. It wasn't the right place for romance with its loud music, blaring TVs, and people occasionally jumping around when their favorite sports team scored.

Not that she could do anything about it. She threw that name out and prayed it would be quiet today. The crowds usually came in around happy hour, which started at four PM. At twelve, they'd get a little privacy to learn about each other. As she rinsed through her hair, the ground trembled below her.

"Oh God, not now..." She turned off the faucet and stepped out of the shower, drying herself off. The shaking continued as she cleaned up and got dressed. This symptom didn't kick in until the house was desperate to eat. Cracks and dead flowers, those were small inconveniences. The house was slightly hungry then. Shanking meant starvation.

"Please hold on." She patted the walls. "Dinner's coming tonight. I'm making eggplant parmesan my way. Just do me a favor and keep Ma away from my ingredients. I know she's going to want to throw her twist into my recipe. Make sure she doesn't."

The shaking stopped right then, a sign that the house understood. She gently tapped on the floor to calm it down. They had that mutual understanding whenever a party was around the corner. The house only shook around her, begging her to feed it. It didn't matter when she fed it. If it got a soul, it stood strong. Their guest list was a good one. People who got away with theft, assault, and murder. They thought no one else cared about their crime. No one paid attention to what they did. Unfortunately, their truth would come out tonight.

We'll take care of this. She reminded herself as she went to the kitchen. The shower worked up an appetite, though she wanted to save herself for lunch.

Radha's heart skipped beats as she drove over to Upper Deck, wondering if Andrew would be able to find it. Nestled in the corner of a small shopping center, only those who lived nearby knew how to get to it. Someone new to town would take their sweet time before finding it since Upper Deck never had a sign out front. Instead, they had a small sign made of lights on their window. The specials scrawled in front often gave them away.

It was no different today as Radha approached it. The sign with today's specials sat out front with their writings. In addition to their usual wings, they now sold egg rolls, tempura shrimp, and a buffalo chicken rangoon. Their beers were also half-off for the day. She smirked at the tiny drawings of little chickens and shrimp in the corners before entering. Entering the restaurant, she stopped right in front of the top scorer board on the side. Even in the low lights, she found her name among the top ten trivia winners and Lata's name written in bold ink for bingo players. The smallest list was the one next to theirs, those who dared to try the Carolina Reaping Sweat and Tears sauce. It required eating ten wings, traditional or bones, drenched in their hottest sauce. They were also only allowed five sips of either milk, water, or their choice of beverage. Those who ate those ten wings without panicking or screaming got their name on the board and won a lifetime pass to the restaurant along with the grand prize of the month. So far, only three people's names ended up on that board.

She checked down at the list to see the grand prize: an all-expenses paid trip for two to the Bahamas. As tempting as it was, she valued her sanity and taste buds too much to attempt that challenge. Sticking to trivia was safer and something she could win. The next trivia night was coming up in two days. If all went well with Andrew, she'd bring him to see her extend her winning streak.

"Hey, there!" She greeted the hostess, a new girl she'd never seen before, who couldn't have been over twenty-one. "I'm meeting somewhere here. Do you know if he's here yet?"

"Let me check..." The girl ran her finger down the list. "I think so. Are you Radha?"

"Yes!" Radha's heart leaped along with her voice. He was here. "I was so worried I gave my guest the wrong directions! It's so hard to find sometimes."

"Don't worry. He's waiting for you." The hostess led her to the table where Andrew sat, in the darkest corner and farthest from the TVs. Somehow, he had the sense to get something away from the crowd up front. He gazed up from the menu as she slid into her chair, leaving her purse and coat hanging on the back.

"Hey! I didn't think you'd make it!" His blue eyes twinkled as she got comfortable. "It took me about ten minutes to find this place. I'm surprised you didn't get here first."

"Oh, parking was a little bit of a pain." She opened the menu to the appetizer section. "That's always been the problem with this place. Great food, but you won't know it if you can't find it. Anyway, I'm glad you were able to get here on time. I'm not the best with giving directions and_"

"Radha." He cut in as she lowered the menu. "It's okay. We made it."

"Yeah." She relaxed her shoulders. "We made it. I know it's not so quiet but..." A loud whoop rang through the room. There they were. That hooting was nothing but the guys at the bar cheering some sports team on. "Sorry. We can go somewhere else if you want."

"Nah, I don't mind it. It's a fun place for everyone. I do like finger foods like this too." He pointed to the pictures of the wings. "You gotta tell me...what's the best kind?"

She cracked a smile at the long list of different sauces. "It depends. How spicy do you like your food to be? Or are you one of those people who can't handle any spice?"

"Oh, I like spice. There needs to be flavor with the spice, though. I don't want it to be like..." He pointed to the very last one. "Carolina Reaping Sweat and Tears. Something tells me not very many people survive eating these."

"Well, no one's died from eating it, but it's really for the experts. Did you see the boards right when you came in? Only three people succeeded in the challenge." She chuckled as she went through the appetizers. "I'm not one of those three."

"I don't think I could do it either. A trip to the Bahamas tempts me, but not enough to eat a bunch of wings drench in Carolina Reaper sauce. I assume that's what they put in it based on the name." Andrew shuddered. "Please tell me there's something that we can both enjoy here."

Radha laughed as she pointed to the specials. "I was thinking about trying the buffalo chicken rangoons as an appetizer. That's good enough spice for you, right?"

"Sounds lovely. I'll let you do the ordering since you know this place so well."

Their waitress arrived to take their drink orders, so Radha threw that Rangoon order in along with a sweet tea. Andrew hesitated over the list of beers before closing it down and taking the same thing. They poured over the menus a little longer as Radha struggled for a conversation opener. This was the worst part: finding common ground. Already, she couldn't talk about careers since they were in two different fields. She knew about the creatures in the oceans, but that was as far as she went. She never went further than a few feet in the sea. Full of inspiration, she painted it many times.

"So…what do you do for fun outside of work?" She played around with the silverware. Immediately, she regretted what she said. Fun outside of work? The man had a job. That took up most of his life as it was. She didn't know how he found time to see her. "I mean…what are your hobbies that aren'tyour work? No, what I meant was...what's your favorite place? No,no, that's…I mean…"

"I get it." He assured her as she calmed down. "I just got into town, so I don't have any favorite places yet. If this place turns out to be good, I might come more often…if you're okay with that."

She picked up the hint then, slowly unwrapping her napkin. Despite appearing charmless, she still caught his attention. "Well, if you like this place, you might also like The Boathouse. They bring in fresh seafood daily." His confused look caused instant regret in her. "Oh, sorry! I forgot! You probably see fish as friends, so you don't eat it!"

"I wouldn't say they're friends, but I'm usually apprehensive with seafood. It depends on the place and their practices. Some places claim everything is fresh, but you look in their freezers and it's a nightmare there." He shuddered. "I'm fine with places like this though. People come here for cheap eats and a good time."

Radha chuckled as she pointed to all the prices. "Well, you'll have a good time, but I wouldn't go far to call it cheap eats. Even the appetizers aren't cheap these days. I'm not sure what place isn't raising their prices now."

"I guess there's only one way to find out." He fiddled with his napkin, dropping the utensils tucked in it. "You must go out and explore, right? You must dig around until you find that right place."

"Right." She relaxed as the rangoons were brought over along with refills of their drinks. The fried food was drizzled with sweet chili sauce and hiding the delicious buffalo chicken mixture called to her. She waited till Andrew took one before she tried it. Crispy on the outside, creamy and spicy on the inside. It wasn't the healthiest item on their menu, but it was worth eating right before the main meal. "Mmmm, what do you think?"

"Delicious." He wiped his mouth with the side of the napkin. "I like the sauce. It's a sweeter sauce than I expected."

"Their infamous sweet chili sauce. They tossed their wings in it too." She took another Rangoon. "Do you mind if I…"

"Go ahead. They gave us six for a reason." He took his second one. "So, while we're here, tell me a little bit more about yourself. I know you like art. I know you can cook based on what you bought. You also appear to be a champion at trivia. Are you good at the music trivia contest they have?"

"Music trivia? Are you kidding? I won three nights in a row!" She joked. "If you really want, you could join my team one night, and we can win a few more nights together. What's your favorite band?"

"Oh, my tastes are eclectic. I can pick anything from Beethoven to the Beatles. In fact, I went to see U2 three times in concert. Once I was in Ireland, the other times were in the US." He pulled apart his Rangoon and checked the inside. "Mmm, not more than chicken, cream cheese, and buffalo sauce."

"Were you expecting something different?"

"No. I just…" He chewed on a small piece of green onion sitting on top of his Rangoon. "I never expected it to taste so good. Anyway, what else is good here?"

"You want more?" Radha chuckled. "Honestly, I haven't heard a bad thing about food on the menu. We come here more times than we like to admit."

The music blasted behind them, nearly knocking her forward while Andrew dropped his Rangoon. Then came a wave of cheers and hooting as the TV blared about a touchdown. Someone yelled for free drinks, which led to more applause. Covering her face, Radha lowered her voice and moved in close enough for him. "I'm sorry about the noise level. It's usually not this bad in the afternoon. I didn't account for the college games though."

"Ah, yeah. It's that time of year." Andrew gazed up as the waitress came over to take their order. "Did you finally decide what you want?"

"Are you a boneless or a traditional wing man?" She

began. "We can do the ten wings, two sauces. Is garlic parmesan and mango habanero fine with you?"

"Let's mix and match, half traditional and half boneless. As for sauces, let's get blue cheese and ranch and those flavors you picked…" He held up an okay sign. Then he changed it to a thumbs up. "Sorry, I forgot I'm not in the ocean. The okay sign is the one you use to show everything's all good."

"I see." She gave him an ok sign. "Is that it?"

"Perfect! So, since I've got you here, I need to know a little more about you." He pushed his plate away. "Aside from you having fantastic taste in restaurants, what else is there to Radha?"

"Oh, I wish there was something exciting about me." Radha chuckled. "I'm your average art teacher…or at least I'm trying to be one. The job market's rough and the art world's even more brutal. Everything is so damn subjective to every single critic out there. You can say it's kind of killed a lot of my desire to create."

"I'm sorry to hear that. If I find out about any jobs at the university, I'll throw word out for you. If you have your resume, I can hand it over to someone that's looking for people. I know we always have jobs at the university." He stared down at the blue cheese dressing. "Are you a ranch or blue cheese kind of gal?"

Radha bit down hard on her bottom lip. She hated revealing that she preferred ranch to blue cheese dressing. The others mocked her for not picking blue cheese, calling her basic for the ranch dressing. She hated blue cheese. There was nothing basic about that. Andrew stared down at her, waiting for a reply.

"Ranch." She finally breathed out. "I prefer ranch."

"Ah, that's great!" Andrew laughed. "I prefer it too

though I'll take both. Everyone's got their favorites. I just wanted to make sure I didn't take anything you liked."

"Oh, we can share!" Radha pushed the ranch dressing towards him. "My mother says I'm weak for not liking blue cheese. I can't help it. I had a bad experience eating blue cheese when I was younger. We went to France once, and my father wanted to try all the French cuisine out there. Let's just say that me, blue cheese, and coffee do not mix."

Andrew snickered behind his chicken wings, nearly spilling sauce down his chin. Radha shuddered over the memory of that France trip. That blue cheese marred her otherwise fantastic memories. Since the mixture messed up her stomach, she steered clear of the blue cheese.Pulling the ranch dressing and boneless wings towards her, she waited until he inspected his food. Garlic parmesan and teriyaki wings. Not a man of spice, which worried her. The one thing her parents emphasized was that her partners needed strong stomachs. If someone crumbled over hot sauce, they weren't worth dating.

Staring down at her mango habanero and hot buffalo sauce wings, she pushed them aside and grabbed a piece of celery. To show she did eat vegetables, she ordered both celery and carrots. He grinned at her as she swirled the stick in her ranch dressing. Behind them, another whoop broke the silence, and then came the laughter. She checked behind her to find people tossing their glasses on the counter and raising their arms. Her eardrums nearly burst once the music boomed behind her. To her side, she spotted a bright pink flyer with musical notes taped up and drawn all around it. The words MUSIC BINGO in bold letters stood out. Oh goodness. Bingo nights were the one night she feared, only because the current champion Lata lost all senses during it. Her fingers dug into the tablecloth over the last time Lata lost. It took hours for Veena to convince the owners not to toss them out.

Andrew followed her gaze. "Music bingo?"

"It's tougher than normal bingo. I've only played it once before. I'm more for the trivia contests." Dabbing her forehead with the napkin, her memory flooded to Lata's screaming and hollering during the games. Her chest hurt over the possibility of getting kicked out next time. The owner warned them to keep Lata calm. Andrew pushed the water towards her, which she grabbed and sipped down. "Thank you. The last time we played this…oh God, it's so hard!"

"We can try that. Maybe I can help you win some of those games." He pushed the napkins towards her. "Let's worry about that later. I have to check my schedule, but I'll call you and we'll see about that bingo night. Maybe I can meet your mother and friends then. They sound like fun."

"I can hardly wait." Her face stretched out, hurting her cheeks. Only one date in, he spoke about meeting her friends and mother. His poor soul would lose it the moment he dealt with their craziness. If her mother didn't insult him, Veena would rub against him, whispering sweet nothings while Lata cluelessly asked questions that she knew the answers to.

"Shall we? I know it's not alcohol, but it's still delicious." He held out a wing. She poked her fork into a boneless piece and brushed that against his. "To a brand-new friendship."

"A brand-new friendship." She tapped her wing against his, slathering bits of mango habanero over his garlic parmesan wing. "I'm sorry. I hope you can tolerate that spice."

Andrew chewed it down, stopped for a second, and frowned, before swallowing. His face changed from confusion to pain and then to delight. He laughed as he wiped his mouth and grabbed his water. Radha relaxed before dipping her wings in the ranch dressing. He didn't cry from the spiciness. That put him one step over other men she brought here. Most ran straight to the bathroom or out the door after the smallest hint of spice.

"That's very good." He chugged his water. "It hits you afterwards, but it's delicious! I can see why you picked it."

"Do you want to try a wing covered in it?" She pushed her plate forward. "It's okay. There's plenty for me to eat."

"Maybe a little later. I need to cool these tastebuds off." He waved his hand over his mouth. "Wow! I'm afraid to try that Carolina Reaping one now! If this is enough to burn my insides, I don't know what that'll do to me."

"Rumor has it, it could set you on fire." Radha sipped her drink. "Though I've never seen anyone spontaneously combust after eating wings. Scream in pain, cry, run for the bathroom, but no flames exploding out of them. Not even with that sauce. Are you sure you're okay?"

"I'm fine." He dabbed the sides of his mouth before going to his wings. "I think I'll stick with mine for now. I drank most of my water over here."

She smiled down into her ranch dressing, dipping carrots and celery into it. He didn't give her a stink-eye upon seeing her drench the wings in it either. Though the heat from the wings hit him, he never got out of his seat or ran for cover. He powered through the mango habanero smears, eyeing the wings in her basket. Grabbing an extra plate on the side, she dumped two boneless wings on it.

"Here you go. I know what you wanted to ask me for them." She handed the plate to him. "You liked it, didn't you? It burned, but you liked it."

"There's sweet with the heat. That helped." He dipped the wing in blue cheese dressing. "Of course, this helps temper the spice too. My taste buds thank you for getting both kinds of dressing."

She went back to her ranch dressing. "My taste buds also want to know what else you like to eat. You can handle some spice, so I could take you to some of my favorite Indian restaurants. Do you love things like tandoori chicken or Gobi Manchurian, or even matar paneer?"

"I love all those things, and then some. I haven't had them in a while though. Making my way around here is like going through a maze. Anytime I think I found a place, I always get lost." He crumpled his napkin, resting it by his plate. "It's amazing that I found this one. I'm more amazed that you came. I thought you'd change your mind.

She swirled up the last bits of ranch dressing with her final wing. A dream. No way could this man be real. He smiled at her, laughed at jokes, and took all her advice. No such man existed. They certainly didn't fall for her. Somehow, he ended up right in front of her. He finished his dish right before her, not dripping sauce or leaving bits of chicken on the bones. He cleaned them out, laying them on a pile. Not a pig when eating. How could she hate this?

Pinching herself, she confirmed she wasn't sleeping. The bright lights, whooping customers in the bar, and spicy food woke her right up. Covering her ears at the next touchdown screams, she relaxed as the waitress came around to check on them. Radha shot her an ok sign while Andrew asked for the check. She went towards her purse, rifling around for her cards.

"Oh no, please don't!" He insisted. "I'll pay for it!"

"You don't have to. I can…"

"I want to." He pulled out his wallet, plucking out a credit card. "You've provided me with such great company. I can't wait to see what else you show me."

"What else?" Radha lowered her gaze. "Are you saying

you want to see me again?"

"I'm that transparent, huh?" The waitress arrived with the bill as he handed her the card. "If you want, you can get a dessert."

"Ah, I think I'm all done now." Radha finished her drink and wiped the small bits off her mouth. "They have a nice, deep-fried ice cream sundae, but I can't put anything else in me. We'll have to get it for another time."

"Like when they have music trivia night?" His eyes went back to the pink flyer on the side. "I saw that when I went to wash my hands earlier. It's music trivia and bingo. Sounds like they'll be playing a lot of old music. What do you think about it?"

"Music trivia night? My friends and mother might go to it." Radha shuddered over those three tagging along. Not yet. She never brought people around to them until a few dates passed by. "Are you sure you'll be okay with that?"

"Of course! The more playing along, the more fun we'll have! It may not be a date like today but…"

"A date?" Radha stopped him as soon as that word popped. "Did you say we're on a date?"

"What else could it be?" He waved at the waitress bringing the card back. "Ah, thank you. I've enjoyed talking to you, Radha. I really want to see more. I need all the help in the world to get around this town."

"Well, I can help with that. I've been here long enough to know all the good places. Are you a fan of museums? What movies do you like? I assume you are a beach person, but what about mountains and lakes? Are you…" With all the questions pouring out, she failed to give him a chance to reply. "Sorry. I got a little curious so…"

"It's fine. Museums, mountains, and lakes are all good. What's the nearest museum here?"

"Um, the history and life sciences museums are right next to each other. We could check them both out." She twiddled her fingers. Her heart raced over the possible answers. Yes, no, I'll think about it? Where was he leading with this? "And the best part is that they're free on certain days! Okay, there are some special exhibits that you might have to pay for. The life sciences museum has an IMAX theater that shows short movies too. If any of that..."

"I'd love to." He cut her off. "That's just my thing."

Her hands dropped on the table. "What is?"

"Going to museums and watching some IMAX movies. I imagine there's a lot to see in them. Even better when they're free." He cracked his knuckles. "Well, I assume the exhibits are free and the movies need tickets."

"You assume correctly. I must check what's available but, if you are really interested..." She reached over and he grabbed her hand, giving it a small squeeze. Every nerve in her body shot up. That jolt woke up every joint in her body and ease all the pains around. "Then yes, I can meet up with you again. Send me a text and I'll tell you all the free times. Also, the movies that are being shown now."

"I'd love that." He didn't pull away despite their sauced fingers. His parmesan garlic ones mixed with her mango habanero ones, not wanting to let go. "I had a really good time today, Radha. I'm hoping that I wasn't boringyou."

"You? I was worried I was too boring! I don't have much going on in my life so..." She let out a deep sigh. "I'm glad you enjoyed it. I'll send you a text about the museum movie times, okay? And next time...I really hope you get to meet my friends."

"I'd love that. If you want, we can meet at your place..."

"No!" She stood up straight, holding out her hands. Andrew leaned away, shock filling up his face. Not wanting to turn him off, she added. "I mean…our house is in the middle of renovations. That might take some time, so it might be better if we meet you somewhere else. I can't tell you when those renovations will be done. The people my mother hired…one minute they're here, the next, they're not. You know how it is."

"Okay, I understand." Andrew motioned her to sit. "We can meet elsewhere. I don't mind if you give me directions ahead of time. I promise I'll be there."

They couldn't let go despite how sticky their hands became. Radha's heart pounded over the possible future dates. He didn't hate her at first sight. He didn't find her boring at all. He wanted to see her again and told her to text him. Her breathing slowed down. She didn't let him go. She couldn't. After years, she finally found someone willing to sit with her and listen. Nothing to take this from her. Not the house, not her own insecurity, nothing. Their shadows on the wall melded together as he gave one more squeeze before pulling back and wiping his hands. He even cleaned up after himself. All of it was too good. More than she deserved. More than she asked for.

She earned this one. She wouldn't let him out of her sight.

CHAPTER 7

Radha returned home to a clean driveway, washed up statues, and a house with very few cracks visible to the naked eye. She didn't spot any of them as she parked the car and walked up to the front door. They faded during her entire date. She stopped to stare at the entire driveway and only found three cars there including her own. None of their guests had arrived yet. It was too early to do anything.

Did they start the party without me? If so, where are the guests? Don't tell me the house ate already! She unlocked the front door, keeping one eye on the demon statues guarding it. They didn't scare most people who came through here. They all figured these were decorations, sometimes speaking to them or even patting them on the heads. Some joked that they held secret powers. Radha didn't believe any of it though, that they held something deep inside. Those empty eyes saw enough souls walk through and not walk out.

She waltzed inside, full from eating lunch and giddy from the lack of cracks in the walls. Closing the door behind her, she touched the walls. "I see you're feeling a little better. Did you get something to eat?"

No answer so she figured it was satisfied with whatever it had. The pictures on the walls stayed in place, which meant no hunger pangs right now. They could cook for the guests without any issues. She left her purse and coat in her room before racing down to the kitchen. Her mother stood in front of the fridge, eyeing everything before her.

"What are you doing, Ma?"

"I'm trying to find where I put my teeth. What do you think?" Swati pulled out a carton of eggs. "I'm starting dinner. Speaking of which, what are you making? Don't tell me it's that eggplant parmesan again. You never make it right."

Radha glowered at her, forgetting all about the ingredients she bought. "What's wrong with making eggplant parmesan? No one has ever complained about it, but you."

"Cause I can't eat it! Your eggplant always turns tough whenever you pull it out of the oven. Oh, and let's not talk about the way you bread that stuff. It's always falling apart because you didn't shake off the excess breadcrumbs!"

Radha refused to argue with her right then. The date with Andrew kept her high above anything else. She found someone who didn't mind her stammering or choices in restaurants. He didn't care that she struggled to find work, couldn't hold down super spicy food, or hadn't been on a date in ages. He liked her enough to see her again. Before her, the roses bloomed in bright red, pink, and yellow on the windowsill. Her happiness spread through the house.

The biggest issue was bringing him home with her. If things went well, that was the logical next step. They'd see each other in more private settings. That also meant revealing more about the house. The guests they brought in never knew anything besides the facts: an 18th century house of stone that reminded them of a castle. It held a garden of flowers and several statues and was nestled far from most of the other houses. They never knew of what lay deep inside. No one knew the house breathed and lived until it was time for it to eat. Then it became too late for the guests. How she could explain any of this to Andrew remained a mystery.

Hopefully, they had a long way before she could bring him here.

It's just one date, Radha. He said he'll call. Don't sweat over it.

"So, why aren't you on your date?" Swati grimaced at a bottle of yellow liquid. "Yeah, this thing's expired. I don't know why you're keeping it."

"Then toss it, Ma. As for my date, I went on it. It's over." She threw another packet of expired food away. "If it's any consolation for you, we had a good time, and we'll see each other again."

"And when is that?"

"We don't know yet. We have to work around our schedules. Well, it's more like he has to work around his schedule. I'm still waiting on answers to interviews." She threw three more packets of expired food. "Now, tell me why the hell we have so much rotting stuff? Four of us, a hungry house, and endless guests, yet somehow we are wasting food."

"How the hell should I know? I didn't make or buy any of it." Swati shook her head. "And your date didn't even walk you to the door?"

"He didn't need to. We met up at Upper Deck..."

"Upper Deck?!" Swati nearly dropped the container she pulled out. "Of all the places in the world, you picked Upper Deck?! I can't believe it. I've raised you and this is how you learned to attract people. Send them to the loudest, biggest sports bar we've got! Just don't tell me a game is going on at the same time. The last visit, I nearly lost my hearing because of idiots screaming in my face."

"It's fine, Ma! We had a great time, and it wasn't so loud today!" Radha threw the last bit of rotting food away. "Look, forget about where we went. The important thing is that we enjoyed it. We had a good time. We'll see each other again.

We just don't know when. It'll be soon though."

Swati wasn't convinced. "I still think you're doing this all wrong."

"You think everything I do is wrong, Ma." Radha stared at the clock on the stove. A few more hours before the guests arrived and she hadn't prepared anything. "I'm going to get changed, then I'll make my dish. Don't touch what I bought!"

"Like I have any use for mediocre ingredients. The maestro works with the very best!" Swati wagged her finger. "You rest your pretty little head, Radha, I'm not touching a thing."

It never failed. Radha stormed towards her room, pushing the door open and throwing herself onto the bed. Ten minutes in and her mother tore into her. She didn't buy that Radha had a date today. So, it wasn't at a fancy restaurant, and he didn't walk her to the front door. He was better than half the men who entered this house. She didn't sense any evil within him. She had to wait until things got more serious between them.

"But will they get serious?" She turned to the walls. "I know you didn't see him, but…it's been a long time since I found someone. I know I'm rusty with dating. I'm not doing too bad, am I?" She pulled herself up and went to change her outfit. "I can't think about that now. Ma's trying to annoy me as usual and she's succeeding. Surprise, surprise."

She turned towards the corner. "Are you sure you don't want to eat my mother?"

The house didn't move at that, but she already knew the answer. Being annoying wasn't a reason to eat a person. Plenty of people becameannoyed for various reasons. That didn't make them a good meal. No, the house wanted a meal it could savor for weeks. Her mother was mostly skin and bones at this point, everything hanging off her rail-thin body.

The house wouldn't last two days if it ate her.

Oh, I can't do it. We need something stronger. She went to the windowsill to check on the garden. Half of the flowers bloomed while the other half started to wilt. The wind swept the fallen petals away as she caught sight of the angel statues around it. Like the house, they also waited for some souls. The cracks were on the walls for now, but if they failed, the artwork started crumbling too. So far, they'd never failed so badly that any statues broke apart. She didn't want to risk that now.

A small knock on the door had her straightening her room up and fluffing the pillows. "Come in!"

Lata pushed the door open and poked her head inside. "Are you busy?"

"Yes, Lata. I take a great deal of time fluffing pillows. I need them extra fluffy, or I can't sleep at night." Radha motioned her to come in. "In case you were wondering, my date is over."

"Well, don't keep me in suspense. How did it go?" Lata closed the door behind her. "Was he nice at least?"

"Oh, he was very nice. We talked about our lives. He's very new to town, so we are going to see each other again. It'll most likely be on Tuesday since he's got a bit of a break during his work. And don't worry, I plan to go somewhere that isn't Upper Deck." She promised. "Though I will say, he did like it. He wants to be my trivia partner sometime, and he'd like to challenge you on bingo night!"

"Well, I'm ready for it! It's been a while since we've been to bingo night!" Lata pumped her fist in the air. "So, I take it that the date was a success? How come you're home so early?"

Radha rolled her eyes. "Why is everyone shocked I'm home early? I only promised to go to lunch with him. We didn't make a big plan. I barely knew him before today. Next time though, I was thinking about taking him to the life sciences museum. Then we can get some lunch when we walk around downtown. It's not too far from his work. In fact, I think it's close to your work as well. I'm sure he'll enjoy all of it."

"He sounds wonderful." Lata eyed Radha for a second before snapping her fingers. "That's it! I get it now."

"Get what?"

"Veena told me that this would be something new for you. It is, isn't it?! It's the first time you've ever been on a date!"

Radha dug her fingers into the bed sheets. "I've been on dates before. It's been a while since my last one, yes, but I'm not new to the dating scene. I'm rusty. I won't lie. I was nervous about the whole thing. Thankfully, Andrew didn't seem to mind. Veena was right. He saw me at my worst when I went to the market. He was fine going to the Upper Deck. I sweated over nothing."

Lata rubbed her arm. "So, when will you bring him here?"

"Here?" Radha turned to the vase full of dead flowers. They cluttered her nightstand, leaving a rather ugly spot in her otherwise spotless room. Combined with the cracks popping from behind her bed, her room reminded her of what was truly at stake. Their home needed some love. The only way to get that was to feed it. Andrew wasn't the food. Judging from his demeanor, he had nothing dark in his past. The house only deserved to eat the worst humans out there. The worse the crime, the tastier the meal.

The latest guests were a motley crew of thieves, abusers, and murderers. All of them got away with the crimes the first time around. They fooled the public with their innocent acts. The police couldn't solve anything, but they didn't count on the house over in the corner. That big house made of stone, a castle on the outside, standing far from the rest of the world. Those rose gardens couldn't feed themselves. Those walls couldn't heal without a little help. Tonight, their home would be fixed with a few new souls. Rotten souls, but they kept the house standing.All of them covered up those cracks, leaving the foundation strong. No strong winds could take this house down. Only a lack of souls.

Lata noted the cracks behind the bed's headboard. "I didn't mean you have to bring him during a party. Just bring him over so we can meet him. Maybe do it when the house is healed and the garden's blooming."

"Eventually." Radha nodded. "I need a few more dates before I can bring him over. Although if you and Veena are desperate to meet him, we can arrange for a big date. It might be at the Upper Deck on trivia or bingo night but…"

"Oh, bring it! I'll whoop his butt at bingo any night of the week!" Lata slapped the top of Radha's bed. "He sounds wonderful, Radha. Are you sure he's telling the truth?"

Radha picked up exactly what Lata got at. "He's still new, so I'm cautious. I don't know his background yet. I don't see any reason to suspect him of anything. The ones we get… they tend to have something off about them. The mask slips after some time. With him, he's not wearing a mask. I know he's sincere about the things he's said."

Lata didn't buy it. "That may be, but you must remember one thing: everything that comes through this house appears sincere. They all talk about the good things they've done. They're never rude to us. They're always good company. What makes you think this man has no secrets? Every person has secrets. It just depends on how dark hissecrets are. Is it something like he forgets to brush his teeth now and then? That's gross, but not a crime. Did he shoplift when he was younger? That's another story."

Radha stopped herself from defending Andrew. For once, Lata made a decent point. The men that came over never showed up as the evildoers they were. They charmed everyone in the room. Never impolite, always willing to help, laughing at all the jokes. They never came off rude to anyone else. Andrew could be like them; a generally nice person who held a dark secret inside. Shaking her head, she turned to her pillows and fluffed them again.

"I guess I won't know that until our next date. I'll check him out." She promised. "I know he works at the university for the time being. If he's on the staff list, then I can find him without any problem. If he's not…well, that doesn't mean a thing. Maybe they haven't put him on it yet."

"That makes sense." Lata patted her on the back. "I hope he is as good as you say. You deserve some happiness in your life."

Radha inhaled. Happiness. Funny how it never came easy to her. Whenever she found a small bit of it, something pulled it away from her. She never held onto any happy moments for more than a few minutes. Those disappeared when unhappy moments pushed their way in. Before she could reply, Lata wrapped her arms around Radha.

"I'll let you get some rest now. You've got some good times coming up."

"You really think so?" Radha perked up. "The whole thing with the good times, is that true? Is my luck turning around?"

"If this guy is the real deal, yeah, I think things are picking up. Hopefully, you get a nice job, and everything will be fine." Lata backed away. "I'll talk to you later, okay? You rest and I'll call you down for dinner."

She lay in bed as the lights dimmed before cutting off.

The Alexa app went off too early though she didn't bother asking it to come on. Two dates wrapped her in a love-filled haze. Strange how one man swept her away. All because he ran into her at the store. He found something in her. Not that she knew what it was. She lacked charisma. Whenever she got feedback for any of work, they always pointed out her lack of charm. She didn't wow people with her art. She threw on colors and shapes though no heart. Those words stabbed her, yet never offered any useful feedback. How could she fix her work if they didn't offer help?

Interviews. She opened her phone to find another rejection. No helpful feedback, just that they found someone else better for the position. Of course. Somehow, they found a person who fit their role of a pottery teacher. Maybe they had more experience, yet it didn't heal her pain. She found love and lost a job opportunity at the same time. If her mother saw her now, she'd come up with a quip, something snarky. Radha couldn't win at everything.Radha was a bit of a failure compared to the rest of her siblings. Why didn't she go to medical school like her brothers? Why didn't she marry a doctor or engineer like her sisters? Why did she screw her life up? Those quips haunted her for many nights. Hopefully, once she got to meet Andrew, Swati would finally ease up on her.

Scrolling through messages, she found a few of them from her siblings. All of them asked how she was, if she needed anything, and if she wanted to see them. She sent a quick "I'm fine, talk to you tomorrow" back at them. Her mind drifted to Andrew again. No awful deeds slipped off him. Most of their guests reeked of horrible secrets when they entered the house. They sealed their fate with that scent. Not Andrew. His cologne swam in her mind.

Despite the date, he didn't inspire anything. No flames,

no paintings, no art that displayed charm. All those colors and shapes floated around the canvas. One day, she'd get her inspiration back. She'd create that work of art to provoke minds and capture hearts. She'd make that one piece of art that could hang in a museum or even in the dark halls of this house. She wouldn't hide them from view. Heading over to her drawer, she found all her paints, brushes, and clothes covered in stains. She forgot she locked these away after she stopped painting. Maybe it was time to start back and create something new. Let Andrew lead her around the canvas and build a new vision.

Finding a blank canvas in the corner, she took her art supplies, laid out the dirty cloth she sat on, and prepped everything. Within seconds, visions flew in of new ideas. Her hands worked away as she squeezed out paint, mixed colors, and washed her brushes. Bit by bit, the painting came into view as her brush ran across the canvas. Colors popped out, shaping into the form of waves. Blue and green, she sparkled some purple and red within them. The waves crashed onto the shore, leaving the white foam against the sand. It fizzled on the ground as the waves rolled in and out. An ocean. She painted another ocean, but one that could hang in a museum.

Where is this coming from? I've never painted this way before. She splashed more colors over the painting, forming darkened clouds rolling into the blue skies. She pictured Andrew out in the middle of this ocean, boat rocking as he struggled to grab the sails. His feet planted despite all the water pouring in, he kept that boat from capsizing in those rough seas. Although she didn't paint him, he was there.

"Maybe I was wrong." She stepped back to admire her new work. Bright blue ocean waves crash on golden sand, leaving its white foam behind. A blue sky with gray clouds rolling to signal danger ahead. Boats off in the distant sea, their steam leaving a trail behind. She didn't bother putting other humans in it, but her heart swelled at the sight. Her best work in a long time. Maybe others might find it simple and uninspiring. Not her. So many lesser paintings hung up on the museum walls. Hers deserved to be there too. Behind her, the house shook and whispered, reminding her she was never alone here. The cold air on her neck caused every hair to stand up, prickling her skin with the next few words.

I guess I'm wrong. He inspires me too.

CHAPTER 8

The party fell into full swing the moment Radha stepped out of her room. Everyone arrived on time as Veena let them in and Lata took their coats. Not that anyone needed them afterwards. Their belongings always went into the feeding room with the rest of them. Every trace vanished off the ground once the house healed itself. They all laughed as Swati led them into the living room for some refreshments. Radha breathed in and out as she stepped down, reminding herself not to blow it.

Within the first fifteen minutes, she pretended not to see two people getting swallowed by the floor. They didn't get a peep out before the ground opened and swallowed them whole.. She only wished she waved at them, while getting a little pleasure from watching them go. It started. Even before they got to dinner, the house began its feast. To the side, she found the cracks forming a small sentence: **THANK YOU.**

"You are most welcome." She whispered, ignoring the group around her. Every party started out this way, loud and lively. None of them would notice the two that disappeared. They barely got out a hello before going into the unknown. Wandering around, she smiled at the statues that were prepared to grab a few more people. They didn't move until Veena began her tour. Maybe they'll start early tonight. The sooner these creeps went, the sooner she'd go back to more important things in her life.

For the sake of the party, she promised not to look at her phone or text Andrew. The party mattered more. Sipping on her wine , she pushed him out of her mind as a few of the guests leaned on the walls. The house didn't take them in right then. It waited for a better moment to come back. She chuckled into her glass as she placed her hand on the wall. Around her, the roses went into full bloom while some parts of the house healed. So far, so good.

Veena appeared at the doorway, calling everyone's attention. "Thank you for being here! I just wanted to let you know that dinner is now served! If you would just follow me, we can get started."

Oh good, dinner. The real fun's about to begin. Radha stood behind several guests and peered over her glass as the walls began to pulse, taking in two more people. Neither got a second to react before they blended into the house. One let out a little squeak, but that died the moment someone else stepped on the creaky floorboards. She smirked in the direction of an angel statue. *Tonight's the night they pay.*

As she went down the dimly lit halls, she stepped on several wilted petals. The low lights and stone walls normally shook up the normal person. If any of the remaining guests saw them, they didn't mention it. Most found the house cool and interesting, chatting about the statues and flowers around. They wanted a tour of every single room, to admire all the vaulted ceilings and shiny statues, and to hear the history. Veena shook her head whenever they asked to go into a new room before the tour.

"Not yet! The tour hasn't started!" She jogged to the front of the group and pushed open the kitchen door. Delicious smells wafted in as the guests went around the tables, grabbing the plates and taking different fried snacks, mixed nuts, and small cups of tea.Radha waited until most had their meals before getting a plate for herself. Though they'd eat in the living room, everyone was to get their meal first.

"And if you have any drink preferences, you can ask Veena to make you one. She's an expert at them!" Lata chimed in.

"It's not the only thing I'm an expert at." Veena winked at them. "Help yourself to whatever you like, then take it to the living room. We'll get a chance to know each other right before the tour."

Get to know each other? Funny, she brought that up when none of them bothered with it. Radha didn't bother to learn the names of the new guests. Some were friendly with her as they handed over their coats and hats. They smiled at her, not knowing that they'd never leave these walls. They acted like her friends, kind and polite, but she could only fake her feelings. She waited for the house to start taking in more guests. In this busy area, it couldn't grab anything as they swerved around and ducked to get their food. Not yet.

Time passed while Rahda daydreamed away. She didn't flinch when two guests behind her suddenly disappeared into the walls. One let out a tiny yelp, but no one else heard them. She tuned it out at the sight of Andrew's text. **Thank you for a lovely time. I double-checked my schedule, and I can't make it Tuesday afternoon. A meeting popped up that I must be at. However, I'm good for Wednesday afternoon. Could we meet then?**

Tuesday, Wednesday…it never bothered her. He wanted to go out again. She quickly replied. **Wednesday is fine. I thought about going to the life sciences museum first, then we could get lunch. Does that sound fine? We can meet around noon if that works.**

She ignored the guests around her, making her way to the living room without any snacks. Her mother occupied herself with juggling all the food, forgetting about Radha and her contributions to dinner. She paid no attention to the foil-wrapped tray in the corner. Her eggplant parmesan came out beautifully. Not a single breaded part of the eggplant fell apart, and the cheese melted all the way through. Even the sauce turned out beautiful, not too sweet, or acidic. Her mother couldn't complain if the rest of the guests enjoyed it.

Her phone went off again with another reply from Andrew. **All of that sounds wonderful. If you could send me the address, that would be great. I need to know where to park. You can pick the place for lunch since I'm still figuring out my way around the area.**

He certainly loved writing long tweets. Not that she minded. The more he wrote, the more anxious she grew. The Upper Deck didn't bother her since they both enjoyed the relaxed atmosphere. The restaurants downtown were far more expensive, built for people who could afford a three-course meal for two hundred dollars. She rarely kept that much in her bank account, let alone carried it with her. The few cheap places weren't fit for romantic dates. Like the Upper Deck, they appealed to the average person coming in for good times with friends, cheap eats, and good beer. Before Wednesday, she had to do research: find a good place to eat that offered a variety of food and reasonable prices. Glancing up for a second, she caught one guest getting hauled off by the statues, never getting a second to scream. It served them right.

One less creep in the world. I think I can sleep knowing that.

Lata came over with a plate of snacks and a cup of ginger ale. "You looked a little hungry. Why are you hanging back here anyway?"

"Oh, it's…" Radha stared down at her phone. "Andrew's texting."

"Texting?" Lata nearly dropped the plate. "This is serious! He's willing to talk to you after a date!"

Radha ignored that last bit and stared at the latest text Andrew sent. **I got word that my late afternoon meeting was moved to the following week. By any chance, are you free tomorrow night?**

Her hands shook over the message. Another date. One coming tomorrow night. Her entire schedule was free, but it didn't bother her. Andrew wanted to see her again even after meeting up at a place like Upper Deck. Despite the shouting in the other room and awkward conversations, he wanted to go on more dates with her. She couldn't answer him right away. Her mind wanted to, her heart told her to send that yes, but her hands didn't budge.

Lata stared over her shoulder, gaping at the latest bit of news. "Well? What do you want to do?"

"Do…Do you need me in the house tomorrow?" Radha bit down on her lip. "The party's happening, I'm not sure what to say. I want to go out…"

"Then say yes! What's the problem?"

"I…" She closed her eyes. "I'm afraid. What if I mess up this time around? I have never had this many dates with one person in a short amount of time. We usually wait a bit. I saw him today, he wants to see me tomorrow, and we're making plans for Wednesday afternoon. That's a lot of dates."

She stared down at the message, the cursor blinking for an answer. A part of her tempted to write no, she couldn't make it. Her heart told her otherwise. A date night. This time, they'd go somewhere nice and romantic. There were plenty of affordable places for them in town. She'd give him a list and let him choose. Her fingers stopped trembling when she sent the next message. **I'll check my schedule, but I think I'm free. I know a few places in town that are good for dinner. Do you have a preference in food? Italian, Mexican, etc?**

Lata checked out the message. "So, I guess you want to go. It doesn't matter what you say, your heart is making all the decisions."

"I guess it is." She nodded towards the guests mingling nearby. "I'll see what he says. Check on our guests and make sure they're comfortable. Ask if they need any refills on drinks. We want them to enjoy themselves."

Lata nodded. Tonight was a night of enjoyment. Their guests ate, drank, and laughed amongst themselves for the next few hours. Before the house got its meal, they needed to eat theirs. The best victims were the ones who never suspected a thing. They hung around long enough for the house to satisfy its appetite. Relaxing on the couch, she put the phone aside and tried to eat some of the cheese balls Lata made earlier.Thankfully, some remained on the plate.

The tour had yet to start, yet already six guests went missing, blending into the house. The others suspected nothing, laughing and moving around the house. The statues attempted to grab them but failed this time. The house became impatient. On the wall, she spotted another message in cracks. **THEY'RE MOVING TOO FAST.**

"I know." She patted the wall. "Be patient. It'll be over for them soon."

In the corner, she spotted her mother stuffing a few of those cheeseballs in her pockets. A guest attempted the same and was swallowed by the ground as they tried to leave. She tried her hardest not to laugh. No wonder Lata ran out of them at every party. The culprit stole them when no one watched her. Radha ground her teeth, wondering what to say. Not that her mother would listen to her. At eighty, Swati figured the whole world catered to her now. Whenever she woke up, it was a day to do whatever she wanted. If that meant stealing cheeseballs for herself, so be it. Nothing Radha told her sank in with her. She went past that age of being told what to do and following the rules.

Her phone went off right then, so she grabbed it and checked his answer. **I'm good with any of those. What's the best place around here? And if you can come, is six a good time?**

Oh God! He wanted more information. Every little thing coming from him, he meant with sincerity. He liked her enough to go out with her again. Her mind scrambled for a decent place close to home. The only thing coming to mind was Carlota's Italian Bistro, only ten minutes from the house. She went there only two times and enjoyed the food as well as the vast drink menu. The atmosphere led to a good experience, be it romantic or casual. Decent food, nice atmosphere, and non-astronomical prices. Andrew wouldn't hate this.

Quickly, she sent him the name. **Let's try Carlota's Italian Bistro. It's not far from the market we met at. Like five minutes away.**

He wrote back right away. **Perfect. So, what are you doing tonight?**

Her mind ticked away at possible excuses to give him. If she told him about the party, he'd want details. Perhaps he'd ask to come over. Only one date in, he'd want to know all about the party she was at. She could lie and tell him she went to the store. Maybe she went out with her friends. She crawled into bed early with a good book. All those excuses were ones she used before.

"Are you going to sit here all day, or are you going to join the rest of us in the land of living?"

She tucked her phone away, moving to the side to let her mother sit down. "I have a headache, Ma."

"Oh, come on! I didn't talk to you until now!"

"No, I mean…" Radha rubbed her temples. "This whole night is giving me a headache. I'm not in the partying mood. I know it's necessary but…"

Swati checked out two men standing in the corner. "I can't say I blame you. These are the most boring guests we've had in ages! All they do is talk about their work and bowling! I have heard everything I can possibly hear about bowling!"

Radha shrugged. "They're talking about what they do and what they like to do. What's wrong with that?"

"Bowling balls aren't that exciting at all. I was relieved when a few of them disappeared." Swati stared down at the cup of ginger ale she held. "For me, they're all heavy balls you throw down an aisle and knock down pins. How much deeper can you get with that?"

"People find something interesting in boring things, Ma. It's how they make connections. I mean, you might not find art interesting, but for me, if someone asks me my opinion on Picasso's *Guernica,* I can go on for ages about it."

"I know that. You've done it before to me." Swati grumbled. "All because I said I didn't find it so special. I still don't."

Radha shook her head. "The point is that people find common ground on all kinds of things. Let them talk about bowling balls." *It's probably the last thing they'll ever talk about.*

Swati noticed Radha's distant look, no longer focused on their guests. Even as a few more disappeared into the walls, she didn't smirk or glare at them. She stared down at the phone as another text rolled in. "He's still talking to you, huh? You didn't blow it!"

"Why would I blow a date at Upper Deck, Ma? It's a place for people to be casual. He enjoyed it very much, and he's even willing to come during trivia and bingo nights. I was thinking that he might like to meet you then."

"That's all good, Radha. Just keep him away from Lata during bingo." Swati shuddered. "We don't want to chase him off when you finally get a decent date!"

"Relax, Ma. It's music bingo. Lata tends to have more trouble with that." Radha glanced up as the remaining guests erupted in laughter. Veena sat between two guys with their arms around her, teasing them and giggling at every word. Lata regaled a few more people with her stories, everyone captivated by what she said. They both held all the charm in the world. Radha couldn't understand what Andrew saw in her that he didn't see in women like them. She itched to reply to his text, but didn't bother. Swati's eyes locked on her.

"You can wait to text him later. I know you're excited, but we have bigger things to take care of." Swati's gaze rose towards the ceiling cracks as she brushed dust off her shoulders. The message FEED ME appeared before them. "I just got this on me. The roof's gonna cave in."

"Don't worry, Ma. It's a little dust on you." Radha blew off the bits of ceiling that fell on her shoulder. "Granted, it's more dust than normal but..."

"More than normal? Most ceilings don't fall apart, Radha!" Swati snapped. Fortunately, not a single person in the room heard her. Veena had everyone wrapped around her while Lata offered to bring over more snacks. "Why can't you be like the other two? They are..." Swati lost her words at Veena giggling while a man regaled her with stories.

Then came Lata bringing over root beer instead of ranch dip for their veggie sticks. "Never mind. Pretend I never asked that question."

"We'll be fine, Ma." Radha got rid of the last bits of dust. In the distance, two more people faded into the walls. "Just stay put, and don't blurt random things out. We don't want to scare anyone."

"When have I ever scared anyone away?"

"Oh, let me count the ways…except we don't have all night to do that." Radha rolled her eyes. Not wanting another migraine, she got up to get a drink, ignoring another guest getting grabbed by a statue. "Look, Ma. I need to get some fresh air. I'll be out in the garden. Do you want anything to drink?"

"Eh, I'm good over here. Don't stay out too long. The show's gonna begin."

Radha smirked as she went to get some ginger ale. The show was about to begin. It wasn't much of a show since they never saw anyone getting eaten. Just screams fading away as the house devoured its dinner. After those ended, they cleaned up the kitchen before heading to sleep. The house healed itself with the new food while they prepared for the next day. A crazy night that ended quietly. She expected nothing less.

As she poured herself a glass, her phone went off. Andrew texted her again. Curious, she checked it out while taking sips of her ginger ale. **Are you busy tonight?**

The smart answer was yes, yet she found herself writing something else. **I'm free to talk if you want. I'm just taking a break.**

Grabbing her glass, she headed to the garden and found a cracked bench to sit on. The grass around it withered, though it stayed in place. Her feet crunched the blades as she placed her glass next to her and started writing more texts. **Are you doing anything exciting?**

He took seconds to reply. **Grading a lot of papers. I'm not sure if you consider that exciting.**

It's more exciting than my current life. She started to text that out before erasing it and writing something else. **Tell me something about your work. I imagine you've seen all kinds of things.**

That did it for him. As soon as that message went out, he replied in detail with every bit of his research. It turned out that his area of expertise were whales, humpbacks in particular, though he loved manta rays and sea turtles as well. He saw many of them in person and loved to play with them. He launched into a long story about his encounter with a friendly lemon shark. The more he went on, the more she wished her life contained similar excitement. In no universe could she get close enough to any kind of shark. She only saw them in aquariums along with the sea turtles and rays. How could she compare to that?

You have a fun life. I wish I could say the same thing.

The conversation didn't turn him away. **Ah, not everyone enjoys my kind of work. It's hard and it takes time to get used to the ocean. However, I do enjoy my quiet nights too. I enjoy just walking around town. Nothing too crazy.**

Walking around town…I like walking around town. She sent him a few more messages about her rather dull life. Bingo and trivia were as exciting as she got. He sent a laughing emoji while she confirmed their next date. Carlota's would be a new experience for both. She'd try a new place, and he'd see another part of the town.

"I can't wait." Her hand fell on the bench, noting the smoothness under her palm. Curious, she checked under it to find no cracks. Veena ran through the tour without her. Everyone who survived the earlier would disappear. Anything there before now, had faded out. She couldn't hear any screams, but the ritual went through. Their were no more guests. Their home no longer fell apart. Next to her, the rosebush came to life with bright red roses. Sniffing one, she admired the beauty around her. This garden, her home, it was going to be fine. Andrew wasn't turned off yet. He sent more messages about his adventures as well as some photos. She admired one of the friendly lemon sharks who eyed the camera. No wonder he liked her; she didn't fear him. She didn't barge into the camera or bare her teeth out. She touched her phone screen as if she could pet the shark. Andrew was brave enough to get this close; maybe she could be brave enough to keep this relationship going.

Leaning back, she let the statues heal themselves around her as flowers grew and grass turned green again. The house ate quicker than expected, so she had time to take it all in. Tonight was a good night, a perfect night. She no longer feared the future as she found someone.

"I think I'll be okay." She whispered to the red rose in the nearest bush. Careful not to prick herself, she held it and took in all the fragrance. "I'm definitely going to be okay."

CHAPTER 9

While the party went by quickly with no guests surviving, the upcoming date to Carlota's became another story. It snuck up on her as she struggled to find something to wear. She couldn't show up in her usual clothes this time. Carlota's demanded sophistication. The very least she could do was change jewelry and fix her hair. She made sure not to ask her mother for anything as Swati would have one million ideas. If Radha asked for advice, she never got it. Only criticism on what she currently had. As a result, she turned to Lata and Veena for help. Those two knew what men liked.

Radha rummaged through her jewelry box for earrings that matched. She held up one golden hoop earring and one pearl earring, wondering why they got put together. Putting them close to her ears, she turned to Veena and Lata. "Well, what do you think I should get? The golden hoops or the pearl ones?"

"The hoops." Lata nodded. "They'll sparkle against your hair."

Veena shook her head. "There's nothing that'll sparkle in that nest there, Lata. We want to be more subtle. The pearls will accentuate those giant earlobes."

Radha frowned. "What the hell is wrong with my earlobes?"

"Nothing! We just don't want to draw too much attention

to them. If you wore those hoops, they'd mistake you for a cow or something."

There it went. Even though she didn't ask her mother, the annoyance came back. Asking her friends for fashion advice always led them to criticize Radha's appearance. She didn't let them get under her skin since she heard worse as a child. She still wanted to look perfect for her date. "You know what, let me skip these two earrings and find something else. Maybe I won't wear any earrings at all."

"Oh no, you have to!" Lata insisted. "You want to appear beautiful and sexy, right? He's seen you at your worst. Show him your best."

Radha's hands went through the jewelry until she finally came across a pair of diamond earrings. Her wedding earrings. That was the last day she wore them. Worth almost a quarter of a million dollars, she never saw a reason to put them on. Not during parties or job interviews. Nothing prompted her to bring them out and try them on again. Yet amid the jewelry mess, this was the only matching pair she came across.

Holding them up to her ears, she squinted as the light reflected off the studs. She wasn't a young bride anymore, but they stood out all the same. They sparkled against her thick black locks, now dyed thanks to an upcoming date. Her mother insisted she style her hair and hide all the gray bits. She appeared twenty years younger thanks to that and the makeup hiding her wrinkles and dark spots. No doubt about it. She was wearing these earrings.

"These don't make my earlobes look gigantic, do they?"

"They're perfect." Veena approved. She leaned in closer, admiring the cuts in the diamond. "Aren't these your…"

"They are." Radha started to put them on. "I know I haven't worn them in ages. They have so much sentimental value to them."

"Well, now's as good a time as any to put them back on. It sounds like you're smitten with this man." Lata pulled Radha's hair back to help her fasten the other earring. "There we go! You look ready for this date."

"Not yet." Veena sprayed some perfume around Radha's neck and behind her ears, covering her in a lilac scent. Radha coughed, waving the perfume cloud away. "Now you're ready! You smell like a woman on the prowl, ready to pounce on your prey like a hungry panther!"

Radha finished putting on her lipstick. "I only want to impress one man tonight; I don't want to eat him. It's the house's job to eat others. Speaking of which…" Her eyes fell on the vase of pink roses, now in full bloom. Last night's meal healed their home. The garden also brightened up with lush grass and trees covered in thick, green leaves. Even their flower buds popped up. Their home would be fine for the next few days. The last couple of guests were an unsavory bunch with multiple crimes in their names. The house would chew on them for some time.

"I think we don't need another party anytime soon." Radha got up to check the water in the vase. Even if the house drank most of it, the flowers stayed in full bloom. "The house seems happy."

"It is happy. Aren't you?" Veena pressed her hand against the smooth walls. "I think things are turning around. My home's standing and Radha's got a date. The only thing to make it better is if Radha gets a job."

"I'm trying every single day, Veena. Trust me." Radha's eyes fell on her folder with all the jobs she applied to. So many interviews and not a single call back. A part of her wanted to create some new art to pass the time. Maybe it was her portfolio that didn't inspire anyone. On the outside, the paintings were fine. Most people liked looking at them. Yet when she stared at her work, she got nothing from it. No spark, no inspiration. It didn't surprise her if this turned all the interviewers off. "Maybe it's high time to create something new. I don't know what."

"Well, let the date inspire you." Lata suggested. "You said this guy works in the ocean, right? Make some ocean pictures!"

"Ocean pictures?" Radha chuckled. "Oh, I don't know. The ocean is so vast and so much of it remains unexplored. There are so many seascapes that look the same. What could I do to make mine stand out?"

"I don't know…paint the sea red to make the Red Sea?"

The question didn't warrant a response, but an eye roll. It explained a lot though; her paintings were banal. She had no life in them because her own life had nothing exciting in it. Outside of the house and the parties, she couldn't paint anything that anyone wanted. The house shivered around her. It still chewed down the previous guests, though it warned her that this wasn't enough. It wanted more.

Radha got up to stroke it. "Relax. You got a meal now. It'll keep you full for a while."

"Indeed. Those were some true scumbags we dragged in." Veena blew on her fingernails and patted the walls. "You gotta be patient. I can't change my underwear that quickly. I need time to bring in the main courses!"

"Speaking of main courses, what are you planning to have over there?" Lata helped Radha pull on her coat. "I heard they have a really nice chicken alfredo."

"Oh, I don't know. I barely got a chance to look at the menu. I doubt I'll be able to eat much. I'm so nervous." She pressed her hands against her stomach to stop the butterflies. Strange. No other man gave her these butterflies before.

Something about Andrew's calm and sincere demeanor got them fluttering. They tossed around her stomach, distracting any sane thoughts inside her mind. How could she get excited? If they got serious, she'd have to tell him the truth about the house. Worse, she'd have to bring him here. How would he react to a house that souls? This house survived by eating the souls of evil people for ages. He'd never buy that it was a living thing. Or worse, he'd buy it and dump her within seconds. Maybe he'd turn her into the police. The very thought of spending the rest of her life in jail forced those butterflies to stop fluttering.

"Are you okay?" Veena pressed down on her shoulder. "You're going on a date to an Italian restaurant. You don't have any other plans, do you?"

"No, but…" Radha remembered the house's hunger pangs. "What if he wants to come home?"

"Then I say you got lucky! What's the problem?"

"No, what if he comes…" She waved around the room. "We don't live in a normal house, Veena! It's alive! I can't bring him when the house is hungry."

"It's not hungry right now. The house only eats those it deems worthy of eating. If Andrew's got no dark secrets, he's okay to come over." Veena massaged Radha's back to relieve the stress hidden there. "Now forget about the house. Have a good time. That's why you're going out right; to get away from the craziness."

Of course. She didn't need to introduce Andrew to her friends and mother right now. It was only their second date. He wasn't the kind of man to rush into anything major. Granted, they were going out again rather soon, but she didn't mind. She didn't have much else going on in her life. No other interviews came in and her inspiration ran dry to create any new art. She couldn't blow her chances on the first man interested in her after a long time. Taking a deep breath, she twirled around to show off her dress.

"Do I need to make any changes?"

"Oh, you look great!" Lata clapped her hands. "I hope you have a great time!"

"Just relax, Radha. You're going to be fine." Veena handed over her purse and the car keys. "Be yourself. That's what he loves."

"Just don't sleep with him!" Swati yelled from the other room. Radha's relaxed mood quickly dissolved one of her nerves. Her mother knew what was happening and had to throw her two cents in. Radha had no intention of getting in bed with Andrew after the second date. She didn't jump into the sack with anyone who came around. For her, a relationship required more than great sex. She wanted someone on an intellectual level, someone who could discuss art and books with her. She wanted a person who liked museums, movies, and spending quiet nights at home. The love making afterwards.

"Of course not, Ma. I don't sleep with men unless I want them to die!" Radha snapped back. "If that was the plan, wouldn't I bring them here?"

"I'm just saying. It's only the second date. Don't blow it!"

Veena waved her off. "Go on! Go have your fun!"

Radha calmed down the moment she got in her car and revved it up, backing out of the driveway. The house would be there with all its walls intact. The cracks on the outside sealed up last night and more roses bloomed in the garden. All traces of their victims went away. They erased out of the driveway and from people's minds. No one came looking for them. No one missed them. All that remained were probably their bones deep in the basement of the house.After some time, they disintegrated as well.

As she got onto the road and flipped on the radio, Radha rolled down the windows to let cool air in. The workday traffic died down, so it became smooth driving for the rest of the way. She ignored the butterflies as the music cleared her head. Carlota's Italian Bistro came into view within minutes, the bright lights greeting her as she found a parking spot close by. For a Monday, it had a decent-sized crowd eating inside. She grabbed her things, locked the car doors, and headed inside to where the hostess stood. The waiting room had no one inside, but each table had a few people chatting and eating. Small candles placed in the middle of tables added a nice little touch to low lit rooms. She admired the fake grape leaves and vines wrapping themselves around the sides of the doors. Above her, some popular Italian songs played so she swayed to the beat despite not knowing a single word of Italian.

"Hello, I'm meeting a gentleman over here. His name…"

"Oh, I know!" The hostess looked down her list. "You must be Radha. He's waiting for you in the dining room. Please follow me."

She found Andrew sitting at a table in the corner, staring out the window. He dressed a little better now in a gray suit with a blue tie covered with waves. That tie was the only bit of color making him stand out from the rest. Such a good man. The house wouldn't want him since he had no darkness in him. Everything he told her was the truth. Maybe this one was it. He was the one she waited for.

Oh, please don't screw up. She prayed though unsure if the prayer was for him or for herself. She came across men like Andrew, always good and true. Yet somehow, they never worked out. They had their dates, they had good times, it always went in the right direction. She never pinpointed the wrong moments, but they happened. Something happened to keep them away from her. If they weren't guests, they would disappear from her life.

Not this time. Now she had Andrew, she vowed to keep him safe. The house couldn't eat him. No one could chase him out. The more time she spent with him, the longer they'd know each other. He'd see she wasn't some lonely, poor art teacher struggling for work. Maybe true love would spark inspiration back in her. She'd create art that pleased everyone, sent messages out that the world understood.

"Hey there!" He got up and pulled out her chair. "I hope you didn't have trouble finding any parking. I'd pick you up myself, but…"

"It's all right!" She cut him off as she took off the coat and hung it on the chair. Sitting down, she hung her purse off the back of the chair. "We're still getting to know each other. There will come a time when you'll pick me up from the house. The problem with my place is that it's so hidden in the back of town. Tons of trees, long roads, no other houses around. It's not exactly in the friendliest neighborhood either."
"Oh, that's fine! I've lived in all kinds of neighborhoods. Big ones, small ones. I've seen everything." He nodded towards the wine glass. "I didn't order our drinks yet because I wasn't sure what kind of wine you drink. Or do you not drink alcohol at all?"

"I drink alcohol!" She held up the wine list and almost died at the sight of the prices. Even for wine, these went beyond her budget. "Um, I'm not sure what to take. I prefer red wines, but everything here is so…"

Andrew reached over and squeezed her hand. Her pulse quickened as his fingers gripped her wrist. All words disappeared from her. "Relax. I know it's expensive, but I'll be paying for it. You pick any wine you want. Any of the red wines or white ones or…"

"You pick it." She closed the drink menu. "I'm good with any red wine. I'm more curious about their food. I've heard it's good but..."

She grabbed the main menu, and her heart almost stopped when she laid eyes on the appetizers. Her bank account couldn't afford to eat here on a regular basis. Just a plate of vegetables and a dip cost almost thirty dollars. She tried not to let the discomfort show on her face, yet her mouth twitched. Even a simple plate of chicken alfredo was too much money. Her entire teacher's paycheck from last year couldn't pay for a week of food here.

Andrew noticed her mouth moving about, and he lowered the menu. "I know it's a lot. This isn't a place you visit, huh?"

"I don't come here at all. Places like Upper Deck are more of my speed. And better for my bank account." She chuckled as she ran her finger down the list. "Do you have any idea what you want? Any appetizers?"

"I was thinking we could get our entrees and forget the appetizers. There's nothing there that I haven't had before. And something tells me the appetizers here will beat the ones at Upper Deck." Andrew went down the list. "Oh goodness, the price for prime rib! I think I'll keep it simple and take the baked rigatoni instead. What do you think about that?"

She checked the description of that, noted that it came with Bolognese sauce, and went back to the five-cheese tortellini. "I should let you know that I don't eat beef. I'm sure it tastes nice but..."

"Oh, sorry." Andrew closed his menu. "Will you be offended if..."

"You can have whatever you want." She waited till the waitress came around with some bread. "I'll take the tortellini tonight, the five-cheese one."

"And I'll have the baked rigatoni. Also, we'd like your finest red wine." He handed the menus over and waited till the waitress left before leaning over. "All right, my dear. It's time to get a little closer to each other." His leg brushed against hers, and she tried rolling her ankle over. "Don't be shy. I want to know more about the art teacher. What's your area of expertise?"

"I prefer painting, but I can make anything. I wish I took more ceramics classes though. Maybe if I had, I'd hear back from the recent job I applied to." She grabbed some bread and tore it in half, dipping one half in the garlic butter it came with. "I do love looking at sculptures though. Our art museum here is free on Thursdays after five o'clock. If you want, we can go to that."

"Mmm, five o'clock is when I get home. Depending on my workload, I might go to the gym later or I might just rest at home. It's okay if we must pay though. I don't mind spending more time with you." He took her hand again, still rubbing her foot. "Come on. There's got to be more to you than art and being good at trivia. Oh, and knowing good places to eat."

"Oh, there's not much." She admitted. "I live with my friends, we like to go out and eat, and I keep applying for jobs. I can't remember creating any art for fun. It's like my inspiration's run out." She shuddered. "I'm sorry. I know it's not exciting to hear an artist with no inspiration."

"Hey, everyone gets into a rut now and then. I'm sure you'll get that inspiration back." He stopped playing footsie and moved his foot away. "Something tells me there's more to you. You're holding back."

"Holding back?" She pulled her feet away. "Not really. I truly have nothing going on in my life. There's nothing strange about me." *Aside from the fact that I live in a house that eats people, my life is bland.*

He refused to accept this answer and only rubbed harder against her ankles. "Are you sure? You're playing with me under the table. You're shivering."

"I'm cold." She waved above her head where the ventilation shaft hung. "See? It's blasting air down on me."

"That's not a cold shiver. You're shaking because you're scared of something." His gaze turned to the window as cars zoomed by. The humming from the engines broke through the music playing right above. Strings mixed in with honking described their town all too well. Plenty of culture and even more crazy idiots on the road.

Radha stopped rubbing against Andrew's leg, the shivers running up her thighs. She bounced on the chair cushion as the waitress came over with their dishes. Thank goodness for the food. Her hunger replaced her anxiety the moment the warm noodles rolled in front of her. Taking her fork, she jabbed into them as Andrew stared down for a second.

"Is something wrong?" She held her fork right before her lips, the steam hitting her face. The smells, dear God, invited her to eat the dish. "Do you want something else?"

"Oh no, I was just saying grace. It's something I do right before eating. One of those old habits my parents instilled in me at a young age." He rolled out his napkin and laid it on his lap, grabbing his fork. "You can go ahead and eat if you want. Don't wait on me."

"No, it's fine. I need to cool this down anyway." She blew on her food before putting it in her mouth. A second later, her mouth burned, and she quickly drank down the water. "Oh God! I didn't cool this enough!"

"Burned the roof of your mouth?"

"Uh-huh." She grabbed one of the ice cubes and sucked

on it for a while. "I never learn. I shove hot food in my mouth and burn it off. My mother's surprised that I still have taste buds."

Andrew pushed his glass of water over. "Here. If you need some more, I can ask the waitress for another one. I know how painful this gets."

She pushed it back. "I'll be okay. The food is good though." The steam hit her face again as she shoved the fork back in. No wonder people ate at Carlota's. The fresh pasta, veggies, and grated cheese gave away how much work went into each dish. Staring over at Andrew's meaty rigatoni, a part of her wanted to get a taste. Even with all that beef in it, she held back the drool in her mouth and kept her fork on her plate. This was date number two. She couldn't beg to try food from his plate.

Andrew caught her eye and started to scrape some beef off. "I'm not sure if the taste lingers, but..."

"Oh no, you eat your food!" She insisted. "I was wondering if...how is it?"

"Delicious. You can taste every component in this dish." His foot brushed against her again, this time not shaking. She calmed down thanks to the burned roof of her mouth. Her fears went back to eating something too hot. Now that he rubbed her ankles, she stayed still. "You feel any better?"

She nodded as she started to finish up the dish. Despite the burning mouth, Andrew nailed the fact that every component hit with freshness. If there was a single thing frozen or microwaved, she couldn't pick it out. The crystal chandeliers, dimly lit tables, and fresh linen reminded her she couldn't bring her mother or friends. Couples came here, married or dating. The restaurant was built for romantics, not single people. As she sopped up the rest of the sauce with some bread, her mind sprang up with different date ideas. The museum was nice, but she wanted more nights like this. Nights where only Andrew's eyes landed on her, no one else.

They both finished their dishes as the waitress checked on them. Radha held up her water glass, which she happily took to refill. Andrew's hands went for his wallet, but she jumped up and grabbed him. "No, not this time!"

"Oh, come on! It's not right for you to pay for dinner!"

"Not right? I still have some money, Andrew! I feel guilty that you paid for the previous meal." She sat back down, arms crossed and huffing away. "We barely know each other."

"All the more reason for me to pay. I don't want to worry about these small things. Let me pay, okay? If it makes you feel better, we can split the bill during that music trivia night. I think I should be good, but I will warn you, my schedule is a little wonky right now. I can be called to go out of town at any given notice." He put his card down as the waitress brought over the bill. "There you are. Put it all on this."

"Of course." She took the bill. "I'll be right back with everything."

Andrew faced Radha, who grimaced as another car zoomed right by. Another idiot honked at it, then another one followed. No one died yet from these drivers constantly at each other's throats and burning rubber on the streets. She forgot all about the bill as a car's tires squealed past the restaurant. Rubbing her forehead, the aches disappeared as the waitress returned with the bill. Andrew wrote in the tips as she went for a peek at how much everything cost.

"Ah, no peeking." He pushed it away from her. "It's nothing unreasonable, don't worry. I expected things to be a little expensive."

"What do you define as 'a little expensive'? I assume it's over a hundred dollars."

"Obviously. A hundred dollars would only account for the wine." He tucked his card away. "Don't sweat on it, Radha. Not on the bill and certainly not on the people driving around."

Radha sat back down, scratching the side of her dress. Thank goodness tonight ended. She hoped Andrew had no more plans after this. A second date didn't mean he got an invitation to everything. Fiddling with her purse, she found a discount coupon from the nearby motel and quickly shoved it to the bottom. Veena gave this to her. She'd be the only one who got discounts from hotels for being a good customer. Radha zipped her purse up as Andrew finished drinking his wine.

"Shall we?" He helped her stand up. "Do you have room for any dessert, or should we save that for another time?"

"Probably another time when we're not as full." She slipped her coat over her shoulders as he held the door for her. "Oh, thank you. Tonight's been a lovely night. I did enjoy every bit of it."

"Would you like to come back here?"

"…I have to check my bank account before we do." She pulled the coat around her body, buttoning everything. The wish shifted through her hair, letting it spill all over. The chills in the temperature pushed her towards Andrew as he draped an arm over her. "Oh, it's gotten colder now!"

"The sun's down, so I'm not surprised. They did say the temperature would fall tonight. But there's one nice thing about cold weather." He pulled her in. "You get close enough to someone you like."

She didn't bother asking if he referred to her. It read all over his face. Burying into him, he led her into the parking lot and squeezed her shoulders. The cold picked up as rain sprinkled over them. Radha glowered at the sky as more drops fell. Of course, rain came right at the end of the day. She never heard the forecast before leaving, so she was praying it wouldn't keep raining on the drive home, which would keep her spirits up.

A part of her didn't want to drive back now. Everyone waited at the house, ready with dessert and listening ears. They wouldn't let her go until she dropped every little detail about the date. Then her mother would remind her once more not to blow it. Not that she could do that anymore. Andrew loved hearing everything from her. He didn't run off when she talked about her life. Maybe this was it. This was her chance at happiness.

"Ah, geez, I wish I had an umbrella." Andrew started to remove his coat, but she stopped him. "What? Aren't you cold?"

"I'll be alright. My car is right there." She pointed to it sitting in the back with several other vehicles. "You know, music trivia and musical bingo are coming up. I was thinking we could postpone the museum trip for the following week. I think too many things at once might drive us crazy."

"I was wondering about that. I agree with you; we need to postpone it. I have a meeting soon, which might take up my time. However, I'll make time for bingo and trivia. I couldn't miss that!"

"Good! My friends and mother will be there though. They love bingo and trivia, so I can't escape them." She shook her head. "Be warned. My friends can get a little intense during the competitions, especially Lata. I'm surprised Upper Deck didn't throw us out after the last bingo fiasco."

"Uh-oh, a fiasco? I'm afraid to ask what that was."

Radha shuddered. "Let's just say…don't let Lata drink and play bingo at the same time. While we're at it, don't let my mother drink either."

"Your mother drinks alcohol?"

"Occasionally. We all do, but on that night…God, I can't talk about it." She burst out laughing. Her sides aching, she rubbed her arms for warmth repeatedly. They had nowhere else to go after this. "Well…I had a very nice time tonight. I should probably get back home."

"Me too. But before I go…" He pulled her into a kiss. Radha's hands went out in front, her eyes closing as her arms wrapped around him. That ocean water scent sucked her in. Her fingers splayed out as she dug into his back, letting him sweep her away. As soon as he pulled back, she opened her eyes and gasped for air. "I had to let you know."

"Let me know what?"

"This is the best night I've had since I moved to town." He brushed the strands of her hair off her shoulder. "I really hope we can have more like them."

Her brain short-circuited for a second as she collected herself. No man kissed her this way. Most either slobbered over her or left her hanging. Andrew kissed with passion. He didn't want to let her go so soon. He wanted to hold her forever if he could. Rubbing her arms, she gazed at the sky as a few more raindrops fell. Her cue came in.

"We should leave now. The rain's falling harder." She held out her hand as giant drops splashed into it. "Next time though… I will see you soon!"

"Yes, next time! Give me a text when you get home!"

She fiddled around her purse for the car keys, unlocked in, and dove into the driver's seat. Though she plunged the key into the ignition, she didn't back out right away. Rain poured all over the windshield as she sat in place, grateful for tonight. She braved the weather and didn't get wet, save except for the wet spots on her outfit. After a few deep breaths, she turned the ignition and the headlights on. As the car roared to life, she flipped the windshield wipers and checked behind her. Andrew's car was long gone while she still couldn't bring herself to steer out of the parking lot. Her hands shook as she put on the seat belt and peered over her shoulder. A few cars drove by before she backed out. Rain spilled all over the back window, fogging up certain parts. Flipping on the defroster, she pushed the car into drive and drove out of the lot.

I survived. She pressed her hands on the steering wheel. *I survived the date and…*

A sting from the wheel forced her to pull away and shake her hand. Thankfully, she paused at a red light and stared down at where that came from. Static electricity? No, this sting only hurt for a second. She pressed her hand in the same area and found it. Tiny, slightly deep, dug into the steering wheel. She had never caught it before, yet she had her hand over it. She ignored it on the way home. It stayed there as she parked and rubbed her palm. That sting. That tiny deep mark. In the dark, she couldn't see it. She didn't need to see a thing to know what it was. She saw them all the time in her room, and now they were in her car.

Her hands brushed against a brand-new crack revealing a new message.

DON'T FORGET JULY 3RD!

CHAPTER 10

Radha danced down the gravel road up to the front porch, ignoring the fresh petals leading the way. Since they retained their color, she figured the wind blew them off. It picked up as soon as she entered the driveway and struggled to close the car door. She tripped over the rocks as she grabbed the doorknob and let herself in. More petals greeted her on the welcome mat, red and pink leading the way down the hall. She brushed a few of them aside as she went into her room and sat down on her bed.

He's real. He cares about me. Her mind couldn't wrap around this. So many men like Andrew lost their interest in her. Not him. He wanted to see her again, even if he moved the time to later in the week. He liked Carolta's very much, though he agreed it was good for fancy occasions, not a casual night with friends. She forgot all about the whole thing about July 3rd. Why would the house mention that anyway? There was nothing special about that date. She couldn't dwell on it while Andrew was here.

"I don't know if I could eat here every week." He admitted as they walked to the parking lot. Radha pulled out the after-dinner mint and unwrapped it. Given how well the date went, she prepared for the next move. "My rigatoni was great though I'm not sure why it cost almost forty dollars."

"Let me guess; you could make the same thing at home?"

Radha popped the mint in her mouth. "My mother says that all the time when we go out to eat. It doesn't matter what we have: she can make it better at home."

"No, although your mother isn't wrong. If I could find a decent recipe for Bolognese sauce, I'd be able to pull this off." He stopped in front of his car, a sleek black Toyota Camry made rather recently. A decal of a dolphin leaping over the ocean waves stuck on the back window. He wiped the dirt off with his handkerchief. "I apologize for the sticker. A student gave it to me cause he thought it meshed with my personality."

"I think it's adorable." Radha's jealousy hit right then. No student asked for a reference from her, let alone gave her gifts. "Well, I guess this is it. We're definitely meeting at Upper Deck for trivia night? And Lata's definitely up to play bingo with you. She promises to wipe the floor with you."

"I look forward to it." Andrew moved in closer as she inched forward. Their faces nearly touched as he whispered. "I really enjoy being around you, Radha. You've helped me make my way around this place. It's been tough doing it alone."

"Well, you don't have to be alone anymore." The lights above them flickered as her lips touched his. For a second, she forgot how to kiss when his mouth pressed against hers. She puckered up, bit down on the mint, and returned the kiss. Thank goodness her breath smelled good enough for it. She blew through, taking his air in. Then she stepped back, not sure if he enjoyed it or not. Her face hot, she pulled her purse up her shoulder and started to move away. "Thank you for a nice evening."

"...You're welcome. I guess I'll see you soon."

"Yeah, you will. We still have a contest to win." Her face burning, she waved to him as she went to her car. Sweating bullets, she got in the front seat, turned the engine on, and put the air conditioner into full blast. That kiss wasn't perfect, but he didn't complain. Next time, she'd prepare herself for better. Maybe put in a little tongue. Clutching her chest, she leaned back and took in the cool air.

We kissed on the second date. He's really into me. She turned the headlights on and started to back out though she wanted to stay longer. Checking where Andrew's car stood, she found the lot empty. He didn't waste time to cool down like her. He probably didn't panic over the idea of a kiss. He moved in at the right moment while she stood like an idiot and didn't realize it was a kiss until he was there. Hopefully, he didn't hate her lips.

I'll be better next time, Andrew. I promise.

Now at home, she slowly undressed and got into her nightgown and robe. Tired but not sleepy, she opted to get a snack in the kitchen. She rarely ate after she had her dinner, but her feelings took over. The best way to shut those up was to feed herself. Hopefully, the others didn't finish off the ice cream and cake in the fridge. She craved all the sweets to soothe her embarrassment.

Walking down the halls, she didn't find any cracks in the walls or doorways. These latest guests provided enough nourishment. She patted the wall, received a little shake in reply, and made her way into the kitchen. No one else was there though she spotted a pile of dishes in the sink. Leftovers from the night before. Given how small the portions were at Carlota's, she came back with no boxes. A pity. Small portions and big prices. The girls didn't miss much.

Opening the fridge, she discovered an unopened box of triple chocolate ice cream. Thank goodness no one found this tucked behind piles of frozen meat and vegetables. Grabbing that along with a frozen chocolate pie, she took her desserts and placed them on the counter.

Scooping ice cream out, she stared up at the kitchen decor on the wall. Unlike the walls and artwork, they never suffered from any shaking. These were all old kitchen utensils that Veena's grandmother used back in the day, made of copper and steel, tacked all around. A few porcelain items such as a salt and pepper shaker shaped like ducks weren't touched. Apparently, the house didn't care as much for the kitchen, not like her mother, who complained about how ugly everything was.

"Why does she need all this?" Swati grumbled as she pushed aside a cookie jar shaped like a cat. "Who'd keep these as family heirlooms? In my family, we didn't have heirlooms. You were given a giant tin plate for everyone to eat off until you left the house."

"Oh, Ma! That's not how things went in your home!" Radha moved her mother away from all the porcelain items. "You did not eat things off one tin plate all the time."

"I didn't say I ate on that plate all the time." Swati shrugged. "On occasion, we ate on the floor as well…provided the mice didn't get to our food first. Our heirlooms were nothing but the dirt that flavored our meals!"

Thinking over that caused Radha to choke on a hunk of chocolate. Her mother's stories of the past grew more and more outrageous. Swati claimed she slept on the floor and ate crumbs, and wore old rice bags as clothing. Deep down, Radha knew her mother lived in a nice house with decent China, a floor that got swept often, and food on the table. She didn't stop her from rambling though; the stories provided entertainment when guests could not.

The guests. There was no need to hunt for anyone plus she hadn't checked the news for any new scumbags. For once, the police did their jobs and caught people before they got away. Of course, the real test came during the trials and convictions. Those took their sweet time, so hopefully their poor house would last that long.She gazed at the flowers sitting in the corners. So far, not a single petal fell from them.

As she dug her spoon into the ice cream, Veena burst through the door, her face flushed. Radha swallowed another bite as her friend stormed in, her robe billowing behind her. "Radha, how could you?!"

"Okay, so I opened a new carton of ice cream. None of you touched, so why can't I?" Radha went for the chocolate pie, cutting off a piece. "You're welcome to have some."

"I'm not talking about the food! I'm shocked! I wanna know all the details, and you haven't told me anything!" Veena huffed, wrapping the ends of her robe around her. "You promised me you'd give me every detail if I helped you pick out an outfit!"

"I just got in the house, Veena. All I've done is change clothes and get my ice cream." Radha pulled out the chair, motioning for her to join. "If you really want to know, we had a very nice time. Carlota's is an expensive place, but he still enjoyed it. I doubt we'll go back there anytime soon though. He'd rather go to the next trivia and bingo night at Upper Deck."

"Upper Deck again?" Veena shook her head. "Oh, I knew it was a bad idea to bring you during the single girls' night. You can't stop thinking about that place!"

Radha laughed as she cut a slice of pie for Veena. Upper Deck wasn't fine dining, but she loved the atmosphere and prices much more. "Come on. Ever since he learned I was good at trivia, he wanted to be a part of my team. It's music trivia next time!"

Veena shook her head as she grabbed the ice cream scoop. "Well, I'm glad he wants to come, but tell me about this date. What else did you find out about him? Was he ever married? What else does he like to do for fun? What are his favorite foods? Surely, he gave you something to work with."

"Well, he's been widowed for ten years now. He's busy with work in general, but he mentioned that he liked swimming, going to museums and concerts, and he loves taking walks around town. He's gone on dates before, but they never really went beyond a second date. Oh, he loves trivia and bingo. That's why he was so excited about Upper Deck's contests." Radha chuckled as she dug into her ice cream. "I know it doesn'tseemlike much, but it's been so long since I went on a date. When we get guests, they're never for the long run. Even if they're like Terry, they don't come back here. I never see or hear from them again. This is the first time in ages that a guy has spent time with me and wants more."

"So, you're going again on Wednesday?"

"I think we'll have to cancel that one and move it to next week, but he is going out with us to Upper Deck on Thursday! I don't know what he'll do on bingo night if he goes up against Lata though."

"Who's going up against me?" Lata pushed the door in, her eyes locked on the sweet feast before her. "Oh, everyone's eating without me! You should have told me you were back!"

"I'm sorry. It hasn't been that long. Truth be told, the date was nice. We enjoyed eating at Carlota's, and it turns out that he's just as lonely as I am. He hasn't found anyone to spend time with since his wife died. I didn't embarrass myself either." Radha handed Lata a plate. "He's dying to play bingo against you on Thursday."

"Oh, I'm ready for it." Lata cut herself a slice of pie, then grabbed a bowl for ice cream. "I hope he doesn't mind the competition. At the end of the day, it doesn't matter who wins. What matters is that we have a good time playing with each other."

"That's very mature of you, Lata." Veena scooped some ice cream for her. "You're becoming a much better sport at things."

"I'm also a terrible liar. I'm gonna cream him!"Lata pumped her fists. "I'm not letting go of my championship that easily."

Radha laughed into her ice cream bowl. Lata's competitive side could be amusing at times, but she sometimes took things to another level. The others had to keep her from climbing tables and screaming at the hosts before things got ugly. The last bingo competition that Lata lost almost got them thrown out of Upper Deck. Swati was able to sweet-talk the owner into letting them stay. He allowed it on the grounds that Lata would never be left alone to play bingo. Radha made that vow that she'd watch her every step.

"Just do me a favor and keep the tables in one piece this time." She warned her. "The last thing I want Andrew to see is you losing it when you lose Bingo."

"I don't lose at Bingo!"

"Yeah, that's not what happened last time." Veena licked her spoon clean. "Oh, honey. Need I remind you of the property damage I had to pay them last time? I'm with Radha here. This is the first time we're going to meet him. We need to make a good impression."

"So, you are coming with me?" Radha's hopes skyrocketed when both nodded. "Oh, that's nice! I've told him a lot about you two. I did bring up Ma a few times as well. Speaking of Ma, she's gone to bed, huh?"

"Yeah, last time I checked, she was out cold. We can tell her about everything later." Lata took some more ice cream.

"Oh, this is exciting! We get to see if he's a real person or not!"

Radha frowned. "What makes you think I made this up?"

"With all due respect, Radha, your luck with dates is… oh, who am I kidding?! You have no luck with dates!" Lata went to put everything away before Radha could snap back at her. The truth hurts them each time. Her luck with dates always turned sour after some time. It couldn't happen now. She couldn't lose Andrew for any reason. "But since you've been out twice, I think it's time Veena and I got to see him. I want to know if he's as dreamy as you make him out to be."

Radha chuckled. "You'll see on bingo night. Just don't hit him if he wins."

"I don't hit people!"

"Yeah, I've got a bunch of people who'd argue against that now. They run to the other side when they see you come in." Veena finished off her dessert. "Don't you worry, Radha. I'll keep her away from him."

"And you stay away from him too." She warned her. "I finally found someone. I'm not about to let him go. Not for you, not for the house. He is mine!"

Veena lifted her hands off the table and pushed her chair back. "So, you've claimed. You can relax, honey. I have no intention of taking your man. I'm busy for the next couple of days anyway. Going on dates, looking for food…God, it's a good thing I've got the stamina of a twenty-year-old. My poor house would crumble without me!"

The house shook slightly as Radha struggled not to laugh. They both knew that Veena alone didn't keep the house standing. They brought the people in together. Sure, she was better at luring them in, but they all ended up in the same place. She crossed her fingers that Andrew wouldn't have skeletons in his closet.

"Can you both do me a favor?" She wiped her mouth. "I want you to find out whatever you can about Andrew Gardner. He works at the university. That should be a good place to start."

"I thought you trusted him?" Lata grimaced. "Are you having doubts?"

"I only want to be sure. I don't want to go too far in case..." Radha trailed off, recalling all her dates going wrong. "If he turns out to lie about anything, if he's got dark secrets, I want to cut it off before it goes too far. I can't afford to get hurt. Not like..."

Veena got it right away. "I'll see what I can find. For your sake, I hope he is clean. I haven't seen you this way in a long time."

The house shivered in agreement, though Radha's soul still twisted around. Everyone had something they hid from the world. Radha hid the secrets of the house. They all did that. Maybe Andrew hid something deep and dark that no one could comprehend. Hopefully, it was a small thing. If he had a minor traffic violation, she'd live with that. Anything else, she never wanted to date again.

Please. She prayed to all the deities around. *Please let this be the one. Let me be happy. For once in my life, let me have what I want.*

As soon as she made that wish, her hopes were dashed. Be happy. Anytime she wished to be happy, she got nothing in return. Sadness filled her days, knocking her down one bit after another. She couldn't get that job she wanted. She wasn't inspired anymore to create art. She didn't have the money to move out or travel the world. With their new job of feeding the house, maybe it was best to keep Andrew at a distance. Going too far led to him eventually coming over here. That meant telling him about the house. Then waiting to see if the house accepted him, and if it didn't…

"No." She kicked the thought out of her mind. Now wasn't the right time to bring Andrew over. They needed more time. They needed to get more into his life and learn about him before revealing anything about themselves. The night at Upper Deck was the place to start. If he enjoyed bingo and trivia like they did, he'd get along with everyone else. Veena smooth-talked any man whenever she got close enough to him. Lata was friendly and sometimes made them laugh, though she didn't intentionally tell jokes. Even Swati got a few chuckles in. When Radha spoke, everyone ignored her. Tomorrow will be no different.

Maybe if he falls for Veena, it might save me the trouble of a potential breakup. She can let him down easier. She twiddled her fingers over the upcoming night. No, she couldn't shove him off to Veena either. She wanted him. Veena got any man she desired. She couldn't have Andrew as well. Radha had to be the one who took care of him. She found him, went on dates, and now she had to prepare for the worst. He'd learn the truth about her and the house eventually. He'd learn about their research, the missing people, and how the house kept them alive for years. He'd find the skeletal remains and traces of previous victims. This was her mess; she'd hold him off while they were still in the early stages.

And one day, when they were ready, she'd have to bring him over.

CHAPTER 11

Upper Deck buzzed with laughter and music when they entered for the competition. Radha went over all the music trivia she garnered over the years. She hadn't gone to see U2 three times in concert, but she was aware of their music and their philanthropy. She brushed up on all her knowledge about the Beatles since this was where she struggled. They had too many different eras to keep up with. As she went further into the restaurant, 80s music pumped out with the likes of Madonna, Tears for Fears, and The Police rang through. She relaxed as they got situated with the other teams. 80s music. She could recognize most of those in her sleep.If they asked questions about popular artists and songs, this was her competition to lose.

"Ah, here we go." She cracked her knuckles. "I hope you recognize some of these songs, Ma."

"Recognize? Your father and I made sweet love listening to half of them!" Swati quipped as they waited for their table. "I'm sure I'll nail some of this stuff, kinda the way your father…"

"Ma!" Radha silenced her as the hostess came over and motioned them to follow, gathering a couple of menus. "Save those answers for the trivia, okay? Let's get seated."

Once they got to their table, Radha let her mother sit on one side while Veena and Lata sat across from them.

Her other side remained open for Andrew. After agreeing to play both bingo and trivia, the hostess promised she'd put their names in, and their waitress would come around with the cards. While they chatted around, Radha kept lacing and untangling her fingers. Every hair on her arm stood tall, either from the cold room, or nerves. Hopefully, no one would embarrass her or themselves over here.

"Promise me you'll be nice to him." She warned them, setting her gaze on her mother. "And no pranks!"

"What pranks? I have never done anything to embarrass you!"

"Oh, really? What about back in fifth grade when I needed to be Montana for the United States pageant at school, and you had me wearing a giant T-shirt that said 'Montana' on it?"

Swati shrugged. "Hey, I've never been there before. I had no idea what the heck Montana was famous for. It was your job to figure that out! Anyway, you looked better than the poor kid who had to play South Dakota. I'm still not sure what he was dressed as."

Radha now faced both Veena and Lata. "Remember, this is Andrew's first major trivia night. We're trying to have fun."

"Not just trivia. We're also taking part in music bingo." Veena pushed Lata back before she could say anything. "Don't worry. I'll keep her from the other players."

"Oh, come on! When did I embarrass you guys?" Lata demanded.

"Honey, if I told you all the times you did that, we'd miss playing any of the rounds." Veena took her menu. "Come on. Let's get some appetizers before Andrew comes around. I'm starved!"

Radha focused on her menu, pretending to scan through the list of appetizers and wings. With Andrew, she knew exactly what she wanted, but with her friends and mother, she took her sweet time with decisions. Swati gazed over her shoulder, clicking her tongue at anything that appeared fatty or sweet. Those were immediate no-no's for eating. After a ton of clicking, Radha folded up her menu, waiting for Andrew.

Please come soon, Andrew. I don't want to spend the night entertaining my mother. She shot Swati a playful smile as her mother eyed all the drinks at the next table. Go figure her mother would ogle the drinks she couldn't have. As long as she said nothing humiliating, they'd be all right. *So far, so good. Andrew should come soon. I hope he remembers how to get here.*

After a few seconds, they settled in with their glasses of water. The waitress handed everyone a bingo card, then smiled at Radha. "Are you gonna do trivia alone or joining forces with someone?"

"Ah, I'm actually going to join forces with my date." She checked her phone as Andrew texted that he was parking the car. "He should be coming in here soon. I'm hoping I can get on the board again tonight."

"Oh, so you're performing for the individual round too?"

Radha nodded, taking a sheet to tally her score. "I studied all night. Let's do this." In the corner, she found Andrew entering and waved to him. "There he is! May I have another board? We're ready now!"

They ordered their soft drinks as Andrew approached them, holding out a bouquet of flowers. Radha leaped to her feet and quickly made room for him to sit down. Her mother and friends gaped at him as he pecked her on the cheek before handing the bouquet over. They knew it now. They knew he wasn't a story she put together, but a living, breathing human being. He dressed more casually for tonight, prepared to eat chicken wings and beer, in a t-shirt with the university's logo and jeans. She started to feel over-dressed in the skirt and blouse she picked out.

"I'm so glad you made it!" She gave him a quick squeeze before introducing everyone. "This is my friend Veena, my friend Lata, and my mother Swati. Everyone, this is Andrew!"

"Hello, ladies!" He shook each one's hands and planted a small kiss on Swati's hand. "My, you must be the lovely Swati. I swear, there is nothing more beautiful than the warm hand of a woman such as yourself."

Swati stared down at him. "Relax! If you marry my daughter, you'll end up in the will! You don't have to push so hard!"

"Oh, ignore her. Are you ready for some trivia?" Radha patted the spot by her side. "I told them we're working together, but I also want to take part in the individual contest. I hope you don't mind."

"Not at all. I was thinking I'd also play bingo." Upon those words, Lata tensed up as she peered over her menu. "Relax. I'm only here to play for fun. I won't try to beat anyone."

"And fun is what we're here for." Radha shot Lata a look, and she covered her face up again. "Well, really, everyone just wanted to meet you."

"It's a real delight." Veena nodded to the waitress. "Do you have preferences on drinks?"

"Oh, I like a good old-fashioned beer, but I think I'll play it safe and get a sweet tea. I've got a lot of driving to do tomorrow." Andrew moved closer to Radha with his leg brushing against hers. Her cheeks flamed up as his hand rested on top of her thigh. Her face turned towards the menu, pretending she was scanning through the entrees. "I've been called away to do some research over the weekend."

"Over the weekend?" Radha didn't pull her eyes from

the menu. "Will you be back by Monday?"

"I plan to be. That's part of the reason I had to change our plans. This popped up at the last minute." He pressed his hand against the small of her back. The little shock spread up her spine while she forced herself to keep reading. "I hope you don't mind."

"No, I don't. I figured you had a lot of work." She ran her finger down the entrées. "Mmm, I think we should get some wings. What do you think?"

"What the hell do you think we're here for?! Hurry up and order the damn wings!" Swati snapped. "You told me I don't have to cook tonight since we're coming here. And while we're at it, don't order that awful Nashville hot flavor. No one enjoyed that."

Radha shot Andrew an apologetic look. "Now you see why I took my time to introduce you."

"Ah, don't worry. I think your mother's right. It's time to order something." Andrew leaned over her shoulder and pointed to the twenty wings, ten traditional and ten boneless, that came in four sauces. Radha noted each one in her mind, ignoring Andrew's breathing down her neck as he read. "Do you want to try what we had last time or pick different sauces?"

"Either works for me." He squeezed her thigh as her face burned. "I'll let you make all the choices tonight. After all, you're still the expert at everything."

"Ma, not a word!" Radha silenced her mother before she could throw out some snarky reply. She leaned against Andrew, focusing solely on him. "Let's go ahead and pick parmesan garlic as one of the sauces. I'd like to add mango habanero as well." She pointed to two of them. "And I think we should try the sweet chili sauce as well as the teriyaki. Does that sound fine?"

"Thrilling." Swait closed her menu. "Just make sure you get blue cheese along with ranch dressing. Real eaters of wings eat it with blue cheese."

"Of course, Ma. Let's get the dipping sauce that always gets between your teeth." Radha nodded to the waitress. "We'll get one of each dipping sauce and get both, celery and carrots."

The waitress wrote that down and took the rest of the orders. In addition to the wings, Radha convinced everyone to try the rangoons for an appetizer along with a side of tater tots covered in nacho cheese. Both Lata and Veena got wings, though their order was much smaller, and Swati ordered the smallest order of boneless wings. Despite all the times she got chicken stuck in her teeth, she still loved them. After everything was placed, a loud boom erupted right above them. Swati nearly dropped her fork, and Veena covered up her ears.

"Oh God, who's running this thing?!" She groaned as a microphone screech came through. "Somebody fix that thing already! My ears are about to blow out!"

Radha turned to Andrew, ready to apologize as her head bobbed up and down. "I'm sorry. I know this is much louder than…"

"ALL RIGHT, LADIES AND GENTLEMEN!" The host boomed into the mic. Dressed in the bright orange clothing that Upper Deck employees wore, he stood in the middle of the room and yanked the microphone around. More groans filled the room as he crossed in front, causing more high-pitched noise. He cleared his throat as he spoke in his normal tone. "Sorry about that, guys. We had some technical difficulties, but enough about them! Who's ready to play Bingo?!"

“Ooh, me!” Lata jumped up and down in her chair. A few other people cheered and threw their hands in the air. Radha laghed as Andrew quietly raised his hand so the employees could hand out bingo cards and tokens to cover squares. Radha peeked at Andrew’s card and noted all the different bands written across it. She swallowed when she realized that this game wasn’t like a normal bingo game. On music night, they’d reveal a song title, and the players had to put the tokens on the musician who sang that song. Lata would have a little difficulty tonight as she knew many songs, but often forgot who sang them.

“This is a little tougher.” Radha reminded her friend as she analyzed the board. “Do you remember most of the people on your board?”

“I think so. They sometimes call out a song I have never heard before.” Lata shook her head. “No worry. As long as they don’t play the song…”

“And to make things a little more interesting, we’ll be playing the tunes, and you’ll have to put your token on the right person…if you’ve got them.” The host winked at the crowd who tittered amongst themselves. Radha’s stomach churned as Andrew cracked his knuckles. Hopefully, he remembered the tunes that some of these musicians sang. The squares she saw were singers with very few hits. If the host wanted to mess with them, he’d play a song no one recognized.

“Good luck, everyone.” Veena whispered. “I’m glad I’m not taking part in this one. I can’t remember much about the 80s since the incident with…” She bit down on her lip as her face reddened. “Oh, let’s just say I don’t like wearing neon colors anymore. For very good reasons.”

“It’s a great story!” Swati jumped in. “Do you remember when…”

"Oh look, Ma! Rangoons!" Radha stopped her as the waitress put their appetizers in front of them. "Chew them carefully, Ma! You don't want that chicken between your teeth!" Andrew opened his mouth to ask, but she stopped him. "You're better off not knowing."

They split their appetizers as the game started. Beads of sweat formed across Lata's forehead as the tunes played on. Next to her, Radha saw that Andrew laid out several tokens, with almost two possible ways of getting bingo. Her heart ached for poor Lata, who put a token down, then removed it. Tonight wasn't her night. If there were just words being called out, she'd never hesitate to lay anything down.

"She's having trouble, isn't she?" She whispered to Veena. "Did she get any of them?"

Veena glanced over at Lata's board and shook her head. "To be honest, I don't think they played any songs by those artists.This is not gonna be her night."

Another song played, and Lata finally dropped a token on her card. Unfortunately for her, someone yelled out "BINGO!" and jumped up from their seat. A young girl danced around as the host came over to verify everything. Lata slumped in her chair as he announced the girl as the winner of the round. To rub more salt into her wounds, the prize turned out to be a free dessert. Knowing how much Lata loved the desserts here, Radha reached over and squeezed her hand.

"I'm sorry, honey. Don't stress over it. They'll play another round, and you might get lucky then."

"I wasn't lucky either." Andrew pushed his card away. "We might do better with the first trivia round. Are you ready for that?"

"I'm as ready as I can be." Radha cracked her knuckles as she pushed some tater tots towards Lata's glum self. "You can have these, honey. If it'll make you feel better, I'll buy you that deep-fried ice cream sundae."

Lata perked up at that. "Do you promise to get it with hot fudge?"

"Hot fudge, whipped cream, and the cherry on top." Radha crossed her fingers. "Let's get through dinner and these next few rounds first. I hope I don't freeze up with my music knowledge."

The waiters handed out the sheets of paper with the possible kinds of questions. In addition to naming tunes, they'd fill in the blank questions with lyrics, questions on the musicians themselves, and questions about the songs. Radha's stomach hurt after she swallowed the last bit of Rangoon. The questions about the songs stumped her. She didn't know the history behind every song out there. Unless she checked Wikipedia, she could only make blind guesses about everything. She nudged her mother, who nearly choked on her tater tots, spilling cheese on her chin.

"What?!" Swati wiped the cheese off her face. "Thanks for letting me drop that delicious bit of cheese there! It's scalding my chin off!"

"Ma, the cheese is lukewarm. Your chin is fine." Radha leaned in. "Do you know much about the origins of songs?"

"It depends on the song. The 80s were a wild time for me!" Swati sipped her water before going for more tots. "I remember once when your father and I were stuck in the middle of a snowstorm at a club! We couldn't get home, so he decided to turn on some music, we got in the mood, and…" She coughed. "Oh, you know the rest!"

"No, we don't. You never told us the story before. What happened next?" Lata leaned in.

"We decided to start a macrame project." Swati snorted before finishing her tater tots. "It was a nightclub in the 80s!

We made love, you idiot!"

"Oh, Ma!" Radha turned to Andrew who struggled not to spit out his sweet tea. She prayed her mother wouldn't go into the details of love making, especially because she'd bring up the house. How its walls shook…and not from hunger. "Please forgive them. This is a regular night for me. Now, you know why I don't let my mother out of the house."

"You're fine." He chugged the tea and wiped the sides of his mouth. As he settled in with his sheet of paper, the rest of the food arrived. "Ah, time for dinner and some trivia. Do you think we're going to get something?"

"I hope so. I love music, but I don't know the history behind every musician and song. Unless it's something super popular, I probably won't get it." Radha grabbed a pencil and pressed her paper in front. The other players around them got ready as the first question, naming the tune, started to play. Radha listened to the tune for a few seconds before raising her hand. The host jogged over to their booth, shoving the microphone into her face.

"What is "Back on the Chain Gang" by the Pretenders?" She spoke clearly with no squeaking. The host pulled the mic away and yelled, "Correct!" as everyone else in the booth cheered. Andrew squeezed her shoulders while she frowned over the answer. The host bounded to her and dropped a coupon for a free appetizer. This was how they rewarded the correct answers: coupons to use for the next time. If she came in the top three, she got something even better, such as getting the whole meal paid for, free merchandise, or tickets to a movie.

"I thought that song came out in the 90s, but no, it's an 80s song!" Veena exclaimed as they got ready for the next question. This was to fill in the lyrics. She closed her eyes and hummed the tune. "Oh, I know this one! I swear I know this one!"

"I know it too!" Lata held up her hand. "We used to dance to this song when I was younger! Oh…I can't remember it at all now! My head's completely blank!"

"What else is new?" Swati muttered as she pulled out a piece of chicken in her teeth. "I remember this song too. It was the night that I conceived…"

"Ma! You're breaking my concentration!" Radha listened closely to the words and started to sing them to herself. Swaying her head to the music, she tuned out the other sounds and went through every word. "I gotta take a little time. A little time to take things over. I better read between the lines in case I need them when I'm…"

"Older!" Veena cut in, snapping her fingers. "Oh, I remember this one now. The next part goes…now this mountain I must climb feels like the world upon my shoulder. Through the clouds, I see love shine…"

Radha's hand shot up in the air as the host ran to her. Without waiting for the microphone, she sang out loud. "Keeps me warm as life grows colder!"

"That's right!" The host exclaimed. "Now for a bonus, can you tell me when that song was released? The year is good enough but if you give me the month and day, I'll turn this into a free meal coupon."

Swati kicked her under the table. "You better know what that is. I want to take Gladys and the other girls from my card club to eat."

Radha vowed not to give this coupon to her mother. The card club was filled with women of Swati's age who spent the afternoon doing nothing but chatting and playing different card games. There were at least twelve ladies in it. The free meal covered dinner for four. Swallowing, Radha thought back to the days when her father played the radio while they drove to school. He sang at the top of his lungs, completely off-key and often getting the lyrics wrong. All the same, she learned a lot from those rides. She looked up the correct lyrics and joined in with him when they went out. He always threw out silly tidbits of information with each song, and now their time had come.

"Would it be November 13, 1984?" She guessed. She knew the year and month. The day was completely in the air because November 13th was her father's birthday. The host cheered with a "Correct!" and the whole room erupted. Radha leaned back as a waitress came around and refilled her water. Everyone else grabbed her hands and squeezed them as another coupon fell at her plate. A free dessert.

"Here you go, Lata!" She handed the coupon to Lata who eagerly scooped it up. "Now you can get that deep-fried ice cream sundae."

"Oh, I'll treasure this forever!" Lata pressed the coupon against her chest. "This is the greatest thing anyone ever gave me!"

"The greatest thing? It's a coupon for a free dessert, not an ice cream sundae made of gold!" Swati grumbled. "We win these things all the time. Hell, you even wonthose prizes at Bingo!"

"I know but…there's nothing better than a deep-fried sundae…except maybe a regular old sundae." She clapped her hands. "I think they'll have another round of bingo soon. I'll try again with the songs. It's hard to remember everything though. My brain doesn't have enough room for it."

"Ma, not a word." Radha put her finger to Swati's lips. "This is a hard competition. We're all taking our sweet time trying to figure out answers." She turned to Andrew. "I'm sorry. It's a crazy night."

"Ah, I don't mind. Good company is hard to come

across!" Andrew chuckled into his drink. "I haven't really been able to enjoy myself like this ever since I lost my wife."

Lata blinked. "Where'd you lose her?"

Radha grimaced. "In the line to ride Space Mountain, Lata. What do you think?!"

"It's okay, it's okay!" Andrew laughed as new bingo boards dropped on their table. As another started, Upper Deck often changed up the boards to add more excitement. Radha stared down at her squares as Andrew stroked her back. "I don't really talk much about my late wife. It's still hard to deal with. I mean, it's been a long time, but she never leaves my mind. She can't, you know?"

Veena reached over and squeezed his hand. "Oh, I've been there. It's hard to move on. Even when you're on your eightieth date, you never forget that first love. That's why I like Upper Deck. So many new people to meet and it's a great way to forget where you are."

Radha sank into the cushion as their food came out. Her appetite faded out despite the delicious smokey smell coming off the wings. As everyone else passed the food around, she stared down into her plate: five wings, some celery and carrots, and her small container of ranch dressing. That could settle her stomach for a few hours, yet she couldn't put any of it in her mouth. The others dove into their food, dipping everything in blue cheese dressing, and chatting amongst themselves. She couldn't jump into the conversation. With Andrew's leg rubbing against hers, she didn't want to talk. She wanted to leave the craziness of bingo and trivia night behind, go home, and spend the rest of the evening with him. Upper Deck with her mother and friends in tow worked when it was just them. With a date, she wished the two of them could play these games together.

Feed me. Her stomach growled as the next round started

up. That voice. It didn't come from anyone sitting around them. It didn't come out of her own body. She knew it because it echoed whenever it got hungry. Their home needed food. They were enjoying themselves, eating and laughing, while it cravedfor something else.

Maybe I can take some wings home. The lemon pepper ones should be fine. She eyed the table next to theirs, a group of friends eating at least forty lemon pepper wings. She enjoyed those just fine, but she preferred the sauce-covered wings to the seasoned ones. Maybe Andrew was the same one. Maybe the house had preferences. Their home waited for them, hungry for something new. A new group of guests? That would take time.

"Radha?" Andrew pushed a plate of boneless wings in front of her. "Are you okay?"

"Huh?" Radha held back the mouthful of drool at the sight of those smoky wings, glimmering under the low lights. A small cup of ranch dressing and a pile of carrots and celery waited for her to start dunking. She rubbed her forehead and grabbed one of the small plates. "Oh, I'm sorry. I didn't realize our food was here."

"You spaced out there. I thought something was wrong." He pushed a different plate towards her, this one full of garlic parmesan wings. "I thought you were tired of playing, or maybe you didn't know what the song was."

"The song?" She found her bingo card underneath everything. "Oh, right! We're still playing! What did I miss?"

"...The last three trivia questions." Now it was Lata's turn to be concerned. She intertwined her fingers, dropping them right on the table. "I thought you had no idea what songs they were playing. You were doing so well earlier."

"Oh!" Radha shook her head and pulled her card out. "Oh, I'm so sorry. I spaced out there for a little bit. What were the songs?"

"I don't know. I was hoping you did."

"Eh, you didn't miss much." Swati waved it off. "You're still a good player even if you're out of it. Just eat up, and you can pick it up in the next round. Just don't drown those wings in the ranch dressing."

"Of course not. I only plan to dunk the wings in them." Radha put a few boneless wings on her plate. "It's the celery and carrots I plan to cover in ranch dressing." She held up the plate of spicy wings and pushed them towards Andrew. "Do you want some, honey?"

"Ah, thank you, but I think I'll stick to the garlic parmesan wings for now." He narrowed his gaze. "Are you sure you're okay? I mean, if you're bored..."

"No, it's not that!" She nearly jumped out of her seat. Around them, an uproar filled the room as those people at the bar celebrated some winning game. She hadn't paid attention to what aired on the TVs, but clearly it was good for all of them. "I just...I think I'm a little hungry. Let me eat something, and my brain will clear up in no time."

She listened to the chanting in the back as she dunked a couple of wings in the ranch dressing. Her stomach grumbled as she finally started eating. Now she understood why the house starved so much. She struggled to focus on a simple bingo game. She knew her music all right. Even if she couldn't get the singer, she'd get the lyrics eventually. Yet with all the thoughts swirling around her head, she couldn't win anything.

The house needs to eat. I'm eating and it's got nothing to chew on. She caught Veena's eye, sending her mental messages. If anyone else noticed the state of the house, she would. It belonged to her, after all. She knew all the house's hunger pangs and cries. As she sipped her drink, she winked at Radha to get the message. They'd feed that house once they got home.

"Oh, I love this song!" Lata exclaimed as a loud pop song cut in. "I can't remember a word of it or who sang it, but I do know I love it! I danced to it years ago!"

"So did I!" Andrew laughed. "My wife and I…oh, I remember we got stuck in a snowstorm once. We were driving to my in-laws, which was a bad idea in the first place. Then came the storm. I wanted to turn back, but she insisted we move forward. My mother-in-law wasn't a forgiving woman. Anyway, we got stuck and the radio played and…" He stopped at the sight of Radha slowly dunking her carrots in the ranch dressing. "This song came on. I remember sitting in the car, praying we had enough gas to stay warm and get back on the road. A miserable moment, but a memorable one too. I keep wondering when I'll have another like that."

The truth dawned right then. He wanted that kind of moment with her. A moment where they'd get stuck somewhere, cold and miserable, listening to whatever came on the radio. They didn't have anything like that yet. They hadn't gone off on their own to visit anyone or get stuck anywhere. They only had a few nice dates together, eating out and having fun. Nothing that would make a fun memory in the future. She had nothing exciting.

Maybe this is a sign. He wants to do something more. He wants something exciting and memorable. How can I give him that?

These were the days she wished to be more like her sisters. Rupa and Manik never feared anything. They could drop all they did, pack their families up, and move on to another area without worrying about leaving anything behind. With such supportive spouses and friends, they worried about nothing. They wouldn't hesitate to tell Andrew yes. They wouldn't take their time to make decisions. Right now, she wantedtohave their confidence.

"Well..." She started to speak, wondering what he'd take from this. "I...I haven't been on a trip in a while."

"It's true." Swati nodded. "I get about two million photos a day from my other children, visiting all around the world. Even in the middle of the night, my phone is going off because my other daughter has no concept of time zones! I had to put her on mute eventually."

"Well, I wasn't thinking about going too far away yet." Andrew admitted. "I'm still working, and I won't have a long vacation for a while. I was thinking that eventually I would like to head down to Italy. Have you heard of the Cinque Terre? Five little towns around the coastline. Such a beautiful area. You must go there one day."

"Maybe I will." Radha relaxed the moment the host announced another round. "Oh, here we go! I need to catch up with everything. No one say a word, I have to listen to the questions. I keep missing things."

For the next few minutes, they all did nothing but eat and play. Radha succeeded in getting the next four questions in a row, though she hugged Andrew whenever they won. With each hug, the warmth between them burned. All at once, she wanted to go with him to that Italian coast and see the Cinque Terre towns. She wanted to spend nights on the beach with him, enjoying the cool breezes and quiet hours. If she got to see Italy, she could spend her hours sending photos to her sisters, bragging about all the places she saw. Not only that, she'd see it with a guy who liked her. Who wanted to date her. They always teased her for being so lonely and boring. Now they'd see she could attract people. Somehow, she attracted Andrew, and he hadn't run away yet. Things worked out well so far.

Feed me.

The house. As soon as it came into mind, she forgot all about Italy and future trips with Andrew. Their house needed her more than he did. The house was a part of her life, as her family loved to emphasize. If she turned on it, she turned on the family. Her heart ached over the idea of turning on anyone. What if she had to turn him away? She couldn't do that. Not unless…her heart ached over the possibility.

I can't let him go. Not unless I find out he did something horrible. He couldn't do something horrible.

He wouldn't.

Right?

CHAPTER 12

Radha thumbed through the pile of coupons from her wins. Free appetizers, free desserts, buy 1 get 1 free entree. Upper Deck would feed them for the next few months. She also managed to win a new mug, a T-shirt, and a chance to take part in the upcoming championships. Thank goodness Andrew knew more about music than she did. She could sing lyrics and forget the singers, but he didn't. He got them into the top three.

The biggest worry now was finding the time. Radha had all of it, of course, since no one wanted her for any jobs. Andrew assured her that he'd be free in the evenings, though he couldn't guarantee things would stay that way. He crossed his fingers as they walked back to the parking lot. He wanted more time with her.

"I had a great time tonight! I know it's not the museum but…"

"Oh, you can go to a museum any old time!" Veena waved it off. "Wouldn't you rather have fun with your closest friends?"

"He barely knows you! How are we now his closest friends?" Swati wondered out loud. "He's dating my daughter for a week, and we're suddenly close?"

"It's all right. I'd love to see more of you." Andrew kissed her hand before moving to Veen and Lata. "It was a pleasure! I don't remember doing anything so fun in a long time! How often do they have these trivia nights?"

"Oh, there's something happening every week." Radha pocketed all the coupons. "It's not always a music-themed night. In fact, sometimes we just have regular nights of trivia and bingo. That's what Lata's the champ at."

"I wish they didn't make it so hard tonight." Lata stared down at the one coupon she received. A free drink. It wasn't the worst thing in the world, but it wasn't what she normally won in these contests. She won the bigger things, such as trophies, giant tote bags, free meals for a week, and occasionally a trip nearby for two. "I know all those songs. I just couldn't remember who sang what."

Radha squeezed her shoulders. "Don't feel bad. That was hard. A lot of people struggled."

"Not me!" Swati waved her money around. "I got a hundred big ones here! I bet against you guys and look what it got me! Now I've got money to gamble with everyone at the center!"

Andrew leaned in close, pulling Radha towards him, making her forget all of Swati's declarations. His cologne wafted over her. She waltzed around, lost in a cloud of his musk. God, this was it. She stood on her toes and tiptoed towards the car. She didn't care that her mother bet money against her. She was in love. One week in, and she fell for this man smelling of ocean breezes and sandy beaches. She didn't know if he picked this cologne on purpose because it swept her away. She almost skipped to Andrew's car, ignoring the smirks from Veena and the confusion of Lata. They understood everything.

"It was so nice to meet you." Lata cut into the silence. "Next time, though, I will have your behind on a plate at bingo!"

Radha almost crumbled from that declaration, but

Andrew burst out laughing. "I'm sure you will! It was great to meet all of you. I think I can make it to the championships, but I'd like to see you again before then. Maybe I can come to your house?"

"NO!" The four of them cut in as he backed away. Radha cleared her throat, pushing away the thoughts of swimming in Andrew's cologne. She fell out of the fog and landed back to reality. Not the house. He wasn't ready for it. They couldn't drag him in while the house healed itself, flowers blooming and cracks closing in. It wasn't time.

"What we're trying to say is that the house..." Radha turned to her friends, waving her hands around for some help. "Our house isn't ready because..."

"We're redecorating it!" Veena threw in. "Painters come in and out all the time, it stinks!"

"Really? I thought it was the smell of decomp...ow!" Lata winced as Swati swatted the back of her head. "Hey, you can't tell me you don't smell that?!"

"Yes, it's really that bad!" Radha cut in before Andrew asked more questions. Lata would blow their cover if her mother wasn't there to keep in check. "I promise, though, once all the decorations are ready, you can meet me there. I'll take you on a full tour."

"Sounds fantastic. I hope the house redecoration wraps up soon." He kissed Veena and Lata's hands. "I hope I see more of you both. And as for you..." He scooped Radha into his arms, and she fell back into his cologne-scented body. Leaning in, he pressed a kiss on her lips. This time, she prepared herself for it. Her body dipped back as he lifted her off the ground. Behind her, the weight of everyone's stares and smiles bore into her. Oh, jealousy hit them hard. She loved it.

About time someone paid attention to me. Every muscle

inside of her relaxed, every nerve tingled. For once, bad luck didn't loom over her. She found something good, something to hold onto. Sniffing him, she took in that strong musky cologne before gently pulling back and letting him squeeze her arms.

"I'll call you later, okay?" He nodded to the others. "Have a good night, ladies. I'll see you later!"

"Bye!" Lata waved at him as he went to his car. The others sent their goodbyes, yet Radha froze. Her lips warmed by his kiss, she leaned against the side of her car to take in the night air. This kiss set everything inside her ablaze. Every cold joint, every aching muscle, everything sprang to life the moment he took her in his arms. Being in a man's arms again gave her that boost in life. The rest of her world came undone, but not the romantic part. She waited until his car drove out before turning to the others, all watching him zip out.

"So?" She held out her hands. "What do you think?"

"Ooh, I like him a lot and I'm jealous of you!" Veena gently punched her in the arm. "Seriously, how did you meet a man like that? I refuse to believe you bumped into him at the supermarket."

"Well, that's the truth. He and I were browsing in the same area, and we bumped into each other." She opened the car's side door for her mother. "I know it's not the type of thing you see in romance novels, but…"

"Who cares about it being from romance novels? Don't blow this one!" Swati snapped as she got inside. "I haven't seen a man this perfect since…hell, I don't think a perfect man exists. Not even your father. The man never put a toilet seat down if his life depended on it."

Radha laughed as she made her way to the driver's seat and waited for the others to buckle in. "So, I'm taking it that you approve of him?"

"What's to dislike? He's handsome, got a great job, very intelligent and kind, and he's the type of man who respects mothers. The only thing that could ruin this is if he hates my cooking. If he says one bad thing about my food..."

"Oh, Ma! He's not coming to our parties!" Radha revved up the car and started to back out. "We save those for the very special people, remember? He doesn't fall into that group."

"That we know of." Lata reminded her. "You've only known him for a week, Radha. What if you dig into his past and find something awful about him?"

Radha nearly screeched to a halt when she got the first light. Thankfully, it switched to red as soon as she hit the brakes. The car lurched forward while she wobbled in the seat. Lata wasn't wrong. One week wasn't long enough to know everything about a person. If Andrew had any skeletons lying around, they'd pop out soon enough. Her hands gripped the steering wheel, praying he showed every true part of him. He worked at the university like he claimed, but what else was true? What else could he hide from her?

Knowing her, she'd end up with someone who wasn't perfect inside. If the house found out about him, they'd have to feed him. No, she couldn't do that. There were plenty of other terrible people in this world. The house could eat them and stay standing for the rest of eternity. It couldn't have Andrew. Not when she finally found someone who liked her. He didn't care that she had no work or that she preferred boneless wings with ranch dressing. No way was she letting him go.

The light flipped to green, and she edged forward. "I can't sense anything terrible in him, Lata. You make a good point, but you met him tonight. He had no problem competing against you in bingo. And let's face it, you both struggled on that. He wasn't angry that you couldn't win. If anything, he's looking forward to the next night."

"Well, I think you should take him to the museum next time. All you've shown him is Carlota's Italian Bistro and Upper Deck. There's more to this place. I bet he doesn't know about the bakery that makes those amazing cakes. Or that little tea shop in the corner. If you want, I know a few places where you can really get to know him." Veena nudged her shoulder. "I get discounts too, so if you want to use one..."

"It's only been a week! Give them another week before you try to send them to your favorite love shacks!" Swati threw her hands in the air. "Anyway, I like the guy. I don't sense anything terrible in him either, not like the other people. A mother knows. I can tell when someone's a scumbag. He's not one."

"All the same, we shouldn't rush into anything." Lata reminded them. "Let's see how things go, okay? Maybe later, when the house is fully healed, we can bring him over. Not for a regular party, but just a small get together."

A small get together. No one remembered the last time they held one of those. The parties were big affairs full of food, music, and good times right before the house devoured the guests. Her mind went to Terry for a second. What if Andrew came on one of the party nights and he escaped? Would he forget all about her?

"It's too risky to invite him now." She decided. "You're right. I have to take him to other places first. Show him around town since he's new. He deserves to know a little more about me. Hell, he deserves to know about all of us."

"We met him already. What more does he need to know?" Swati shrugged. "Look, if you want the truth, he seems decent. Far more decent than some of the duds that walked through our door. He had no problem hanging out with us. Hell, he was willing to pay for the whole thing! I'd say he's a keeper!"

"Your mother is right, Radha! I don't meet men like this often. I'm jealous you managed to reel one in." Veena chuckled. "Charming, smart, handsome, and he likes playing trivia with us? They don't come around all the time. Hold onto him."

They drove down the road, taking in the quiet scenes around them. From the craziness inside Upper Deck to the lonely darkness ahead, Radha turned up the heater, so the car warmed up. She turned on the windshield wipers to get rid of any excess dirt and leaves on it. Tonight went well. Andrew got along with her friends, and her mother behaved for a change. If their next few dates went well, she saw a long relationship ahead. Perhaps even marriage. After a string of losses, she deserved a win.

"You have to bring him to the next bingo night. The regular one." Lata reminded her. "I want him to see me win. Tonight was hard, but next time...oh, maybe we can all go see that new movie! You know, the one about the dog who wins a marathon? That might be nice."

"I'll do whatever I can. You know, he talked about the Cinque Terre in Italy, and I remember Rupa showing me photos of it. So many clear beaches and tiny little cafes...the houses nestled up in the mountains...she complained it was a lot of hiking, but...whoa!"

BAM!

She slammed the brakes with a screech, lurching everyone forward. Before turning into the driveway, she caught sight of the house, and the darkness swept over her. Their home. The entire time they had fun, their home suffered.

Quietly, she eased the car down the driveway, her eyes widening at the damage. Dead petals flew in the wind, brushing against the windshield as she flipped on the high beams. They were no longer on the main road, so she used them to get a better look.

"Oh boy!" Swati whispered. "This is…This isn't a good sign. What the..."

"Were we robbed?!" Lata unbuckled her seat belt and tried to stand up. "Radha, I can't see anything! What happened?!"

Radha couldn't answer as she processed the scene before her. Their home came into view. yet the darkness couldn't hide any of the cracks sticking out. Dust crumbled off the roof, sailing down to the ground as they parked the car. She unbuckled her seatbelt and cut off the car engine, switching everything down before getting out. No, none of it was a dream. A piece of the roof sailed down as more cracks appeared on the outside. In the thick stone, jagged lines broke up the beauty. The bushes up front went from lush green to rusty brown. Sticks on the ground broke once they stepped on the ground. Even the grass, once long green blades, turned brown and crunchy. Radha tiptoed towards the front door and ran her finger down the cracked door. They weren't robbed since it remained locked, yet the house suffered. While they enjoyed themselves, it came undone.

"Oh God." Veena stepped up to the door, brushing off the dirt on the sides. "This is worse than I feared. The last party wasn't enough."

"What do you mean?"

"I mean…it's still hungry. We can keep feeding it guests, but that's not what it wants." Veena closed her eyes. "It's only happened one time in the past, and it took us weeks to satisfy the house. This time, it's craving something specific."

"Something specific?" Radha repeated. "Well, what happens if we can't find that something in particular?"

A piece of roof crumbled and smashed into the ground. Veena stared down at the pile of dirt and new cracks forming around them. This answered all the questions. The house wouldn't settle for anything. It wanted something special, something that could take weeks to find. It demanded food. Each wall cracked with more dust falling. It started. The hunger pangs grew as they entered their home, assessing the new damage. Broken vases, broken stairs, everything falling apart. They didn't need a party. They needed the special something.

Without it, the house would die.

CHAPTER 13

The damage turned out to be minimal, though it didn't ease anyone's pain. All the cracks and dirt would take time cleaning. They checked all their valuables to find nothing out of place. By some miracle, all the paintings and sculptures stayed in their places. Radha shuddered as several angels stared at her, dragging her with their emptyeyes. These days, she hated them over the demons. At least she expected evil glares from them. These cherubs, all made of white marble, judged her as she walked down the halls. They didn't like something.

"Stop staring at me." She grumbled as she went into her room. To her relief, that remained mostly untouched save for so many flowers and petals lying around. She went over to bed and checked the headboard. Nothing. The house suffered slight damage after starving. After a few pieces of meat, it would heal itself.

But, what if it's not enough? The frosty air around her gave the worst sensation in her stomach. The house wasn't happy at being kicked aside. It didn't like it when dinner came too late. She patted the wall. "I'm sorry. You'll get your food in a few minutes. Just hang in there."

Another hunger pain shakes. It forgave her, yet remained unhappy. How could she forget about it? How could any of them not feed the house? Here they were, laughing and eating, while it sat here, waiting for something. When it didn't get what it wanted, it crumbled. Her bed creaked as she pressed down on it. Terrific. Now it affected the furniture. This would take a long time to fix. The petals on the ground swirled despite no wind blowing in. Once all together, she saw the sentence.

FEED ME NEXT TIME.

"Of course." Kicking aside the pile of petals, Radha fiddled with her phone as Andrew's text popped up. At first, she didn't check on him, but as another text chimed in, she opened it up. **I had a good time meeting your friends tonight.**

Breathing normally, she ignored the cracking wall behind her and sent a reply. **I'm sorry we can't see each other this weekend. I still want to see you next week at the museum. Is that fine?**

He took only a second to send a thumbs up and a 'yes' emoji back at her. Then he confirmed the same time and place as they originally planned. Pressing the phone against her chest, she fell on her bed, her head hitting the fluffed pillows. Hair spilling around, the cracks in the house reminded her of the bigger things. Their home no longer craved the old guests. It wanted a guest to sustain for years. As another petal fell off, she stroked the walls.

"I think you want him, but I can't give him to you." She whispered. "He doesn't have anything terrible in him." Another crack split right above her headboard. "No, you can't do that! I'm willing to give you anyone else, anyone but him! You can have my mother! She's old! What does she do besides cook and complain?" The house stopped cracking then. "No, you're right. It's no different from when she was younger. All she's ever done is cook and complain. That doesn't make her a decent meal."

Her eyes fell on the picture of her and her father from years ago. These lonely nights brought out the same old grief inside. He died well before she moved into this house, yet she talked to him as if he stood right by her. He listened to her problems with everything. Unlike her mother, he approved of her desires, encouraging everything she did. The only other man besides Andrew who gave her that little bit of happiness.While her mother dragged her for every little thing she did, her father stood by her side. He didn't always like everything she did, but he took time to understand her. Even after he passed, she kept all his advice and followed through with it. A small part of her wished he was here with them. He usually got her mother to calm down. Unfortunately, she didn't get that little support system anymore. Dad was gone, so she dealt with her aging mother on a regular basis.

"I can't lose him, too, Dad." She whispered. "I know the house needs souls. We feed it all the time. But, I don't know if I can bring Andrew here. It's a dangerous place for him. If he found out the truth…he can't. I've already let go of plenty of people. Not him either."

Not that her father could give her an answer. If he were listening, he'd laugh and tell her not to worry so much. All Radha ever did was worry about life. That's why nothing really happened to her. That's why she never got a decent job or went anywhere fun or did cool things. She worried about things that never happened. Andrew wasn't coming to the house. They hadn't seen each other long enough for her to bring him around. For now, he was safe.

Don't think about what isn't happening, Radha. Focus on fixing yourself. Fixing what's around you. Dwelling on the future won't get anything done in the present.

A knock on the door formed cracks in the frame as more

petals fell. Shaking her hair, Radha stretched out on the bed, grabbing her book on the nightstand. "Come in!"

Swati pushed the door open, already wrapped in her robe and nightgown. "I can't sleep in my room."

"Your room's cracking too, Ma?"

"No, I can't sleep thanks to me losing fifty bucks in the latest bet I made with Gladys." Swati sat next to her, spotting the picture of her late husband. "Don't tell your father that, though. He always gripes about money around me."

"Yeah, well, I doubt he'll do anything." Radha fixed her father's photo before sitting back down. "Where did you get fifty dollars anyway?"

"Your purse. Where else would I get it?" Swati grabbed a handful of petals, rubbing her fingers against their pillowy softness. "You too, huh? I'm walking through a field of these things. I can't see the floor underneath, let alone find my slippers, cause I'm surrounded by petals! We gotta do something for this house."

"What do we do, Ma? The same old thing? It's not enough." Radha threw her hands in the air. "I don't know how to drag people in here. You were right. I can't attract anyone with anything. No one is good enough anyway."

"Hey, you attracted Andrew. I haven't complained about him!"

"But the house..." She got up as she inspected the rest of the cracks. Each one grew longer and deeper with the steps she took. No, not tonight. Not Andrew. "I can't bring him here. Meet him outside, fine. But the house? No way."

"Why not? Are you worried he'll find out the truth? He's gonna know what goes on. If he wants to be part of our family one day, he'll have to get used to it." Swati's face fell as Radha turned away from her. "You're not thinking about cutting it off now, are you? You haven't had a relationship that lasts longer than a week. This guy likes you, Radha. I don't know what you said or did to him, but he wants to be around you. Isn't that enough?"

"It's not that, Ma!" Radha slammed her hand against the one smooth part of the wall. The house shuddered at the blow, so she stroked it gently. "I'm sorry. I just…I'm scared of him finding out. We're not exactly holding bake sales in this house! People have died here. People have been dying for generations, something we've kept from the public. This is moving faster than I thought. And I like spending time with him. I like our talks, no matter how simple they can be. I like him. Is that crazy?"

Swati shook her head. "The crazy thing would be if you had no sparks between you. I saw everything tonight. He's rubbing up against you, wrapping his arms around you, laughing at everything you say. No matter how stupid it is, he's engaged with you. Why do you want to let a good thing go?"

Radha stared up at the ceiling as the creaking settled in. They rarely headed upstairs where dark halls and empty rooms lay. She hated going to them as Veena claimed the spirits of their family lingered inside. Lata claimed she saw their ghosts wander down these halls, always appearing disappointed. They weren't satisfied with the souls they got. Veena also claimed her husband's spirit lingered up here, which was why she spent more time here than anyone else.

Creak! She jumped back as the floorboards above squeaked. Not a ghost this time. Was someone stomping there? She moved away from the noisiest part and moved into a corner.The creaking continued as she waited for it to slow down. *Creak…creak…creak…*

Her mother wasn't wrong. She couldn't afford to lose Andrew. No man listened to her the way he did. Yet she expected something to pop up and derail the relationship. Making her way back to her bed, she plopped down and spread her hair out. Swati split it into pieces to braid. "I guess I'm scared of the future. What if he hates me for something later?"

"He wouldn't hate you unless you did something stupid. So far, you're nailing this. That's a first." Swati tightened her grip on Radha's hair, yanking on her scalp. Radha gritted her teeth as her mother continued to braid. "Hold still! This is why I tell you never to use a hair dryer! You've got split ends and your hair's falling out!"

"That's not the reason, Ma." Radha winced as her mother wrapped her hair around. "Gently! Are you trying to rip out the rest of my hair?"

"I'm perfecting it." Swati bit down on her bottom lip as she braided everything. "Have you ever thought about getting a haircut? It might help you maintain this mess."

"I don't think it's a good idea, Ma. My hair never…ow!" She dug her nails into the mattress as her mother pulled more hair back. "Easy, Ma! What are you doing to my hair? Are you trying some new hairstyle?"

"No, I want to see if that guy on National Geographic was right about hair being used as a musical instrument. Of course, I'm styling your hair!" Swati grumbled. "At least I'm trying to style it. You have so many knots in here, you'll make sailors jealous!"

Radha gave up arguing with her mother, leaning back, and letting her work away. After a few seconds, Swati's hands loosened up and she moved the hair around, braiding it. Her mind drifted to older times when they sat together with her mother constantly combing or styling her daughter's hair. Only Radha sat still whenever Swati wanted to braid something. Rupa and Manik preferred doing their own hair and her brothers never stayed in place long enough to do anything with their hair. No matter how much it hurt, she sat there so her mother had something to do.

"This takes me back." Swati grabbed the hair ribbons and tied up the braid. "Remember those days, Radha? When I did your hair?"

"Oh yeah." Radha chuckled. "I think I may have been six or seven when you started doing my hair. You always liked to play with it."

"Eh, it's more like I was bored and wanted something to do. Your sisters decided that they didn't want my advice. They grew up before I got a chance to raise them. You, on the other hand, took a little more time, which I liked. It gave us time to get to know each other. That's why I'm worried about you blowing this thing. It's the first guy who likes you, Radha. I mean, he really likes you! Why are you struggling to show him the same affection?"

"I'm not! It's just that…" Radha pulled away, her braid swinging back and forth. Don't blow it. That advice came from her parents and grandparents when she was a child. Don't blow it on final exams. Don't blow it on asking people out. Don't blow it on job interviews. Yet somehow, she managed to blow it on everything. Her mother was right; she couldn't blow this one. The house couldn't eat Andrew. "I'm scared of getting too close."

Swati moved to the side so Radha could sit up with her. "Come here. I get that you're scared of feeding him to the house. Don't sweat that, we'll find something for it. Now, the question is…what do you feel for him?"

"Feel for him?" Radha stared down at her toes, digging them into her sandals. The slightly long nails reminded her of her bi-annual pedicure appointment. Andrew hadn't noticed these monster claws, thank goodness. She only wore shoes covering these toes. "Well, I think we get along. We have a good time whenever we're together. I do think he could be the one to spend the rest of my life with."

"But?" Swati prompted her. "Something's holding you back."

"But nothing, Ma. I don't want us to go too fast. I normally didn't bring guys to meet you until a few weeks had passed. And even then, I was never sure."

"Big deal. You weren't sure the two times you brought guys over to see me." Swati shook her head. "Look, Radha. You're well into your fifties now. I could help you with these troubles when you were a teenager. Hell, I could help you when you were in your thirties. At this point, you're not dating to start a family. You want someone to grow old with. Ask yourself if Andrew's the one. Is he the one you see sitting with you on the front porch and watching the sun go down? Is he the one you would go on vacations with, make romantic dinners for, and stand by through thick and thin? If so, then you gotta do what your heart's telling you to do."

Radha let those words sink in. Her mother never got this deep about relationships. Most of the time, she turned down the men that came through the door. None of their guests gave her a good vibe. Neither did the random men they dated. Seeing that Andrew got her talking and thinking about the future, Radha found brighter days on the horizon. Maybe it was meant to be. Maybe a few more days, she'd know for sure what she wanted.

As she turned to thank her mother, she found her going through her cellphone. Swati shook her head as she swiped through photos. "Your sisters spend way too much time going everywhere. Look at this…souvlaki in Greece! French fries in Belgium! Macaroons in France and beer in Germany… oh, what the hell?! Tell me your sister isn't feeding her kids beer! She goes out of the country and thinks no rules apply to her!"

Radha squinted at the screen. There was Rupa waving around all the food she and the kids were eating. She wanted to hate them for this, hate them for going around and spending so much money, yet she couldn't muster up the strength for this. She couldn't get angry at her sister for living the dream and traveling all around. Rupa begged her to come a few times with the family, but Radha declined. As tempting as traveling was, she didn't want to be the burden in that group. They'd enjoy themselves out in the sun, trying new foods and exploring small villages, while she dragged her feet behind them. For those reasons, Radha turned down her sister's offers to come along.

Going with Andrew? She could do that. He wouldn't mind if they spent some time alone, enjoying the quiet nights in the villas and the lively nights in the cities. They'd be together, experiencing each country to the fullest. She glanced over at Rupa's latest photo with the family all sitting by the beach. Those crystal blue waters reflected the same seascapes she created. Granted, they sat on the floor, but one day, when the house healed itself, she'd hang them on the wall.

When the house heals itself. When will that be?

Radha continued to play with her phone, going through all her sister's photos. Hearing Andrew talk about his wife sank her heart deeper. She couldn't fill that void for him. She couldn't get lost with him in a snowstorm, listening to 80s music while praying they had enough gas in the car. His eyes twinkled when talking about his late wife. He laughed at the memory, no matter how miserable it might have been. She didn't have anything of that sort in her life. Even memories of the past never made her laugh this way. No one in her family sparked that kind of joy. She loved them all, yet never went beyond that obligated love. Not even her mother, who continued to pick away the lint on her body, got that sweet love that she craved. Nor did she give it in return. Neither of her parents knew what real love was. They assumed doing things for their children covered it all.

No wonder I can't figure any of this out. Radha frowned at her sister's photo, where the family was standing right in front of the Colosseum in Rome. That marked five out of seven wonders of the world that they'd seen. Five more than Radha ever saw in her lifetime. She never got the chance to see the Taj Mahal in India, since she ended up sick the day everyone went to Agra. They never went back after that, so she lost her chance. She gave up going back since no one else was willing to travel there again. Plain, boring Radha stayed plain and boring with no exciting stories to share.

Maybe this was another chance. Andrew came into her life to bring some excitement. He saw so much while she remained in one place. Now it was time for them to share and enjoy moments together. Their next date could be a vacation at the beach or in the mountains. She didn't exactly have anything waiting back here. They could go away for a long time, get to know each other, and just be together.

The house shook then as Swati pulled away, lights flickering around. "Oh boy! What's next?"

"It's probably hungry." Radha stood up. "I think Veena will feed it in a second. I'm not sure what happened, though. We gave it enough to eat last time."

"That's what you think." Swati plucked the last bit of lint off Radha's clothes and flicked it away. "Geez, you catch more of these things than a dryer does! Anyway, don't worry about the house, and don't worry about Andrew so much. Everything's gonna be fine. The house has gone through worse in the past and we came out in one piece. It'll happen again."

"What makes you think I'm worried?"

"Please! I raised you! You get tense in the shoulders whenever you're stressed out." Swati turned to the wall with a few new cracks. "Though I really do hope Veena feeds the house soon. I don't want it to cave in on you."

Radha nodded though her mind went back to Andrew. The floor shivered and she sat down on the bed. Andrew. Any time she thought of him, the house shook. It wanted something. Curious, she decided to try an experiment. "Andrew!"

Swati turned around. "What about Andrew?"

Before Radha explained anything, the house shivered and proved her point. Snapping her fingers, she got up. "That's it! That's what's causing the shaking."

"What are you talking about?"

"Whenever I think about or mention Andrew, this house shivers. It starts cracking again. See?" She pointed to fresh cracks on the ground. "I think I know what it's craving right now. It wants Andrew."

Swati blinked. "Your boyfriend? But don't we…"

"Yes, Ma, I know. Andrew's not the typical type of food." Radha gulped. "He shouldn't be a guest here. I can't bring him here, but…" The floor cracks widened as she stepped over them. "I don't know what to do, Ma. He and I get along great! I want to go farther but…"

"But what?" Swati waved her hand around. "I think you're overthinking this. You're exhausted and it shows. If you're worried, just keep him away. Don't bring him here, and he'll be safe. Go on a bunch of dates. Go to the museum, the movies, restaurants, go to the beach! You'll still have a great time without coming here."

"What if he wants to come here, Ma?"

"Make up a damn excuse! Tell him we're redecorating and…" She waved her hand over the cracks. "Believe me, that is close to the truth. You can't have him over cause the house needs some repairs."

She relaxed right then. Of course, she could use the redecorating excuse. Veena and Lata did that all the time with men they liked. They'd meet in other places, still enjoying the company and not concerned about bringing them home. She could do the same. "You're right, Ma. I'm stressing out over something so simple. I have to keep Andrew…" The house shook around her. "Sorry, I have to keep him out of here. Even if he asks, I'll tell him not now. Not while we're in the process of fixing this place up."

"We're always fixing this place." Swati shrugged. "Every other week, we have to fix this place. At least you won't be lying."

"I guess not." Radha calmed down. "You're right. Maybe I'm overreacting to all this. I just met Andrew. I'm still learning all about him. I need to relax and not jump to conclusions."

"That's what I've been saying for years! You always panic over the smallest thing, and you always get through." Swati squeezed her shoulder. "Now don't sweat over this anymore. Andrew's not in danger. He's got no reason to be in danger."

Radha returned the squeeze even though the nagging feeling never left. The house's shivers always scared her. She never knew what it really wanted. The only thing she hoped was that her mother was right; Andrew was not in danger. All this was in her head. She panicked only because she finally had someone.

"He's not in danger." She repeated as she laid her hand against the wall. "I'm overreacting. Nothing's going to happen. Andrew will be fine."

The house shivered as new cracks popped out of the wall, a reminder that it listened. It knew everything. The house heard her every word...and it didn't agree with anything she said.All over the walls, she found the same date written repeatedly. The house screamed at her. It wouldn't do this without reason. Still, she couldn't understand the importance of it. Even as it swirled around, she didn't get it.

JULY 3 JULY 3 JULY 3 JULY 3 JULY 3. REMEMBER JULY 3.

CHAPTER 14

Radha spent the next few days trying to coax the house towards another meal. This whole July 3rd thing got out of hand. She found nothing of importance about it save that there were Independence Day parties all around. That didn't mean anything awful. Save for loud noises and fireworks and maybe some idiots getting in fights, it didn't mean he committed a crime. No, there had to be more to this.

She researched each day for a new evil soul it could munch on and heal itself. Sadly, most of the people who came across them were walking around for minor offenses: shoplifting, writing bad checks, causing a small brawl in the bars, everything of that sort. The house wouldn't eat them. If it did, it wouldn't stay satisfied for long. It wanted the worst offenders of the law.

"I'm failing at this." She tripped over the sidewalk as she checked herself out in a store mirror. Andrew didn't cancel this next date, assuring her he wanted to go to the museum. Her mother played around with her hair, yanking it and tightening it into a high ponytail. With all the pins in place, Radha couldn't take it out, but she loosened the hair tie and let it hang low. There! Dabbing a little perfume behind her ears, she calmed down and headed towards the museum. People wove in and out of her, half busy on their phones and the other half rushing through. She nearly stumbled into someone who texted while walking. The man apologized without looking at her, went on his way, and continued to type away as she cursed under her breath.

Next time, she promised to pick a less crazy time to go downtown. Every day, people wandered around along with all the tour groups and buses driving through. The blaring horns and squealing tires gave her nightmares of the night at Carlota's. The only thing to ruin such a quiet night were those cars. Now, they were about to ruin her museum as well.

Can no one drive in this place? She fumed as she punched the crosswalk buttons. A group of people congregated behind her, all talking at once. At her feet, a cute corgi gazed at her with its big brown eyes and whimpered. A part of her wanted to kneel to pet it, but she resisted. She dealt with unkind dog owners and their equally unkind dogs as a kid. They never wanted her near their precious babies, even when she claimed she wouldn't hurt them. She stepped away from the corgi, hands dropped at her sides. She wasn't petting him right before lunch. The light flipped for them to cross, so she took several steps behind the corgi before moving.

"All right, don't blow this." She took a deep breath as she pulled open the museum doors. A crowd already gathered in front as she went to grab a map. Not that she needed it. She preferred wandering around museums without the maps or audio guides. They always dragged her down, taking up too much time, when she wanted to learn on her own. Tucking the map in her bag, she breathed again to start the dating. So far, she hadn't tripped over her feet or stumbled over words. She couldn't mess this up.

Andrew waited for her in the museum lobby, checking out the IMAX theater prices and times. She walked up to him and tapped his shoulders. He turned around with a smile, pointing to the posters of fungi, dinosaurs, and the ocean. "Hey, I'm glad you made it." Leaning in, he pecked her cheek. "I thought we could watch one of these shows. I'm particularly interested in the ocean one, but I'll take anything. What about you?"

"I don't have a preference. Fungi, ocean, dinosaurs…I'm sure they're all interesting." She checked the time for the ocean movie, which would start in thirty minutes. The others would follow right after. "Uh, we have some time right before the movies so I was thinking we could explore the bottom floor? It's got all your favorite ocean creatures in here."

"Oh, really? I don't remember telling you my favorite ocean creature."

"You didn't. I figured you loved them all." She led him towards the exhibits. "There are some small creatures in tanks, but they're mostly statues of the animals. Maybe some skeletal remains of whales and creatures from the past. I hope you're okay with it."

"I'm fine. Everything came from something in the past. I can't tell you how old some creatures in the ocean are. Going down there, it's…well, it's like another planet." His eyes glazed over at the tank of jellyfish swimming around. "These guys are what I'm talking about. I did a lot of research on jellyfish a few years back. It's like seeing dinosaurs in real life."

"Dinosaurs? Aren't they reptiles for the most part?"

He laughed as they stopped in front of another tank, this one full of seahorses. She stared at them floating along the fake coral reefs and seaweed. "You're right, but what I meant was jellyfish have been around longer than we have. Longer than the dinosaurs themselves. It makes you wonder what they've seen. If they could talk, what could they tell us?"

Radha wanted to laugh at the idea, but his words sank in. These creatures in the ocean saw more than most people had. They knew everything going on around them. No wonder he found them so fascinating. She also caught the subtle message in his words. "You really want to see that ocean movie, huh?"

"I can't help it. The farther I'm from the ocean, the more I crave it. I wish the beach were closer. We could go there almost every day." He moved from the seahorses to several crustaceans wandering around in their tank. Radha shuddered as they crawled around the fake sand, their little legs digging in. She never liked these guys, even though Andrew eyed them in fascination. Their bodies sent shivers into her so she moved to another tank filled with fish. Checking her phone, she noticed they had ten minutes before the ocean movie started.

"Hey, if you want to get tickets, we should go now." She nudged him. "Your favorite movie's gonna start."

"Right, right." He followed her to the ticket box office, bright red in the face. "I bored you, didn't I?"

"Bored me? No way! I'm still standing next to you, right?" She whipped out her credit card before he could reach his pockets. "Um, two for the 11:00 showing of Oceans: Past, Present, and Future, please."

"Oh, Radha, you didn't have to." He moved back as she took her card and the tickets. "I could have gotten that."

"You've paid for dinner the last three times. I can afford to pay for a forty-five-minute movie." She waved him off. "I may not be working right now, but I still have money. This is nothing. Now come on." She led him towards the auditorium. "After this, we can finish exploring the museum and go for lunch. I don't have any preferences."

"Neither do I. Everything you've picked has been incredible." He stepped into the dark auditorium where several people searched around for seats. Spotting two in the back, he grabbed her hand and led her up to them. "Granted, you've only taken me to two places, but I've enjoyed both of them."

"Then I hope you enjoy Rosarita's…provided you like Mexican food." She twiddled her fingers. "I rarely come downtown, but that place always has the best drinks and food. Ma can't resist eating their chips. One time, she…" She cut herself off once they got to their seats. He let her go in first while she silenced her phone. Only her mother sent a text demanding Radha pick up some after dinner mints and napkins for the next party. They ran out of them at the last one.

Next party. So far, they hadn't made any plans for another party, yet her mother loved to be prepared. The house cracks lingered in her mind. Their house crumbled while they had fun. No, that couldn't happen. This was their home. A place they shared memories and love inside. They spent nights talking in the kitchen, walking around the halls, and admiring the roses in bloom. Even those sculptures, be angels or demons, had their place in the house. She walked by them with their empty eyes locked on her. They knew the house needed to eat. Sooner or later, she needed to bring in more meals.

The house can wait a little longer. I'm not running off. Not when this is the first man who's shown interest in me.

They settled in their places as people crowded in. Radha rested her purse by her feet as Andrew draped his arm around her. She sniffed the air, catching the scent of ocean water and tequila. "You haven't been drinking today, have you?"

"Oh, no! This cologne…" He sniffed behind him. "That's the last time I trust anyone behind the store counter. I asked for the most popular scent. This is what she gave me. I'm supposed to smell like a moonlit beach at night."

"Instead, it smells like a New Years Party hangover." Radha finished off for him. The doors closed as the room darkened. She rested in his arms, ignoring the strong stench. "Don't worry. I'm sure it'll die out by the time we leave this place."

The movie rolled while people silenced themselves, and Radha lost herself in the narration of the oceans. Andrew had a point about them holding so much mystery. Layers of the sea remained unexplored. As vibrant colors shifted around on the screen, showing the different stages of the sea, Andrew's foot got right next to hers. Tapping her toes on the dark linoleum floor, she waited until his hand fell on her knee. She inched her hand close to him, yet pulled back. He always wrapped his arms around her and rubbed against her knee. Why did she hesitate so much? They got this close in a short amount of time. She dropped her hand back on her lap. No, she couldn't move this quickly. This relationship zipped by, but she wasn't ready to take the next few steps. She wasn't sure how to approach this.

As they watched a humpback whale leaping out of the water, droplets splashing everywhere as it went down, his arm dropped down and his hand squeezed her thigh. She bit down on her lip and gasped as the whale landed, flippers waving in the air. Even from this screen, she couldn't peel her eyes away from this beautiful creature. Andrew's eyes glazed over as the scene moved to one of humpback whales swimming in the bright blue ocean. No wonder he wanted to watch this: the IMAX experience gave them every bit of what happened down there.

Radha stared down at her feet to find Andrew inched a little closer. He pulled his hand off her thigh and pulled her back towards him. The air conditioner blasting through destroyed that horrible alcohol smell. Now, all she got off his body was the ocean water. Relaxing her shoulders, she leaned in her chair as the movie slowly came to an end. She didn't move out of the seat until the lights came on and other people started to leave.

"What do you think?" Andrew helped her stand up. "Aren't those whales something?"

"They're beautiful. I've never seen one in person though, just on TV and movies."

"Oh, God, they're even more magnificent in person! There's a tiny bit of fear when you swim right by them because they're so huge. Yet at the same time, you can't help being in awe of them. Watching them on that screen, that humpback whale...nothing can ever compare to the emotions rushing through you when you see it."

She couldn't compare it, but listening to him waxing poetic about whales burned her soul. The fire grew once they started walking around the ocean exhibit. He stopped a few times before the statues of various whales, their descriptions polished in gold to identify them. Pointing to a statue of a humpback whale, he waved over it.

"Can you believe that I've swam next to these guys?"

"I believe it." She nodded. "I believe everything you claimed to do. However, I..." She checked her phone as another message from her mother came in. Once more, Swati demanded the mints, though she forgot to bring up napkins. Instead, she mentioned wanting Pringles chips to give their guests. Radha shook her head, dropping her phone in her bag. Those Pringles weren't going to be anyone's but Swati's alone. She only mentioned this so Radha picked them up. Her headache mounting, she headed towards the elevator for the next floor.

"Radha, wait!" Andrew followed her as she pressed the up button. "Were you bored down there? I'm sorry, I just…"

"No, it's not you." Radha clutched her purse. "My mother's texting in the middle of our date. Demanding I bring things home. Somehow, she thinks I'll have time for shopping afterwards. I don't know how she can't get a hint that I'm busy!"

"Hey, no big deal. We can pick up those things for her on the way back. It's not much, is it?"

"Only three things." She shrugged. "Let's worry about those later. Tell me more about whales."

"Okay then! You're one of the few people who've asked for that." Andrew pulled her in close. "Did you know what humpbacks are best known for? In fact, they're known for many wonderful things, not just singing. I bet I could fit everything I know about them in this museum."

"I bet you could." She pushed her hair aside and moved in closer. "Tell me more about them. Did you have any crazy encounters?"

"Oh, I couldn't count all the encounters with both hands. Most were friendly, though. Maybe a little too friendly. In fact, I should tell you about the time I encountered one that thought I was its calf. That was an experience I can't forget but wish I could."

Radha let him drone on about whales for the next few minutes, her mind shaken up with excitement and dread. She nodded at everything he said, even if she didn't get all the facts about whales. They didn't matter when there was a hungry house waiting for her. It wanted her to bring him over. It wanted that little taste of him.

No, he can't go. He can never go. Ma said not to worry,

but... Radha pretended to listen and pay attention to the exhibits. They ogled the giant statues and fossils of creatures from years ago. She admired how much everything evolved throughout time, how all creatures adapted and grew with their changing environments. She'd listen to the audio at each exhibit while absorbing all the information.

As of now? She knew nothing except that Andrew loved humpback whales. Sure, she remembered the little quip about them singing, but the rest blurred in her mind. Here she was, walking around and acting like nothing horrible waited for her. She was enjoying exhibits and movies, having fun like a normal person, when she was anything but. What if he learned about the dark secrets? What if he researched missing people and came across their guests? What if he learned about her house, that family home that stayed for generations? Could he? Every trace of them disappeared after a party, yet what if they missed something? She wiped the sweat forming off her brow as they went into the next room.

"Isn't that something, Radha?"

Radha blinked as Andrew turned to her. "What is?"

"Your friend's over here!" He waved behind her. "I had no idea Lata was showing up. You didn't tell me she was coming!"

"That's because I'm not expecting anyone to join us. Are you sure it's Lata?" Radha followed his gaze, wondering if he mixed Lata up with someone else. Her blood pressure spiked at Lata waving back. Despite the small crowd behind them, she made her way towards them. "What a pleasant surprise."

"I wonder if she wants to join us. That could be nice."

I'm sure she will. She's only here for one reason. Radha inhaled over why Lata came over. She wasn't a museum goer by any means. Maybe her mother was ill, and taken to the hospital. Maybe something happened to her relatives overseas. Her blood froze over the house cracking and coming undone. It wouldn't fall apart now. They still had time.

Oh, please. She prayed as Lata got closer. *Please tell me you're here because of good news.*

Please don't tell me something's wrong with the house.

CHAPTER 15

As happy as Andrew became, Radha's stomach lurched over the possible news. Her friend came here to give her news and would do it once they got a free moment. She didn't enjoy walking around and observing exhibits. She asked all the obvious questions whenever they went on museum tours to the point where no one asked her to join them. For her to walk over here meant she wanted to see Radha for something.

The house. Something's either wrong with the house or my mother. And given that Lata's faking her happiness, it can't be something wrong with my mother. The sharp pain in her side dug in deeper at Lata's smile curling up. A fake smile. Their home was in danger. Those cracks finally gave in and brought it down.

That can't be though! We keep feeding it. She tapped her foot on the ground as Andrew waved his arms and beckoned Lata forward. He had no clue how bad things were, the poor thing. The cracks on their home walls, the wilting flowers. He knew none of it. All Radha could do was continue to act normal. Lata wouldn't reveal anything in front of Andrew. She knew better than to spill the secrets of their home in public.

Be calm. Be cool. Nothing's wrong yet. You're going to be fine. You're just meeting your friend over here. Don't let poor

Andrew think you're out of your mind.

Lata waved to them as she bounced over, nearly knocking over a few children getting in her way. She weaved through the lines of them, apologizing for all the bumping. Brushing past other visitors, she stopped right in front of the skeletal remains of the triceratops. Andrew waltzed right over, holding out his hand while Radha thanked every deity that she didn't cause a scene. Most of the children wandered off without a second thought, too busy admiring the dinosaurs and doing the interactive exhibits. They didn't care that Lata bumped into them.

"Hi, Lata." Andrew pecked her on the cheek. "I'm surprised to see you here today. Radha says you work during the week."

"Only part-time. It's basically office work." Lata explained as she admired the triceratops before them. "We have one of these things back at home."

"You've got a display of the triceratops?"

"No, this banister." She rubbed her hands against the gold banister, squeezing it. "Feels just like home. That's the main reason I like to come here. Well, that and I love going up to see the insects. Did Radha take you inside the butterfly house yet?"

"Not yet, Lata." Radha moved them away from the exhibit. "We're slowly making our way around the floors, then we're off to lunch."

"Would you like to join us?" Andrew cut in before Radha could signal Lata to leave them alone. Her friend came here for more than the exhibits. Lata never showed up at museums unless she brought news with her. Of course, with Andrew around, she couldn't reveal that news. She'd follow them until the moment he stepped away for some reason. Now he asked her to lunch, she prayed Lata said no, that she had to go back to work. She could drop her news off later. Not during a date. If only she'd…

"Oh, I'd love to!" Lata ignored Radha's gaze as they moved towards more dinosaur exhibits. "Where were you planning to go? I know a nice little cafe just a block from here. Many of my coworkers get lunch from it."

"Sounds nice! I don't think we had reservations anywhere, did we? Radha mentioned that Mexican place but I'm sure a cafe is fine too." Andrew checked with Radha who grit her teeth and signaled Lata to stop. He caught her with her teeth slightly out. "Is…is something wrong?"

"What? Oh no!" Radha forced herself to smile. She couldn't show those off to him, looking no better than the dinosaurs they stood around. "I just…I was hoping we could go somewhere a little quieter. That's why I suggested Rosarita's earlier. At this hour, it's not too crowded."

"The café's quiet, Radha. Most people don't eat there, they just grab their lunch and go." Lata explained. "They serve mostly stuff like sandwiches and salads, healthy and easy to eat. But, if you would like something more…"

"It's fine." Radha cut her off. "We can try a fancier place for our next dinner date. I think sandwiches would be okay for now. As long as it's not Upper Deck again."

Lata snapped her fingers. "Speaking of Upper Deck, there's another bingo night on Sunday! And it's regular bingo this time!"

"Sounds great!" Andrew clapped his hands. "I am free on Sunday for once. I look forward to our rematch, Lata."

"I look forward to kicking your keister at bingo." Lata grinned tight enough to redden her cheeks. "If you don't mind, I need to hit the ladies' room for one second. Do you want to come, Radha?"

There it came. Lata found the perfect opportunity to

drop the news, and they couldn't waste a second. Radha eyed the ladies' room in the corner, completely free of a line. She nodded as she squeezed Andrew's hand. "I could freshen up a little bit. Wait right here, honey. We'll be back."

"Take your time. I'll sit over here when I'm done." He pointed to the bench against the wall as some people got up, leaving it empty. "Afterwards, you can take me up to see the butterfly house."

"Trust me. You won't want to miss it!" Lata led Radha into the bathroom and quickly checked each stall in case anyone lingered around. Radha opened each door, found a few toilets unflushed, and slammed them shut. Of course, half the people using the restroom didn't bother to flush anything. With toilet paper all over the floor and an overflowing trash bin, it didn't surprise her that there was no line. Leaning against the sink, she faced Lata and narrowed her gaze.

"All right, the coast is clear. I don't see any cameras around either." She checked above them. "Nope, just ceilings. All right, what do you need to tell me?"

"It's the list." Lata began. "We don't have enough people. I've been going through my phone and there's not many we can drag in here. I've sent messages out to the ones I did find. Half are either ghosting me or turning me down. The other half say they'll think about it. The ones I found…it won't be much of a party."

"Well, how many do you have?"

"Three so far. That's not the biggest problem though. The house doesn't want these three." Lata gulped. "You know how it shivers when it likes something? Well, it didn't like anything we picked out."

Radha never noticed those shivers, but the lack of them worried her. "We can still have a party with three guests.

That's not a terrible thing."

"The house doesn't want them. It wants something else. And…" Lata swallowed. "I have a bad feeling I know what it really wants."

"You do?" Radha's face fell when Lata started to walk away from her. "What aren't you telling me, Lata? What is it that you really came here for?"

"It's him." Lata kept her eye on the door in case someone burst in. "Andrew. I think…this morning at home…the house shook every time one of us brought him up. Veena said it's the normal hunger pains. This is when the house wants something specific. It's craving one big thing."

Radha swallowed as Lata's words came together. "What does the house want?"

Lata stared at the door. "Make a wild guess."

Radha blinked, her face contorting over the idea of leading Andrew down that hall. "Oh no. No no no, you cannot do it! You can't be right! I suspected it, but I was hoping I was wrong! I even told Ma about it, but she said not to sweat on it, that I was imagining things. I wanted to imagine it. I wanted to overreact. But no, I can't do it! I'm not sacrificing Andrew to the house! He hasn't done anything wrong! At least…I hope he hasn't done anything wrong."

"And that's just it. The girls and I researched all morning for anything weird about him. There's nothing. You mentioned July 3rd, and we didn't find anything unusual. He does work at the university like he said. He's got a lot of awards for his work. And his social media is clean. Mostly pictures of him visiting different places. He's even got one of us up now, talking about enjoying a new place with new friends."

A new place with new friends. Her shoulders heaved over the possible pictures he posted. "Has he mentioned anything about me?"

"Not really. I guess you told him not to post about your dates. And if you didn't, maybe he's being respectful. He might ask you if it's okay to post stuff." Lata moved away from the wall and grabbed Radha's arm. "We should go now. I hear someone getting close."

As much as she loathed it, everything came together. Plenty of people deserved their punishment. Why would the house want Andrew, who showed no signs of awful deeds? He hadn't treated anyone poorly. She noted every single move, every breath he took. From her friends to the waitresses to all staff at the museum, he treated all of them with kindness. Even if there was a problem with the bill, he never lashed out at them. He kept a quiet tone that stayed serious about the issue. That wasn't an awful person.

And even if he was rude to staff, that's not a reason to bring him to the house. The house doesn't care about people flipping off waiters. Her head spun as the automatic dryers went off. Of course. This bathroom had everything go off every five seconds: toilets, sinks, and dryers. Lata motioned her towards the door, yet she wasn't ready. Grasping the sink behind her, Radha braced herself for more conversation.

"I hate being right. The house is craving him for a reason. We might have to dig a little deeper into his background. I don't know if I can ask him about it yet. It hasn't been that long since we've started dating." She whispered, praying no one would burst in to use the bathroom. "Until I get some time for research, we'll have to stall the party. Forget those three guests. We have to feed it whatever we've got. Beef, pork, chicken…heck, if you can lure a rabbit into that room, that might work."

"A rabbit?! But…But it's a living thing!"

Radha's skin stood on end. "And what do you think all our guests were, Lata? Zombies? Look, this is a tough situation. We're desperate over here. We can't let the house crumble. Just feed it like you'd feed anything else."

"So, throw a hunk of beef into the room?"

"Veena's done that before when we've had slow times." Radha walked towards the door, listening for any footsteps growing closer. "Okay, I think we overstayed our welcome. Even the bathroom's telling us to get out."

"Really? I didn't think bathrooms could…"

"Just move!" She pushed Lata out of the door as the toilets went off again. "I don't want to leave Andrew waiting!"

They avoided an incoming group pushing in for the toilets as Radha's mind went to the house. Lata wouldn't lie about this. There were days the house craved certain things. One party could be filled with people who got away with murdering their spouses. Another could be corrupted police officers who let crimes take place under their noses. It never picked out one person to eat.

Andrew's not hiding anything, is he? Her stomach churned as she headed to the bench Andrew sat at. The house wouldn't crave someone for the hell of it. Often, it found out someone's dark secret before her family did. Did he hold something deep inside? They hadn't found it through all their searching. He gazed down at his phone, going through several photos, when she tapped his shoulder from behind. He took her hand and pulled her next to him, waving the phone in her face. A photo of the night at Upper Deck danced before her.

"I was just updating my social media apps. I hope you don't mind this picture." He showed her a shot of all five of them, taken by the waitress right after Radha won a game. Swati brought her glass up to her lips, Lata's mouth opened slightly, and Veena glared at someone behind the waitress. Only Radha's face glowed under those low lights, with

Andrew holding her close. The smile on her face beamed as she struggled not to laugh. He clearly picked this to impress her. To show her in a better light. It didn't matter if the others weren't perfect. For once, she was.

"I love it." She admitted as Lata sat down on the other side. Andrew continued scrolling through several photos of the ocean and the creatures living in it. The house couldn't eat him. Maybe it wanted one of the creatures on it. They never fed it fish, but maybe it craved that. "Listen, Andrew. We go out a lot, but I haven't had a chance to look you up on social media."

"Oh, it's not a big deal. My social media handles can easily be found if you look up my name. I'm sure there are plenty of guys named Andrew Gardner, but I'm the only one working at the university."

"That's not it." Radha eased into the next part. "I keep thinking we're going too fast. I love spending time with you, but I feel like I barely scratched the surface."

"Well, there's not much else to me, Radha. Everything I've told you is all there is to me." Andrew held out his arms. "And I'll admit I haven't talked a lot about my late wife. Chantal and I had a wonderful marriage. I can't say I don't miss her. I think about her all the time, wondering how she'd feel about this. She wanted me to be happy."

"And are you?" Lata pressed on. Radha shot her a look as she went on. "Are you happy hanging out with us?"

"Absolutely. Chantal wanted me to find people to hang out with. To make new friends and move on with my life. She would have loved to know all of you." He squeezed Radha's hand. "Don't worry. I'm sure she'd have loved you. She'd approve of you."

The pit in Radha's stomach grew as she remembered their home. If Lata's suspicions were correct, she could never bring him over. Even after several dates, he couldn't set foot in their house. Worse than that, she got the name of his late wife. He trusted her enough to reveal it. Shaking, she found the nearest bench and sat down, processing everything. Andrew got stuck in a snowstorm with Chantal. He listened to music with Chantal. He knew all about Chantal and, based on the little she got, she was the absolute opposite of Radha. His eyes twinkled with every memory of her. How could she compare?

Maybe he'll get tired of me, and the break-up will happen quicker. She winced as Andrew laughed over one of Lata's jokes. *I guess there might be a few perks to being boring and dull. He won't lose his life if he grows exhausted by me. I'll do all the usual things I do: read, go to movies, visit nearby cafes. Nothing extreme. He'll tire of me in no time.*

"What do you think, Radha?"

Radha pulled herself back into reality as both Lata and Andrew stared at her. "Think about what?"

"Your friend was saying that we should go to the history museum as well. I do have a lot of work waiting for me at home, so I'm thinking about making it another date? How do you feel about that?"

"I, uh…sounds good. I'll check and see what my schedule is like later, then give you a call." Every nerve in her body swayed back and forth. More dates. He wasn't bored of her yet. He wanted to see her again. Her stomach growled, reminding her to eat as well as the house's hunger.

"Well, I'm glad we settled that!" Lata wrapped her arms around them. "I don't know about you guys, but I think we can get some food now. What do you say?"

"I was about to say the same thing. Let's finish up and then get some food. We can try the Mexican restaurant next time." Andrew winked at Radha, who smiled in return.

"What do you say?"

"I say…that's a plan." Faking all the enthusiasm hurt her. Here they were, having a grand time enjoying exhibits and planning the future, while she sweated deep down. Lata's warning didn't leave her. Her worst fears wouldn't erase themselves. Somehow, saving Andrew meant saving the house. As he laughed and walked around with Lata, she knew he wouldn't pull away quickly. She had to force him to go. For the sake of his life, she had to break him.

Even if it broke her in return.

CHAPTER 16

Radha didn't sleep for the next few nights as the house continued to shake and crumble. She'd wake up to dust on her pillows and covers, all falling from the ceiling. The only thing keeping it standing were the pieces of meat Veena fed it every night. They worked for the time being. Beef, pork, chicken…all that healed it for a few hours. Lata still couldn't bring herself to lure a rabbit in, so Swati and Veena worked on that. Letting animals in for the house to gnaw on. That animal meat only healed for a second. Humans filled it. Humans kept everything standing.

She daydreamed about the previous parties, how guests filled the room and slowly but surely disappeared from existence. One minute, they'd sit on the couch. The next minute, they fell through the floor or dissolved into the walls. The crunching sounds got to her before they bothered anyone else. It wasn't enough this time. Anywhere she turned, she saw that date. July 3rd. Even with all the research on recent things during July 3rd, she came up blank. Why was the house fixated on it?

The lack of sleep led to more research. Andrew's social media contained nothing suspicious, just plenty of photos of the ocean, his coworkers, and Chantal. There she was, his former wife, bright brown eyes and a smile wide from ear to ear. In every photo, she broke out in laughter. Andrew remained by her side, either holding her or leaning in close, his skin brushing against hers. With each photo, Chantal grew more beautiful. She was gone, yet in these pictures, she came to life. No wonder he fell in love with her. No wonder he talked about her with fond memories. She belonged to him, and Radha couldn't replace her. She had nothing that Chantal had: charisma, beauty, or a clean record.

That was the other thing she checked up. Even if Andrew did nothing, perhaps Chantal had a darker side. He might not have been aware if she did anything in secret. Radha went through everything about her, hoping to catch some hints on Chantal's personality. Someone like this couldn't be happy all the time. She and Andrew had to have bad moments aside from the snowstorm. They had to have dark times.

Yet all the searching led to nothing out of the ordinary. Chantal lived a relatively normal life despite all the adventures she had. She died happy, the way most people wanted to die. She got to live a full life with the one she loved. Next to her, Radha stood no chance. Andrew couldn't use her to fill a void. At the same time, she didn't want him to get eaten. The house healed from the last few bits of meat, but not all cracks healed. The ones in her room remained right above her head, warning her that they'd come down any second. The moment she least expected, that roof would cave in.

"But, you can't have Andrew!" She scolded the walls. "Look, we've done our research. There isn't anything wrong with him! I looked up everything on July 3rd. There's nothing! He's not a criminal who's escaped the law. He didn't commit any crimes and got away with it. Lata's right; the man doesn't even have a parking ticket! The worst we saw was he forgot to turn in a video rental several years ago. Even still, he paid the late fee! How can you crave him?"

The house didn't respond, though she knew it took every word in. The girls spent all night looking for something about Andrew, anything that could explain the house's desire. He told the truth about his work, what he enjoyed doing, and they even found his social media. He had plenty of friends, though no other dates outside of Radha. Through years of pictures, they found him at parties, bars, boats, and camping in the woods. They found photos of his late wife with captions talking about how much he missed her. He kept his promise and didn't date until now. He had nothing wrong with him.

Then came the words. She turned away for a second to find the same words repeated all over the walls. Again. The house was doing it again.

JULY 3 JULY 3 JULY 3 JULY 3 JULY 3

"July 3rd. You keep bringing it up. What about July 3rd?" The walls shifted again to reveal more words cracking out. THE DAY BEFORE INDEPENDENCE DAY. Radha groaned as she whirled around, her head aching. "Yes, I'm aware of what July 3rd is. What else is so important? How does Andrew tie into July 3rd?"

She grabbed her phone and began to search for anything regarding July 3rd. It popped up with many articles about several incidents on that day. Independence Day festivities. Sales on that day. The movies coming out around that time. She even scrolled down for any major events on that day. Aside from mentions of festivals and concerts, she came up blank. The same old things she saw before were there.

I'm probably doing this wrong. She rubbed her eyes, hoping the words would go away. They stayed in place, taunting her with the obvious fact. The cracks began to shift, forming new words on her. "The day before independence day. I need a year. It's clearly not last year or this one."

JULY 3, 1984.

There it was. The house gave an exact date. Her fingers trembled as she typed in Andrew's name along with July 3, 1984. The pit in her stomach widened on the first article popping up. The picture of a car accident with a totaled car up front forced the bile up her throat. Then she zeroed in on the title: 1 DEAD, 3 INJURED IN CAR ACCIDENT.

"One dead, three injured…oh please…please…" She pleaded as she clicked on the article. Skimming through the first article, she learned about the victims who came home from a party when they crashed into another car. The driver of the other car got away with a broken arm and minor cuts. As she read on, she prayed Andrew's name wouldn't pop up. They kept mentioning the driver, but no name.

"It can't be." She shook her head. "They don't say his name! They don't mention him at all! It could be some other person."

The more she attempted to convince herself, the less convinced she became. The next Andrew Gardner article led to more information on the accident. The driver who crashed into them wasn't of right mind, completely high on cocaine. The police didn't know where he got the drugs from, but they were enough to impair him. No one stopped him before he got on the road. No one questioned him before he got behind the wheel. No one tried to help him.

"Oh God." She checked out the address on top. Forty years ago. She wasn't living in the house back then. Her family lived nearby, visiting on occasion. Her father told her stories about the grandparents and the magic deep inside. The house that saved them.

"That's it, right?" She asked the walls. "You knew he killed someone. Granted, it was an accident, but…you knew."

A petal from the flower vase landed on her nightstand. That was her answer. He killed someone while high on cocaine, and somehow, he evaded justice. She couldn't bear to go through articles about the victims. The only things she learned were that they were young, home from college, and ready to party. They were all too young, hence why Andrew got such a small sentence. 18 months. A year and a half for taking a life, even if it was an accident. Maybe he was sorry for it, maybe he was clean now and never touched drugs again. Maybe he learned to be a better man, and others forgave him.

But can I forgive him? If this is true, how can I look at him the same way? Her phone went off at that moment with messages from all her social media networks. To her sadness, Andrew posted photos for the whole world to see in Facebook. Even worse was the caption in the main post.

A great night with great new friends. Thanks for welcoming me into your town.

Radha's heart broke with the photos of them together. Andrew finally got around to posting a few pictures from Upper Deck, where they shared a drink together. How could this be? How could the same posting these pictures have killed someone? The house craved him because he got away with the crime. Even if the judge agreed to the sentence, not everyone else did. Radha turned green over the whole year and a half of prison part in the articles. No, the house was right. He deserved to pay for this, but maybe she could extend his life a little bit. There were plenty of other offenders out there. The house would be fine with them. All she needed was a party theme.

"Let's see…do we have any birthdays coming up?" She checked the calendar on her wall, which remained blank save for the dates with Andrew and upcoming interviews.

Those still gave her shivers when their dates approached. With some new paintings, she hoped they'd inspire the interviewers when they gazed through her portfolio. Some of the spark returned. A burst of life erupted in her when she painted now. They weren't dull splashes of paint, but photos in acrylic. She picked up the ocean painting and held up to the wall, hiding a few cracks. If she put it up now, no one would notice all the marks around it.

"No." She decided as she put the painting down. She'd hang it after the next few interviews. "I won't let you have him. We have another date coming up." The bright orange words BINGO NIGHT on Sunday reminded her it wasn't exactly a date. "Well, okay, Lata insists we go for bingo again. She wants to get her title back. Not that she ever won music bingo in the first place."

The house shuddered, giving the cue that it starved for meat. Radha went to the kitchen to find a giant slab of uncooked steaks in the fridge. They loaded up on beef when the house started to crumble since no one came up with a party idea or new guests. She grabbed the meat and unwrapped the plastic, letting the meat slide off the Styrofoam tray. All the blood stains dripped down on the counter as she took the meat to the feeding room. Going down the hallways, she imagined all the guests who came in them, ignoring the statues around them. The low lights and small rooms added a little extra comfort. Her feet glided across the petal-covered floors as she faced the feeding room, which was closed tightly. Her hand fell on the knob, knuckles tightening to turn it. She rarely came here as the noises in the room unnerved her. She never knew what lay in there. Just a dark spirit who craved souls, waiting for food every night.

"Sorry. I know you want more, but this is going to have

to do for now." She turned the knob and carefully opened the door, throwing the meat in the open darkness. She listened for the gnawing before closing the room up. It snarfed down everything, leaving only spots of juice on the ground. Every few weeks, Veena cleaned those spots up so the room was tidy for the guests. She didn't want anyone to come in and find a bloodbath. A clean room appealed to people more, even if it was darker. Turning her gaze to the vaulted ceiling, bits of dust came down as the cracks healed up. It ate the food, satisfying the growing hunger for the time being.

"It's hungry, huh?" Veena spoke up from behind. Radha clung to the empty plate with the meat's juices still swirling around. "I know. I've been waking up in the middle of the night anytime I hear the floorboards creak. I woke up to three new cracks right above my headboard…which I didn't cause. I haven't had anyone in my bedroom in days now."

Radha let the moment to make sarcastic comments slip by. Veena's worries mounted along with hers. Their house couldn't survive off slabs of beef for long. "We need to throw another party, but what kind? The house isn't interested in random criminals anymore."

"Of course. I know the whole story since Lata wouldn't shut up about last time. It wants to eat your boyfriend."

"It can't!" Radha stormed away from the door as cracks formed under her footsteps. She slammed down harder so the house understood no meant no. Until she got to the truth of July 3rd, she couldn't let it snack on Andrew. "This is the first time in ages I've dated. Not only that, he likes me too! I keep begging the house to…" She slowed down. Telling her cousin would give her some comfort. "Maybe I shouldn't beg it."

"What do you mean?"

"I keep thinking about why the house wants to eat

Andrew. I did some digging of my own and…well, I think he may have gotten into trouble with law when he was in college." Radha went into the truth with ease. She didn't want to drop the bomb without leading up to it. "I mean, college students do all kinds of crap, right?"

"Well, yeah. What could he have done back then? Forget to turn in a rented video? Got a parking ticket? Smoke some pot?"

"It's…close to smoking pot." She breathed out. If Veena figured it out on her own, she could spill the rest of it without problem. "You know how it is. He got a little reckless and…"

"You don't need to tell me." Veena patted her shoulder. "I've been there, done that. It's no reason to send the poor guy to his death. If it happened years ago and he hasn't done anything wrong since, we don't have to worry." She then patted the house's walls. "As for you, you can't be stubborn about your food. It'll come. Give us time."

The house had no answers. Radha raced to the kitchen and put the plate in the sink, rinsing the juices off. Veena was right at her heels, knowing very well that Radha didn't say everything she wanted to say. She tapped her foot as Radha went for the hand soap to get the beef residue off. She scrubbed till that red residue slowly washed away. As she ran her hands through the warm water, the stench grew worse. No surprises. That stench lingered on all of them when the parties ended. Once those screams died, the smell followed everyone. Radha took long showers to scrub every area, though the efforts were in vain. They took part in these deaths. They planned it all out.

"I don't know what to do." Radha wiped her hands. "He's a different person now, right? He's a changed man. Who I was in college is different from who I am today. That's the same for him. If he doesn't do anything wrong..."

"Then you have nothing to worry about." Veena checked the calendar on the fridge. "Hmm, next weekend is busy, but maybe I can plan a party for the following weekend. What do you think? Would you like to..."

"I can't do it!" Radha rubbed her head. "I'm trying to understand it, and I can't! I don't get this man at all! He was perfect! He was the one for me and..."

"Okay, so he's not perfect. No man is. He got a parking ticket, or he was speeding or maybe he smoked pot. It's nothing like murder, is it?" Radha paled as Veena's face darkened, the truth hitting her. "Oh God. He didn't...he couldn't..."

"I'm not sure if this is completely accurate. It's all the articles I've seen so far. They all say that Andrew got high forty years ago and hit another car, killing one and injuring three others. There's not a whole lot of information about what happened with him except that...well, he got a year and a half of jailtime."

Veena blinked. "Excuse me? He killed someone while high, and he gets a year and a half in prison? Tell me you're joking."

"I'm not." Radha inhaled. "I read those words repeatedly. It's true. He went to jail for eighteen months. He did his time, and he got out. I guess he cleaned up and turned his life around. Still, I get why this is..." She shuddered. "God, what am I going to do? He never told me about it! What's next?"

"Well, if he's a killer, that makes it easier to break off with him." Veena pointed out. "Call him out on his crime. Tell him that you know, and you can't be with a murderer. Even if he did clean up his act, he kept everything from you."

"Yeah, I wish it were that easy. I should break up with

him. After all, I wouldn't date any of the guys we invite. Why should he be different?" Radha went to the fridge and found leftover ice cream along with their newest chocolate cream pie. "What do you want to eat? Finish off the rocky road or dig into the pie?"

"Both." Veena rummaged through the cabinets for bowls and spoons. "Honestly, I should text Lata and ask her to bring two more ice cream cartons, a chocolate cheesecake, and another chocolate pie. We are in a crisis here!"

"...And the only way to solve the crisis is to eat our weight in chocolate and sugar? Sounds like a plan." Radha placed the cartons on the table and went to grab some knives. "Oh, I'm so confused. I don't want our house to fall, so I guess I could let it eat Andrew. Yet at the same time...I don't know if I want to do that."

Veena cut into the pie and handed Radha a slice. "Well, the idea of him being a killer never crossed my mind. He seemed so kind, and he is! But why did he hide all that from you? If he's clean and all is good, why keep the truth?"

"I guess he didn't want me to think less of him. I mean, would you be happy dating a killer?" Radha grabbed a fork and dug into her cake. "That's the thing. I could break up with him for other reasons. He's too clumsy for me. He tastes his food with his fingers. He wears white after Labor Day. I could live with all that. But this? I don't know why I'm hesitating. I always thought I could dump someone when they revealed something so dark. And yet...a part of me doesn't want to believe it.

"Well, until you are sure of what you want to do, we have to keep him from this place." Veena glared up at the ceiling. "Yeah, you heard me. Our family made rules here. You don't eat any of the good people."

"Well, it's more like people who are good now. Maybe

not in the past." Radha glanced at her phone, where Andrew sent another message. He reminded her of bingo night, another trip to the museum, and he looked forward to another round of wings. Her fingers wavered over the screen, wondering how to type out her thoughts. Veena was right; to protect Andrew was to break up with him. Two weeks was long enough for them. Better to snip the bud now than let it grow too high.She couldn't wait for herself to make a mistake. Let him down gently.

You can do it. Below her, the table formed another crack. It started now. After the walls, the furniture came apart. Then went all the other things like pots and photos. She covered the crack up with her plate. While not big enough, it didn't disappear. *And I wish this house would stop doing that. Save your cracks for another time. I must send a message.*

Despite all the courage she mustered up, she didn't break up then. All she could write was 'yes' and a promise to see him on Sunday. This wasn't the right time. She had to face him, take his hands, and let him down. As she finished up, Lata arrived with a giant pink box and bags full of ice cream. Veena clapped her hands asshe placed the box in the middle of the sweets, as Lata put out more plates and spoons.

"What's all this?" Radha wiped her mouth with her napkin. "I'm not sure I can eat more."

"You'll have to make some room then. I had a craving for a double chocolate cheesecake today." Lata opened it up to reveal that thick chocolatey goodness waiting for them. "I don't know why, but something inside told me we needed it. That we had things to talk about."

"Oh, we do. It's about Andrew." Veena handed her a plate. "Radha's having a crisis."

"About Andrew? I don't see what's so wrong." Lata joined them in the frosted feast, cutting up the cake. "He was very sweet when I saw him last. He didn't mind me tagging along. He doesn't even mind it when I play bingo!"

"That's cause he didn't see the worst. It was a calm night for all of us." Radha poked away at her cake. Much as she loved cheesecake in general, especially the chocolate ones, she lost her appetite. She couldn't bring that piece to her mouth, though she licked the top. Sugary and thick as she liked it, but it didn't fix her crisis. "Still, there's a bigger secret here. As it turns out, Andrew has a dark past."

"...Where?"

Radha couldn't entertain that question with a sarcastic reply. The news on Andrew warped her mind to places she couldn't fathom. "It turns out that he hit someone when he was high on cocaine. He got behind the wheel, had no clue what he was doing, and then rammed into another car. It happened forty years ago, right before Independence Day."

"Oh my God." Lata's hands went up to her mouth. "Are you sure it was him?"

"I didn't believe it either. I read the articles that popped up for July 3rd about forty years ago. It's all the same thing. Andrew was a young college student who got high and hit another car. One of the passengers of the other car died. He didn't spend that much time in jail for it. I don't know why. I guess the judge saw him as a young man who made the worst mistake of his life. What do you think about it?"

"About him killing someone? It never crossed my mind." Lata shrugged. "I wouldn't have guessed looking at him. Everyone's holding a secret, including us."

"Our secret is tied to our family, though. Our house is important." Radha reminded her. "What would you do in this situation?"

"Well, I'd ask myself a few questions. Is this the man you want to be? Can you live with that?" Lata pressed on. "Can you go through your life knowing that he killed someone? Even if he did his time, will you be okay with it?"

"I…I don't think so." Radha swallowed. "I know the right thing is to break up, so I'll do that. I'm not sure how. We haven't gone too far yet. Just the movies and restaurants, and museums. It shouldn't be hard to let him go."

"But what will you do if he wants to take things further? What if he decides to marry you? What if he wants to move in?! He'll want to see where you live, at least once in his lifetime." Lata shrugged. "Maybe we can just show him the outside. The garden is beautiful when the flowers are in bloom. I saw them right before leaving. All the rose bushes have buds on them! I'm sure that would be a nice place for you to hang out."

"Eh, it wouldn't be enough. It would be like showing him the Louvre from the outside. Sure, it's beautiful on the outside, but that doesn't mean you've visited the place. Besides, the beauty of our home is on the inside. The garden's nice, but the heart of the house is in here." She stared at the walls, now slowly healing up. The house finished eating, so she peeked under her plate, and the crack faded out. "I have to do this by myself, girls. Somehow, I have to hurt him."

"Technically, breaking up with him is hurting him." Lata reminded her. "Why don't you two just be friends? If you're not ready for a relationship, you can say so. Tell him that things are going too fast. Be friends. Friends don't always go to each other's houses. It'll also give you time to deal with the news of him being a criminal."

"A former criminal." Veena corrected her. "Remember, he's done his time. Even if it isn't fair, he followed through with the sentence."

Radha pondered over the idea for a second. Being friends kept them together, and it kept him safe. He'd be less inclined to come over and get too close. They could still have fun with each other, going to all the places they wanted to go. They'd still have good times. Rubbing her arms, she remembered all the warmth of Andrew's body. How he laid his hand on her thigh. The way he kissed her under the stars. Even now, his lips remained on hers, the memory of that kiss. Her hands went straight to her mouth, rubbing around the sides. Friends didn't kiss this way.

"I can't." She shook her head. "Even if I keep a distance, even if I tell him I'm not ready, I'll still want him. I can't stop wanting him. I'm angry and I want him at the same time. It's tough!" She pulled her hands away, wishing Andrew stood right by her. She craved his touch now. His hand on her body, his lips on hers, anything. "Oh girls, what can I do? I've never felt this way about anyone before. Not even when I was younger. I haven't been with someone like him in… well, never. How can you break up with someone like that?"

Veena dug her fork into her cake. "Well, I can't say I've been with someone like Andrew. Many men came close, but he's something special. You can't just use him like a Kleenex, throw him out after you're done. You must be delicate. Men's hearts are fragile. One small slip, they fall apart."

"Tell him you're angry at him. You don't have to be harsh with the breakup. Let him down gently." Lata added. "Tell him you're not ready for a relationship. That'll give you some time to get over him."

"Not ready for a relationship." She snapped her fingers. "That's right! I'll tell him that we're going too fast, and I need some breathing space! People will respect that, right? I'll tell him that when I'm ready, I'll start dating again! Yes, that'll work!"

"That's more like it! Now, let's finish all this and clean the place up. We have a plan."

Radha took one more piece of cheesecake, yet her work wasn't over. All she had was a plan. Executing it was the actual delicate part. She rehearsed the way to let him down. The right time hadn't come yet. Her courage hadn't built up. Hopefully, it came around quickly. Her toes brushed the floor, coming across a deeper crack. Soon.

It would be over soon.

CHAPTER 17

Radha's emotions went on a roller coaster over the news. July 3, 1984. She hadn't looked through those articles since that night, but they spoke the facts. A car accident in the middle of the night. The perpetrator begged law enforcement to go easy on him, he never meant to hurt people. The articles depicted him as a young man who was high on drugs, yet incredibly emotional and sorry for his actions. That sounded a lot like Andrew, begging people to let him go for a mistake. Yet this was not any ordinary mistake. She read on about the victims who agreed that Andrew wasn't evil. What he did was wrong, but they weren't going to hate him for it. They wanted to help him move on and clean up, as that's what their children would do.

They're so much more forgiving than most people would be. Radha put the phone down. Maybe that's why Andrew cleaned up: the people he hurt forgave him. They were okay with him moving on, not wanting to dwell on the past. Why couldn't she do the same? Her mind still frazzled, she went to the kitchen where Lata was sitting and doing more research. They hadn't planned another party, but she still went to look for updates on unsolved cases and wanted criminals.

"You don't look so good." She noted as Radha came in, searching for something to eat. "Do you need something?"

"Actually, I do need something. Can you do me a favor?" She nodded at Lata's phone. "Did you read anything about the case from forty years ago?"

"Forty years ago?" Lata repeated, the pieces slowly coming together. "You're talking about Andrew's case?"

Not in the mood to give a sarcastic remark, Radha only nodded as she grabbed a cup and poured herself some coffee. "I keep reading the articles because I don't want them to be true. I don't want to believe he did this. Yet the more I read, the more convinced I become. It's hard to deal with."

"Well, it would be hard to deal with. We all liked him. For once, you found someone who liked you right back. You don't want to think he'd do anything wrong. He was perfect for you."

"Now, he isn't." Radha slumped down in her chair. "I know you're right. I wanted to believe that he was perfect. I didn't see a reason to dig into his background. That's probably what was wrong." She grabbed the coffeepot and poured herself a cup. "I got too into him that I didn't pay attention to the obvious. I don't know what to do now. I could live with this if he committed a fraud or shoplifted or something like that."

"That would be easier to deal with. I think the house would forgive that too. We've had relatives who stole things." Lata went through her phone, reading the articles Radha couldn't bring herself to go through. "Oh God, the victims were all college students. The one who died was only twenty-years old. He went through the windshield."

"Oh God." Radha buried her face into her hands. She didn't want the details behind the death. The wreck pictures burned into her brain. Andrew, being this reckless and getting behind a wheel while high, wasn't on her mind. "Why couldn't he shoplift something? I'd live with that! I mean,

Ma shoplifted stuff when she was a girl, and the house hasn't eaten her...unfortunately."

"Look." Lata put the phone away, closing the article. "It's tough to deal with. I like Andrew too. I have no doubt he's a changed man. I don't think he's getting high and getting behind the wheel anymore. He probably learned his lesson."

"That won't matter to the house. They see him as a criminal who got away." She rubbed her eyes. "And the thing is, it's right. He did get away. Since when is 18 months a fitting punishment for manslaughter? No matter how many strings his lawyer pulled, it still doesn't feel right to me. The house doesn't find that to be justice."

"It doesn't sound like justice, but that's what they decided on." Lata got up from the table, squeezing Radha's shoulder. "Come on. I want you to be on your best behavior, though. It's bingo tonight, so I don't want to see you gloomy."

"Bingo night?" Radha rubbed her eyes. "I completely forgot about it. I don't know if I want to go. I'm not really in the mood to play."

"It might take your mind off things for a bit. Just be calm. We'll get through this."

"I hope so." Radha couldn't shake July 3, 1984 out. Even if the house didn't taunt her with it, she saw it all around her. The house was right. As always, it was right when it found victims. She touched the wall, rubbing the sides. "I'm sorry I didn't believe you. At the same time...I'm not sure what to do."

LET ME EAT HIM. The cracks formed. PLEASE.

She couldn't reply to that. Instead, she went upstairs to putter away in her room and practice breaking up with him. At this point, that still sounded like the best option. She couldn't reveal house secrets to him, and she couldn't see him as the same person anymore. It would take ages for her to get that old feeling back.

This should be easy. I can do it. I can let him go.

Bingo night at Upper Deck arrived quickly, with Radha wishing to turn back. Her courage to break up hadn't come around. With all the excitement pouring in, she forgot about it until they left the house. Driving down the streets, she didn't know what to say to Andrew. No doubt he'd sit right next to her so they could play footsie or hold each other. Breaking up with him in the loud chaos of Upper Deck wouldn't work. He'd never hear her or reply.

Just relax. She focused on the road ahead, careful not to run into any cars or people. While her mind wasn't entirely there, she couldn't forget about reality. They put her behind the wheel for a reason. No matter how spaced out of her head she was, Veena knew she could trust Radha to drive over all the others. The other two pointed it out as they headed for the night.

"I'm sorry, but Radha's going behind the wheel." Veena locked the door behind her. "She's the one driving."

"Why?" Both Lata and Swati demanded as Radha unlocked the car doors.

"Because she's the only one who's not going to hit something because she feels like it."

Lata and Swati conceded that point as Radha let them in. Hopefully, she wouldn't draw too much attention to herself tonight. She didn't have the same luck in bingo as with the trivia nights. Bingo came down to luck and having the right card. Somehow, Lata ended up with all the lucky cards and the prizes from winning. She inhaled sharply over the upcoming excitement. No doubt, Andrew would either be impressed or terrified.

Maybe Lata's winning might scare him off. Make my job easier. She began to calm herself as the traffic thinned out.

Turning on the radio, she switched to more current music and rolled her window down.

Once they got in the parking lot, the bright lights outside and a large crowd got under her skin. The nerves intensified as she stepped towards the pub, as music kicked in. This time, they played all kinds of classics to get blood pumping, and everyone hyped up for bingo. Swati grimaced as they weaved into the entrance, getting right in front of the hostess.

"We got five for bingo today." She glanced behind the hostess' shoulder. "Preferably a place in the back. The last time, you guys threw me near the bar, and some guy tried to toss me like a football. You can't make touchdowns with an old lady with false teeth and bad knees!"

"My apologies, Swati. We'll make sure to get you a nice place in the back." The girl promised, grabbing several menus and checking the open spots. "Okay, I think we have one getting cleaned up right now. I'll get you over there in five minutes."

"We won't miss a minute of bingo, will we?" Lata asked.

"No, it hasn't started yet. We're still getting everything ready. And speaking of bingo…" Her eyes narrowed. "Please don't curse the other players out if they win. We want to create a calm, fun environment here."

"Oh, what makes you think I'll curse people out?! I've learned my lesson!" Lata crossed her fingers. "I promise no one will get yelled at, hit, or maimed while I'm playing."

Radha shuddered as the hostess finally signaled them to follow. So far, the only noise came from the music blaring above. None of the people at the bar erupted in cheers or screams. There weren't too many games playing, but those TV screens droned on, pushing another headache onto her. They got to their booth in the back while a waitress brought over some water and napkins. She calmed down everyone settled in, grabbing menus though they knew what they wanted. Her eyes fell on the old appetizers, wanting some mozzarella sticks this time around. Her mother glanced over her shoulder, squinting to read the tiny print.

"Ma, you have a menu of your own. Why don't you use that?"

"I can't read the damn thing! The letters are too small!"

"Then why read mine? It's the same print." Radha pointed out the appetizers. "Look, a giant pretzel with beer cheese, mozzarella sticks with marinara sauce, garlic knots, spring rolls…"

"Okay, okay, I get it. Let's get a pretzel! But not the beer cheese, that gets stuck to my teeth." Swati reminded her. "You try washing that out of dentures every night. It's not a pretty sight."

"Fine, I'll get you a pretzel with mustard, and the rest of us can have some mozzarella sticks."

"Mozzarella sticks?! That's good for a ten-year-old, but we're women. I think the ahi-tuna nachos sound so much more sophisticated!" Veena threw in. "Think about it. They're a little pricey, but I've heard they're worth it."

"Ahi-tuna nachos? Boy, they put everything on everything these days." Swati shook her head. "I still want my pretzel!"

"And I want the spring rolls!" Lata threw in. "Everything else makes my hands too greasy to play bingo. I can't leave grease stains on my bingo card!"

Radha laid her head down on the table. Andrew hadn't come in, yet the arguments started. Then came a cheer from the back room, which pounded down on her skull. People filled up the booths around them and added to the noise. Her relief only came when the waitress arrived to take their order for drinks. The others gave their orders, and it came down to her. Lifting her head, she shook out her hair and turned towards the entrance. No Andrew yet, but plenty of whooping and hollering men heading into the bar. The party became too much. A regular Coke wouldn't heal her.

"A Coke, please…with Jack Daniels." She muttered down at the menu. "Lots of Jack Daniels."

"Lots of Jack Daniels, huh? I hope you don't plan on getting behind the wheel afterwards. Veena made you the designated driver." Swati warned her. "I've taught you not to drink and drive because it will…"

"Lead you to a road of destruction. I'm aware, Ma. I'm sorry, but I'm a little anxious. I just don't know where Andrew is." She tapped her foot on the ground. "He knows where it is! Maybe he's just running late!"

"That's all it is, honey! You saw all that traffic out there!" Veena waved at the growing crowd. "Everyone's here for bingo night! He might be looking for a parking spot. I'm not sure why we didn't just meet him at his place."

"We can't!" Radha rubbed her forehead. The headache throbbed and snapped away at her. "You know this better than anyone else. The moment I go to his house, he'll want to come over to our place! I can't bring him over!"

"Well, lie to him." Lata suggested. "Tell him that our house is being renovated. In a weird way, that's what happens after every party. It gets renovated."

Radha inhaled as she stared at her phone. No messages from Andrew yet. It wasn't like him to ignore her. He promised to be here tonight, yet the room filled up without him. Did he sense the breakup coming on? Maybe he took one step ahead and decided to drop her without a word. That would have been the easiest for both; leave without finding out why. Let him disappear like all the other people.

Breakup without saying a word. Not her first choice, but her aching soul could heal faster if she never heard from him.

Maybe he's tired of me already. It's for the best. She grabbed the table, clinging to the tablecloth. If he chose to end it, she wished for a sign. Anything to tell her that it was over. End it quickly. End it before she ended it.

Andrew finally arrived at their table, handing over bags of gifts. His face flushed as he leaned over to kiss Radha's cheek. "Hi, everyone! I'm sorry I'm so late! I got home a little later than intended, and traffic was terrible! Hope I didn't miss anything."

"Ah, we're just deciding what to have for appetizers. No one's really up for the rangoons this time around. We're torn between the pretzels, spring rolls, and ahi-tuna nachos." Radha moved over so he could sit. Grabbing the hand sanitizer on the table, he cleaned his hands before grabbing a napkin. "What would you like?"

"Hmm, do they have anything in the form of a sampler here? I didn't really check the appetizers last time."

Lata smacked her head. "Of course, we have an appetizer sampler! We can get the mozzarella sticks, pretzel bites, the spring rolls, and…oh, they don't have the ahi-tuna nachos as a choice."

"It's all right. We can get them and the sampler." Radha suggested, turning over to her mother. "It's going to be pretzel bites, Ma. I'll still order the mustard for you."

Swati shrugged. "Eh, a pretzel is a pretzel. It all goes in the same place, comes out the right place, it's all good."

Radha shook her head and leaned into Andrew. "I'm glad you were able to make it. I was just about to text you."

"I'm sorry, honey. I should have texted you sooner, asking if you wanted a ride since I was on the road. You could give me directions to your house…"

"It's all right! I'm the one who told you to meet me here." She patted his hand as waiters came around to disperse bingo cards. "There! You're here, I'm here, we're all here, and on time to play bingo. I hope we have a great time tonight."

"Oh, we will," Lata promised. "I swore I wasn't going to climb on tables, scream, cry, or threaten to jump anyone while we're playing." Andrew turned to Radha who shook her head, warning him not to ask about these things. The less he knew, the better for his health. "As you said, this is a fun night. We're all here to have a good time. It doesn't matter if we win or lose, what matters is that we tried."

"That's very mature of you." Veena complimented. "I'm surprised you are taking this well."

"I'm also lying through my teeth, but why ruin it for everyone? I want to keep coming here and winning." Lata pretended to zip her mouth shut. "You won't hear any complaints from me."

"I hope not." Radha turned to the menu. "What about our main courses? Should we go for wings as usual?"

"Not me. I want a veggie hot dog this time!" Swati read down the menu. "With everything on it. Sauerkraut, onions, vegan chili, mustard…no ketchup though! And I'll take fries with it."

"Fine, one veggie dog with the works. What about the rest of you? The usual wings?"

They both nodded, and Andrew pulled her in close. His musky cologne got into her head once more. She couldn't break up with him right now. With the loud music and cheers, it wasn't the right place. She promised to take her time with it, telling him when things got terrible. She didn't want to lose him to the house. It ate meat to hear for a couple of hours before it broke again. Veena covered up the holes on the siding with tape, though they never held together. All the imperfect spots in the house were her reminders. Break up with Andrew. Give him the cold shoulder. Ghost him. These days, people disappear without saying a word. She could block his number, go off the grid, maybe even fly over to someone else's home for a bit. One of her brothers could hook her up with a decent hotel. Get away from Andrew.

Let him go, Radha. For his sake, let him go.

His hand dropped down her back as her heart broke. No, she couldn't ghost him. They spent a good amount of time in two weeks for her to act like it was nothing. He wouldn't forget her, not after all they shared. The breakup had to come at a time when both of them were too vulnerable to do anything. Right now, a smile beaming across his face and eyes twinkling, she couldn't break him. Her mother warned her not to blow it. Telling him now would ruin any future chance of being together.

If we even have a future together. She shifted her weight to let his hand fall as the bingo games started. The host called out numbers and letters, which she didn't have yet. Her eyes lifted towards Lata, who put two markers on her board. Then she peeked at Andrew's board with one token. Veena and her mother also had one. So far, all had gone well. The host also checked up on Lata, who rubbed her hands gleefully. She stayed put in her chair, sipping her soda while staring down at the board. Their waitress arrived to take their order, writing down everything over the noise. Once she promised to return with their appetizers and drink refills, Radha relaxed her shoulders and let Andrew wrap an arm around them.

Cool and calm. How could she stay that way when a break-up was around the corner? The house didn't stop trembling at the mention of Andrew's name. It chewed on its meat with the desire to eat something more. She still didn't understand what it wanted with Andrew. He was just an ordinary man with nothing in his past. Lata eventually found two parking tickets that he paid for, but they never took people in for that. What else could he hide?

He's too nice. He's got nothing bad in his life. Yes, his wife died. Yes, he's forgotten to return movies. That doesn't mean he deserves to get eaten. Her eyes fell on the shiny surface of the table. She couldn't do it. She couldn't hurt him by breaking up or sending him to the house.

The appetizers arrived as Swati dove down to grab the pretzel bites. "Oh yeah, come to me! And mustard! My old friend!" She took a few on her plate, dipped one in the sauce, and popped it in her mouth. Her eyes widened as she chewed, flashing a thumbs up. "Great as always! My compliments to the chef."

"I'm sure Walter already knows you already love them. You tell him every other week." Radha laughed as she grabbed a mozzarella stick and broke it in half, letting the cheese stretch. Holding up one end, she handed it to Andrew and nodded at the marinara sauce. "Want some of that?"

"Actually, I had something else in mind for this. Put your end in your mouth."

Radha stared at her end before doing as he asked, gripping the mozzarella stick with her teeth. He put his end in his mouth and stretched it. She leaned back, letting the cheese stretch a bit before he pulled in and kissed her. Their mouths smashed into the melted mozzarella and crusty bits around them, but she gave in. Biting his bottom lip, she took in all the crumbs off it. In the corner of her eye, her mother hoarded more pretzel bites while Veena chugged down Lata's drink.

"Hey!" Lata's exclamation pulled them away from each other. She pushed her bingo board away to grab her glass. "I was drinking that!"

"I know, but didn't you see what happened? There is passion in there! There is heat and love and enough sweat to drown a man at sea!" Veena grabbed pretzel sticks, much to Swati's dismay, and dipped them in the mustard. "Oh, how I've longed to do the cheese stretch with someone!"

"The cheese stretch?" Andrew blinked. "I just thought it might be fun. I saw other people doing it."

"Fun?! Oh, honey, you wanted to do more than kiss her. You stretched the cheese. You know what that means, don't you?"

Radha frowned. The host walked around their table, reminding everyone bingo would start soon, while she regained her composure. "Stretch the cheese? It's a fun little game, Radha. We're not trying to start anything!"

"Well, I hope not! These tables aren't the most comfortable if you get my drift." Veena went for Swati's drink, yet pulled away when Swati's hand came down on the table. "Forgive me, I just drank my entire thing and I'm still thirsty."

"Then call the waiter over and ask for a refill! Keep off my crap!"

Radha ignored them before grabbing a mozzarella stick and dipping it in the red pepper sauce. She loved the marinara as well, but the red pepper sauce had a slight kick that elevated a regular stick. It also held sweetness to balance some of the acidity. She held it up, moving it towards Andrew. "Want to try some of this sauce?"

"I would, but let me take my own." He followed her example, dipping a stick in red pepper sauce. "If you like it, I'm sure I will."

"Oh, come on. You're already a great guy, and I approve of everything you do. You don't have to keep doing things to please my daughter." Swati stared at her half-eaten mustard.

"Though don't lay your hands on my mustard!"

Andrew moved away from it. "The mustard is yours. Now, let's get ready for some bingo!"

As they sat and listened for numbers being called, Lata's hands moved towards Andrew's thigh. In record time, it landed on top of it, and then his hand fell on hers. Her heart skipped a beat over his fingers grasping hers. Breathing in and out, her other hand covered up the numbers getting called. In front of her, Lata was one square away from the bingo. Next to her, Andrew also came close to it. Any second, one of them would win. She squeezed his hand as her eyes closed. The food wasn't there, yet she sweated like she down all the Carolina Reaper-flavored wings. The beads lined her forehead as she grabbed a napkin and wiped herself up.

"Are you okay?" Andrew checked her face. "Your face is so red!"

"It is?" Radha checked around for a reflection, but did not have time to see herself. The final letter belonged to Lata who leaped out of her chair and threw her hands in the air with a "BINGO!" The people around gave her room as she danced and nearly knocked the table over. Radha leaned into Andrew as the host came over with her prize.

"Well, congratulations! Let's get a quick look…" He checked her board, going through each square. "Yeah, I called all those. And your prize is…" He nodded at the hostess, who came over with a brand-new mug with UPPER DECK written in black and orange letters. "This mug! I hope you enjoy it!"

"Oh yay! My third one!" Lata showed it off, pointing to the orange plate of wings on the side. "Best wings in town. What do you think?"

"It's nice." Radha nodded. "Just promise us you won't panic if one of us borrows it to drink coffee."

"I've allowed you to use my mugs before!"

"Yeah, and then you threatened to break it over my head when I heated my tea in it." Swati snapped. "It's a mug, dummy! It's probably not more than five dollars at this place! Heck, they've got a store where you can buy more."

Andrew checked behind him. "Is that true?"

"Yes, honey. They sell merchandise in a store in the back. We can check it out later." She patted him on the shoulder. "Come on, another round of bingo is about to start. Let's see if we can win this round."

"Good luck." Lata nodded at them. "I hope you guys do well!"

Radha smirked. "You don't mean that at all, do you?"

"Not a single word."

The next few minutes led to more excitement and eating as Radha kept catching Andrew's glances. He noticed her as well, shooting her small winks and smiles. She waved at him as they continued to play. Even after all their dates, simple as they were, she still didn't have anything like the ones he talked about with his wife. The most exciting thing was the little cheese stretch, which any idiot could have pulled off. It was nothing compared to being stuck in a snowstorm or playing with a lemon shark.

Why me? She dunked some of her wings in ranch dressing. A huge plate sat in front of her that she barely touched. She wasn't even sure when they came in, yet here they were, waiting for her to eat. *How could someone like him want me? If it weren't for the house, I'm still not going to be a fun person. I really need to cut him loose.*

"Radha, they called your numbers." Andrew nudged her. "You missed three of them."

"They did?" Radha never got a chance to figure that out because Lata yelled 'BINGO' into the room, causing a ton of groans. She sank back in her seat, relieved that the round ended right then. "It's all right, honey. I don't feel like playing anymore."

"Why not? Are you not feeling well?"

"No, it's more like…" The house popped into her mind, opening its door and begging for food. *Feed me. Feed me. I'm hungry, so feed me.* "I wish we could leave. We need to talk."

"About what? Are you upset?" He leaned in and gazed into her gaze. "Come on, Radha. Tell me. If you'd rather go home…"

"It's not that. It's…" The others paid no attention to them, so she went on. "I'm wondering if you're enjoying all this. I mean, it's no humpback whale experience."

He chuckled. "And I thought you weren't paying attention."

"Well, I paid half-attention. Does that count?"

He pulled her into a hug. "I'm enjoying myself. I don't need everything to be a great big adventure. Sometimes, a quiet night with friends is enough. Just you, me, and…" A loud whoop in the room disrupted his next few words and they both burst out laughing. "Okay, it's not a quiet night but it's fine with me. If you don't play anymore, you don't have to. We've won enough!"He braced himself as Lata came around and danced with others. Then he leaned in and whispered. "You don't have to stress over anything, Radha. I'm glad to be with you."

That did it. Those words broke her even further apart. The time to dump him hadn't come around, so she snuggled against him and tried eating her food. These were times she enjoyed as well. Even if she didn't win, she had fun with them. He liked them. He didn't mind that she wasn't going crazy over bingo tonight. He was fine with her the way she was. Which made the upcoming breakup harder to endure.

CHAPTER 18

After some time, Radha got some food in her and decided to play trivia after all. The reassurance from Andrew boosted her energy. All the knowledge she forgot came right back to her. Andrew clapped for every correct answer, eager to be part of her trivia team. The entire time, he never strayed from her side. Despite this, she didn't clap for herself or smile during the competition. She couldn't enjoy any of this. Win or lose, it was shaping up to be one of the worst nights of her life.

"We can do this." He reminded her. "I'm right here if you need me."

"I'll be okay on my own." She tried her best not to appear frosty, yet the words slipped out. "I can handle it. I've done it before."

"I know that, but I'm just offering support." Now he grew concerned. "Is everything okay, Radha? Things seem off lately."

"I'm fine." She put her focus on the trivia contest, not bothering to look at him. "I'm just getting into the competitive spirit right now. I need to concentrate."

"Well…okay. I guess I should do the same."

He didn't get it. Even when she appeared cold, he tried to get close. How could he do it? How could he move on with his life so easily? She wondered about Chantal. Did she ever know the truth? Did he hide that from her? If not, Chantal was a strong woman to live with a man like this. She married him, lived with him, and loved him despite what he did. She was a lot stronger in that sense. On the side, he found Veena and Lata shooting her looks to keep cool. This wasn't the place to accuse him of anything.

I'll keep playing. If I play, I won't remember what he's doing.

Their team trivia round went well, with both winning second. Radha's pop culture and social media knowledge weren't up to date like some of the other knowledge. When they asked for names of popular TikTok influencers, she went blank and turned to Andrew who also had no idea. In the end, they both made all the wrong guesses and lost the first-place trophy by a few points.

"Social media influencers. Those were the one group of people I didn't want to interact with." Radha polished her trophy, a little smaller than the first place one. In addition to that, the two of them got two free meals the next time they came in as well as two Upper Deck T-shirts and an Upper Deck mug along with a gift card for their gift shop. Not a terrible prize to get after going through several rounds. "I'm sorry I'm not up to date on certain things."

"Neither am I. If there was a category on oceanography…maybe about humpback whales or manta rays…we'd have this in the bag." He nudged her. "I'm sure you remember everything about our museum trip. I dumped a ton of facts on you. Did you know that a humpback whale can sing? Unique, beautiful tunes."

"And let me guess, you have their album." Radha nudged him back. "What's it called, Shamu Sings the Blues?"

Andrew burst out laughing. "Shamu was a killer whale, Radha. They're not the same as humpback whales. Though did you know that orcas, or killer whales, are more likely to…"

"I'm aware, honey. I was just messing with you." Radha caught her mother dozing off in the corner,mouth slightly open and body swaying back and forth. Anytime someone started to drone on a subject she didn't care about, Swati dozed off. She couldn't contribute to it, so she let herself go. Radha poked her mother, who almost fell over, still asleep. "Oh, she's out cold. Let's change the subject. You'll have to regale my mother with your tales on whales another time."

"Fair enough." Andrew picked up the message. "In any case, it was fun again. I'm glad you loosened up a bit. I like trivia nights, but I was never that good at them."

"Because they never asked questions about whales singing?"

"Well, partially that and partially because I had no one to play with. My wife wasn't big on doing trivia in restaurants. In fact, she didn't enjoy them at all." He lowered his gaze. "I wish she went once, though. Maybe she'd change her mind."

Radha stroked his arm. "It's okay, honey. If you had fun, then…"

"I did!" He reached over to hold the trophy. "I mean, look at this! It may not be first place, but we won some nice stuff! Next time, I'll brush up on my social media knowledge. Then we'll get that trophy."

"Speaking of trophies…" Radha spotted Lata dragging her gigantic trophy from winning bingo, laughing and admiring how it sparkled in low lights. "Brace yourself, honey. We're going to deal with this for the next three hours."

"I see what you mean." Andrew let out a mighty sigh as he leaned closer towards her. "I'm bracing myself, all right."

Lata waved her trophy around. "Read them and weep, everyone! I'm still on top!"

"Congratulations, Lata! You're one fierce competitor."

Andrew admired the trophy as she held it over her head. "I've never seen anyone get bingo that quickly, but there's a first time for all things, right? You did well."

"Well? I beat everyone!" Lata exclaimed. "I creamed them! I deserve more than congratulations!"

"Oh, honey, you've got free meals for a month, free dessert for the rest of the year, and tons of free stuff from their store. What more do you want?"

"A few more free desserts wouldn't hurt."

"Oh, really?" Veena joined them, shaking her head. "Sorry for all the fuss, Andrew. She gets this way all the time. It's kind of sad."

"That's not true. The last time, I didn't win any free desserts. That was sad." Lata reminded her. "Oh, I'm so excited you got to witness this, Andrew!"

"I'm glad I witnessed it as well. In fact, if you're up for it, my friends in the biology department throw a bingo night for staff and students every other Tuesday. Others are welcome to join if you know someone at the school, and well, you know me, so…"

"I say yes!" Swati tossed in. "Let's go kick some students butts at bingo!"

"Ma!" Radha groaned before turning back to Andrew. "Forgive them, honey. That sounds lovely. I figure it won't be as big as Upper Deck…"

"Definitely not." Andrew shook his head at the giant trophy. "The most you might get is a gift card to a place like Panera or something like that. It's no trophy but…"

"Eh, we'll settle for it. I could use one of those charged lemonades." Swati waved it off. "The last time I drank one, I got the buzz of a lifetime! I went from a senior citizen to my twenties all over again!"

"Ma, the last time you drank one, you thought you were

in the Winter Olympics, and you were attempting to ski jump off the roof." Radha shuddered over the memory of dragging her hyper mother off the roof while Swati yelled about going for the gold. Thank goodness they had no neighbors nearby. It took them nearly three hours to get her away from the ledge and back in the house to get the lemonade out of her system. "Seriously though, if you go, you're going because you want to have fun. Not for prizes."

"Eh, that's a load of bull." Swati snorted. "I'll see you at the school's bingo night, Andrew."

"I'd love to see all of you there. You're all my friends." He took Radha's hand as her heart started slipping down. Friends. How could she hurt him? He deserved so much better, given that he tolerated all of them. Laughed at their jokes, listened to Veena's wild escapades, played along with Lata, and even endured Swati's random zingers. Right now, he found his car in the parking lot and waved his keys. "Well, ladies, it's been a great night again! I'd love to hang out a little longer but I gotta wake up early tomorrow. Gotta take care of some work-related things." He leaned over to kiss Radha's cheek. "I'll see you soon, I hope."

"Of course! We can see each other before that bingo night. When will you be free?"

"Ah, I have to check my schedule. I don't know if we'll have another big night together but…" He gazed down into Radha's eyes. "Maybe you and I can meet up for a little bit. I might have one free night next week. We can try a new place for dinner. Maybe a movie if we have time?"

"Maybe." Radha agreed. "You know I'm completely free. No interviews have come in."

"Ah, I'm sorry. If I get a chance, I'll check the art department and see if there's anyone who needs help there. We're almost getting new job openings at the university. Though most are for students, I know there are a few spots opening for others."

Radha beamed. A job at the university would settle her down. Granted, she never taught college students, but they'd probably be easier to calm down than younger children. At least she wouldn't worry about them trying to eat paste, wetting their seats, or screaming at others for stealing their paint. "Are you sure? My resume may not be…"

"I can have a colleague look at it. We'll discuss this next week, all right? I really have to run." He waved to the others. "Ladies, it's been a pleasure as always! Have a good night!"

After all the goodbyes, Radha's mind went back to what he told her. The university always had new positions popping up, yet nothing ever impressed her. She already went on their website to check them out. The art department opened positions for students, but never any teaching positions. Still, if Andrew could pull strings, perhaps she had a shot. A boyfriend and a job. Maybe life turned around for her.

No, no, stop thinking about him. She scolded herself. Andrew was no ordinary boyfriend. An image of the house popped in, dark with the lights flashing on and off. The door flung open, swinging back and forth. The walls cracked open, and everything split apart. Hunger. *How can I protect them both? Either way, one of them will lose.*

Walking to the car, she found Veena right next to her. She nudged her shoulder, tossing her dark hair to the side. "So, how will you do it?"

"Do what?"

"Oh, come on! You are going to break up with him, aren't you? You want to protect him from the house!" Veena spotted the car all the way in the back and unlocked it. "Face it, this isn't going to work out. Either you tell him the truth, or you let him go. It's up to you."

"Tell him the truth? He'd never buy it." Radha shook her head. "Come on! How can I tell him about the house? He'd think I was crazy. Even if he came here, he wouldn't believe it!"

"Actually, he might." Veena sucked in her breath. "The house might not eat him right away like the others. It's craving him, so it wants to devour him slowly. It hates the ones who escaped years ago."

"I already know all that."

"No, what I mean is…if he were to see you in the house, it won't wait till you bring him to the room. It'll start draining him out on sight. If the house tastes his blood, he'll pass out. Then it'll suck him dry until there's nothing left. You can't let him spill blood in there."

"Spill blood? How is he going to do that?"

Veena shrugged. "Don't remember when I accidentally cut myself a few weeks ago while trying to chop an onion? The house shivered, but it wasn't hungry. It knew I hurt myself. It didn't hurt me since…well, it's me. If I were someone else, I probably wouldn't be here."

Radha's mind went back to when she hurt herself hard enough to bleed last time. She remembered trying to shred mozzarella cheese with an old grater and ended up cutting her finger. She panicked as she ran towards the bathroom, desperate for ointment to soothe the wound. Not once did she pay attention to the house itself. Her head spun as she scrambled for a band-aid. Back then, she assumed it came from the sight of blood. Now with this new information, perhaps their house held more power.

Feed me. I'm starving. I want blood.

"Has it been shaking a lot?" She stared down at her finger. The wound healed ages ago, yet she still remembered the fresh red line popping out. Panic set in as pain followed. "If so, then we need to..."

"Not yet." Veena shook her head. "It's not time for a party. There's no one I can invite right now. I haven't had time for research. I'll keep feeding the house with what I can find at the store. You must remember, though: Andrew's done something terrible. The house has a good reason to eat him."

"Please don't remind me." She rubbed her chest as the burning filled up. "I swear, was it something I ate or is it more? I mean, I did eat a few more wings today..."

"It isn't indigestion. Your pain is coming from the idea of breaking up."

"No, I think it might be that new spicy sauce." She rubbed her stomach. "I should have known better than to try something labeled "Death Grip". Really now, how many habaneros did they put in this thing?"

"Radha..." Veena narrowed her gaze. "You can't fool anybody here. I know your tolerance for spicy food. This goes beyond that; you're in pain over what's to come."

"Maybe I am. What's it to you?"

"Everything! You're so scared, you keep shaking whenever Andrew says anything. When he looks at you, you want to run away. You are afraid. For good reason though. You don't want to let him go. That's why it pains you so much; you're letting him go to save him." She squeezed Radha's shoulder. "Relax. He'll be better off without you around. The house will heal. Everything will get better."

I wish I believed that. Radha reached around and squeezed Veena's hand on her shoulder. Her cousins didn't want this either. They understood the predicament she found herself in, but they weren't her. The time was coming. With more cracks appearing on their home, time screamed at her to cut

Andrew loose now.

Let him go…even if it breaks your heart.

"You're right." She nodded. "We have to do this not for myself, but for everyone. Think about those victims. Okay, they were forgiving. It still doesn't change anything he did. It's not about how I feel now; it's about keeping everything we have. I'll do it."

"You'll do it?"

"Next time I see Andrew, I'm breaking up with him." Each word dug into her soul, yanking another piece out. "It's over."

CHAPTER 19

Radha planned her breakup over the next few days. The house continued to shiver and break as she put together the words to say. Letting him down gently was the only way to go. She called Andrew a few times, but he always had something to do. One day, he had to go out of town. Another day, he got stuck at work due to his students and endless meetings. He dragged every second out as if he knew it was coming. Maybe he sensed her urgency was bad news. He didn't want to deal with it.

"He's purposely doing this. He knows something around the corner." Swati told her as they went out for a walk around town. Since everyone came home early and had nothing better to do, they opted to see things around downtown. It was a quiet day for them, very few people wandering about. Once she parked the car, Radha let everyone out so they could stretch their legs. Sun high in the sky with cool air balancing it out, it was too good of a day to break anyone's heart.

I hope you're still at work, Andrew. I hope you have a lot of work. I still haven't figured out what to say. I'm upset and confused. Radha practiced her lines, though none came out naturally in her mind. She'd never broken up with anyone since they did it for her. Maybe he figured she'd never learn the truth about him. Seeing other couples around them only shattered her. These couples walked around, linked together, engrossed in each other, not caring about the rest of the world. If they ever broke up, it wouldn't be because one of them committed manslaughter. Manslaughter. That word alone should have been enough to cut it off, yet she still hesitated to bring it up.

"I can't do it." She peeked into the window of a café before moving forward. "I can't face him."

"I don't think he wants to face you either." Veena pulled her away from the café window. "Men tend to do this when they want to avoid something. Maybe he was worried you'd find out the truth. Suddenly, he has a million plans. I've seen it before. You want to talk, oh, they can't talk. They're too busy to talk. That's all this is. He's not busy. He's avoiding you because he knows you know about him."

"That's it, though. I don't think he knows." Radha paused in front of a bakery, light shining down on the cakes and cookies in the window. Her stomach growled as she closed her eyes. "He's giving me time to come up with a good way to do this, though. I can get this done when I do see him."

"Let's hope we can see him soon though." Lata eyed up ahead and pointed to a group blocking them. With people on all ends, they didn't see a way around. "How are we supposed to break through? They're everywhere!"

"I think…let me see…" Radha stepped in front to check out the crowd, growling and screaming at a building. Most of the group looked like college students, though she found people of all ages standing around. No police stood around, so she didn't see anything getting out of hand. "I think… maybe if we…" She turned one direction to find a swarm of people blocking her. "Okay, let's try…" The other direction had a different swarm. "Maybe if I…" She never got a step in as more people filled in. "All right, I have a feeling we'll have to cut through them. Let's get a closer look."

"Oh great! We're never getting out of here!" Swati groaned. "What's going on anyway?"

Before anyone answered, someone screamed about the oceans, and a chant for protecting them rang through. People started singing and waving their signs around, vowing not to stop until changes took place. Radha sank back, admiring all of them. Here were a bunch of people who knew what they wanted. They tackled a problem straight ahead and didn't think about any consequences. They didn't hesitate to stand up for what they believed in, even if they got arrested or hurt.

And I need to do the same. She clenched her fist, getting closer to the crowd. She pulled her mother away, getting her behind. "You know, we could probably go the other way. We're in the middle of…"

"A protest!" Veena gasped. "It looks like…oh, they're protesting those who hurt the ocean."

"And how'd you know that?"

"Cause that's what's written on the sign." She pointed to several signs waving around, throngs of people shouting down the streets. They all crowded the streets, screaming for justice and protection. Radha squinted into the group, noting the ages of protestors. They went from young children all the way to senior citizens. She supported them and their desire to protect the environment, yet didn't understand why the demonstration was here. They weren't close enough to the ocean. Whose attention were they attempting to grab?

"Let's barge through them!" Swati started to head in, but Radha grabbed her and pulled her back. "Oh, come on! They're protesting for the ocean…away from the ocean! How effective will that be?"

"It's not just that." Lata moved in closer and glimpsed

at the building in front. "Oh, this must be a restaurant! I've heard about this place. They had to close since they violated a bunch of health inspection rules. Then I heard the fish they sell isn't really fish."

Radha gulped. She wasn't sure where Lata was leading with the story, but she could put all the pieces together. "Honestly, if any place deserves a protest, it's this one. Still, it can't be because of health violations. People don't protest until…" She caught all the signs of whales all around. Though she couldn't read them all, the pictures of whales injured and dying gave it away. "Oh! We should probably go away. We're going to bother them."

"Thank God!" Swati groaned. "I can't imagine why you'd want to be here. It's a mad house!"

"Well, it's a good cause." Lata pointed out as more people joined in, flanking their sides. "I'm not sure what the cause is exactly. They're all screaming and blocking the way. Maybe I can try…" She attempted to move forward as someone blocked her view. "Okay, let's try…" The others joined her to turn left, which immediately filled up with people. "Let's try the right…" Another group blocked them there. "Oh, let's try to go back!" As they turned their heels, more people filled up that area. "Let's give it up, girls! We're not going to make it."

"Maybe we might. If I show a little something…" Veena tried to move around as several people crowded her. "Oh, excuse me… please…can you form an angry mob away from me?"

"Eh, we're never getting anywhere in this place." Swati shook her head. "Come on! Let's get out of here before…"

"Radha! Ladies! Over here!"

Swati's mouth dropped as the voice cut through the crowd. Radha grabbed her hand to squeeze and ended up grabbing a fistful of air. Lata and Veena froze in place, unable to react. Swati wiped her mouth before she started to curse. "Oh great. I knew he couldn't be perfect. Something had to be off! Now's your chance!"

"Ma! How does that make him imperfect? He's protesting for the good of the environment!" Radha hissed before turning around and holding her arms out for Andrew. "Hi, honey! What a nice surprise! What are you doing here?"

"Technically, I'm teaching a class." He kissed her before waving to the others. "We've been studying a lot about how outside factors have a great effect on our oceans. As you can probably guess, they're in a lot of danger." He frowned at the building. "No thanks to these people, of course…if I can call them people."

"Tell me about it. I keep hearing those commercials on TV." Swati swerved down as someone walked by dressed up in a giant net. "Uh…what's the point of that?"

"Oh, I've told them about the days when creatures used to get caught in nets. How careless people used to be with throwing their trash. When they heard about the latest place polluting the oceans, they decided to act. The best way to get the word across was to give it to people straight. Tell them what you really feel and shout it from the rooftops. Or, in this case, shout it from the streets. I'm so proud." He waved at a group of students who called out to him. "Keep at it, guys!"

"You tell them the ocean's polluted and they're willing to protest? Sheesh, what power do you have, and can you lend some of it to me?" Veena joked. "You must feel strongly about this. You're willing to come out here and fight the big man!"

"Oh, I don't know if I am fighting anything. I just want to prove that one person can make a difference. The more you push, the quicker you'll see change."

He's protesting for the good of the world, though. Protesting big businesses harming the oceans. She stepped away as more people joined the crowd, yelling at the windows above. The lights out, they knew someone listened behind those walls. Nudging Andrew, she gazed around for some hint behind the protest. "You gotta give me a little more information, honey. So, they're harming the ocean. Are they throwing their trash in there?"

"That's part of it. This place dumps their waste where it doesn't belong. The gunk that they make pollutes the waters, destroys the ecosystem, and harms everything living in it. I didn't tell you much about my trips to the beach, but what I've seen…" He shuddered. "I can't tell you how many fish, turtles, and birds I had to free from plastic and garbage. Not just on the beach itself, but under the ocean. I thought people learned not to do this, but…"

"People never learn." Swati patted him on the back. "Believe me, I've lived long enough to see the same old thing happen repeatedly. You're fighting a good fight, Andrew. Trust me. The problem is I don't know if it's enough."

It didn't make sense at all. This wasn't a killer. Even if it happened years ago, he couldn't be so careless. The house had to make a mistake. He cared too much. His heart. She didn't have the will to break that heart. Covering her face, she let the chanting take over her thoughts. Let them fill her up instead. Anything to stall this breakup.He came over here, right when her courage built up. Now it wavered.

You can't be with this man. He kept something horrible from you. So, what if it happened in the past? He killed someone. How can you be with him? Chantal may have forgiven, if she knew, but you don't have to. Let him go.

Something brushed against her, getting all the hairs on

her arm to stand up. His warmth. He stood next to her, his body overshadowing hers. If he noticed her uneasiness, he said nothing. The heat radiating off him was enough. How could she let this go? How could she break such a sweet soul? He nudged her for a reply, so she calmed herself down and glanced around the area for a quiet place. Despite knowing every corner around the downtown area, she drew blanks on a place where they could talk.

"I was…I wanted to see if you wanted to go to Panera." She smiled tightly enough to hurt her face. "I mean, I do have a gift card from a few months ago. I never used that. There's one down the street if you are hungry."

"And we're gonna get that charged lemonade?" Swati grinned.

"No way in hell am I letting you climb on roofs again, Ma. It's plain old lemonade for you."

"So, I was a little overcharged. No one got hurt, did they?" Swati frowned. "The bottom line is I hope we win again next time."

"I'm sure we will." Andrew leaned over and kissed Radha's cheek. "So, does that sound good? You guys come visit me this time around? I can show you my office and where I can get free food from campus. Not even the students know about that spot."

Radha smirked. "Secret spots, free food, and bingo at your work? My, you know how to show a girl a good time."

He kissed her again, sniffing her hair. She thanked every deity around that she broke out the passion fruit scented shampoo and conditioner. Veena gave it to her as a birthday present, reminding her to use it when necessary. It drew all the men in. Not that she wanted all men, only one, to smell her hair. "I really have to go now. Thanks for another lovely evening."

"Likewise." She returned the kiss, her heart dropping lower. How could she do it? How could she break him when they came this far? Her eyes darted towards her friends, who waited for the next move. They didn't want to see this either. They didn't want to break him to protect him. He couldn't pull away from her, planting a kiss on her neck. "Don't… Don't you have to leave now? You'll be making out with me all night. Is there a part of my body you haven't kissed?"

"Quite a lot, but you're also right. I can't afford to spend the entire night here." He checked his phone. "I'll call you when I get home, okay? Have a good night, ladies, and take care."

As they waved him off, Radha leaned against the wall as strength drained out of her. Fear gripped her over the upcoming breakup. Soon. The moment crept up on her, reminding her of what lay at stake. Andrew's life. Their home. What mattered the most, what to save, all rode on her decision. Let one go. Let one of them fall apart. One of them needed to go. One of them needed saving.

Let him go.

Seeing they couldn't move forward in the crowd, they opted to go back and get some food from Upper Deck. Not wanting to risk her mother's health and not wanting to go further, everyone agreed sticking with the old place was best. With another bingo night, Radha expected more excitement, though this was excitement they'd all get behind. She opted not to play this time around, letting everyone else disrupt her thoughts. The lively crowd at the bar already took her concentration away. As she sat down with her drink, she began to unwind.

"Ah, this is better." She sipped her sangria while the others decided on food. Since she still sweated over the talk, she allowed them to make the small decisions. The whooping and hollering from the back got inside her head. She laughed as the waitress came over. "Oh, that's great! I feel so much better already. I forgot about him."

"Andrew." Lata reminded her.

"Oh, I know his name, honey. I meant I forgot about running into him."

"No, I mean…Andrew's here." She waved to someone in the crowd. "How did he know?"

A headache sneaked up on Radha as she faced the same direction. Lata was right; there was Andrew making his way through and waving at them. "Why…Why is he here?"

"He loves bingo." Swati shrugged. "And he's hungry like the rest of us. Why else would he come here? It ain't gonna be 'cause he loves sitting on these broken chairs! You think he loves getting splinters in his ass?"

Radha ignored her mother as she made room for Andrew. "Hi, honey!" He leaned over for a kiss. "How did you know we'd be here?"

"I didn't. I was craving some wings, and unfortunately, there wasn't a great spot out there. My students wanted to stay a little longer, but my legs gave out. I told them I'd see them later. Anyway, I'm starved. What do you guys want to eat? The usual?"

"Sure." Radha forced herself to tune everything out. The others ordered the food while she drifted from one moment to the next, eating in between. She didn't know what she put in her mouth, just that it burned. She sipped her drink, let that cool the sides of her lips, before going to the next meal. The entire dinner, she ate in a trance. Even when she got up, she remained in that trance.

Tell him. Now is the right time.

Wobbly and aching, she started to walk away from the loud noise erupting out of Upper Deck. The others caught her strange movement, flanking to her side for support. Veena helped her up, getting her on solid ground. In her head, the noises rang and banged against the sides. A migraine popped up, reminding her that she carried no pills. That headache would ring through until she got home. Step by step, she found her footing. Lata walked right behind her, rubbing her back.

"You couldn't say anything to him." She whispered. "I think you're going to have to do this without us."

"Yes, I know. I hate to break up with him while there's an audience. In fact, I don't want to break up with him at all." Her shoulders slumped down. "What do I do, Lata? I don't want this. I wish I never met him. Maybe then…" She stopped herself. She didn't really wish for any of this. "What does he want? I thought he left by now."

"Well, whatever it is, this is your moment." Veena reminded her. "He's giving you the opportunity."

"The opportunity? I'm not sure…"

Veena nudged her. "You have to do it, Radha. Now's as good a time as any to tell him. He's calling you over, so you'll have to let him down gently. Don't run away. Don't insult him. Just tell him it's over. You can't be with him."

"What if he wants to know why?"

"Then lie to him. Make up some excuse. The quicker you pull this off, the quicker you can both get over each other." Veena pushed her towards him. "He's giving you this opportunity. Don't let it go to waste."

Radha walked forward despite hating all of Veena's words. Lie to Andrew? No, that wasn't her style. It wasn't something her parents taught her to do. Both told the truth, even if it led them to earn a lot of flak. Andrew deserved the truth as well. The problem was that he'd never believe this. He'd never buy that the reason she couldn't see was because their house wanted to eat him. Keeping her gaze low, she joined him for the walk.

"It's a nice day, isn't it?" He asked. "Seeing all of you again, helping my students, and now I'm walking with you. It's the perfect day."

"Is it?" Her mind wandered away. He remained so blissful and lost in himself. He didn't know the darkness lay ahead, the sadness he'd get in seconds. Radha tried not to engage with him. The less they spoke together, the easier she could let him down. Do it as gently as Veena suggested. Pull it off the same way she pulled a band-aid off. It would be painful, but over with.

Andrew continued talking about his work while she worked up different ways to let him down. She had to work around the truth about the house. Maybe tell him that things were going too fast. A few dates, and they were acting like they'd been together for eternity. The only thing he hadn't done yet was propose to her.

Oh God, what if that's why he called me here? He wants to marry me! Her face burned over the image of Andrew on one knee and asking for marriage. The last thing she wanted was to break up with him while he proposed. *Oh please, I can't go that far! Then he'll want to move in! And I can't let him move in since the house wants him! And I can't...*

"No!" She burst out. "No, you can't!"

Andrew paused as she raised her arms into the air. "You don't want me to take my students on a field trip?"

"Huh?" She relaxed her shoulders. "Oh, you can do that. I thought you asked something else."

Let him go, Radha! He's not worth it! Let him go now!

"Anyway, what do you say?" Andrew nudged her. "How does this weekend sound?"

"Huh?" She blinked. "I'm sorry. I didn't hear what you

asked. You want to take them on a trip this week?"

"I was thinking about us, actually." He chuckled, waving at the groups around them. "I was thinking that after a few protests, you and I get away for the weekend. We won't go far, maybe just down to the shore. Stay a few nights, enjoy everything the beach has to offer. The weather will be great! Maybe we could go sailing or, if you're feeling brave enough, we can hike…"

That did it. The final burst of confidence came out, and she jerked away. "No!"

"No?" He backed away from the sudden shift in her behavior. "What's wrong with hiking? Is it…"

"It's not that." By now, her strength to confront him returned, and she started to storm out of the area. Leave him. This was the time to leave him unless he wanted to be devoured. "Oh, I can't drag this on anymore! I can't be with you. Not after what you did."

"What I did? Protesting? I mean, it's just a protest. It's not a…"

"I don't care about any protest, Andrew. I'm talking about a long time ago. You didn't tell me about what you did when you were younger." As soon as those words left her mouth, Andrew's face fell. His past came back in full force while she kept walking, hands folded over her chest. "You didn't tell me of those three people you hurt. And let's not forget the one person who died! They died, Andrew!"

"I know, Radha!" He grabbed her arm to slow her down. "I know about what happened. You don't need to remind me cause I'm reminding myself of it every day! For the last forty years, I'm haunted by it no matter how much I try to move on! I don't want to live with it, but I have to! I have to…"

"Let me go!" Radha yanked her hand away, heels digging

into the ground and raising up to her full height. He stood taller than her, but her glower weighed down on him. "You have a lot to tell me. How did all this happen on July 3rd?"

"I don't want to…"

"Don't!" She cut him off. "You know exactly what I'm talking about. July 3rd, about forty years ago, when you killed someone cause you got high and you drove while you were high!" Her glare burned down on him as he processed everything. "Did you think you could hide that from me? You probably wiped it all out, but you can't hide from all that. You lied to me!"

Andrew shook his head. "No. I never lied to you. I just didn't tell you everything about me. What happened on that night…it happened forty years ago. Back then, I was a college student who struggled his way through everything. I couldn't do well in school, I had no friends, I didn't always have enough money for everything…it just piled up on me. Even though I passed my classes, they didn't come without their share of pain. I got out by the skin of my teeth. Then came the depression, dark moments, and anxiety that followed me around. Awful thoughts ate away at my mind. I couldn't afford to go to a psychiatrist cause I had no insurance. I couldn't talk to anyone on campus who understood me. It got to the point where I didn't know what to do. I had no one to turn to."

"So, you turned to drugs."

"It's not something I'm proud of. It wasn't something I planned on either. I would never hurt another person on purpose." Andrew covered his face as he recalled every moment. "I wasn't a drug user, Radha. Up until that night, I never touched anything. All I did was go to a party that night. I wanted to…check out of reality."

"Check out of reality." Radha couldn't believe him. "You

went to a party and did drugs to check out of reality? I don't get it! There were a million other things you could have done to feel good."

"You're right, there were. I realize that now that I'm much older. Back then, though, it was a time when everyone was doing drugs. You know that." He inhaled as he started to pace around the area. "I'm sorry I didn't tell you about it sooner. That's only because it happened so many years ago. Back then, the stress got to me to the point where I needed to go out. I had to find something to calm myself down. So, when I saw this party happening nearby, I figured I'd go there. It was just before Independence Day, one month before I went back to college. Just for a little bit, I wanted to escape. I didn't know there would be drugs until I got there."

"You expect me to accept that? You said so yourself! Everyone was doing drugs back then. I got tempted and a desire to fit in, but I thought you'd be smart enough not to drive while high." Radha rubbed her temples, her brain screaming at her to run away. He wasn't who he claimed. The house wanted him for that crime he got away. He killed someone, yet he wasn't in jail right now. "What the hell were you thinking?"

"That's the problem. I wasn't thinking." Andrew turned away from her for a second. "The party started out fine. Everyone had a good time and, even though they brought out drugs earlier, it mostly just pot. I swear I expected to smoke that, and nothing more! We had fun until the cocaine came out. One by one, they started taking turns and I pushed myself to try it. All I wanted to do was try it."

"Andrew, trying means using a little bit. You got high to the point where you weren't lucid anymore!" Radha started to walk towards him, then backed away. Every bit of her wanted to bring him to the house and let it devour him.

Let him fall through the floor, mesh into the walls, having the ceiling smash down. He was no different from the other creeps that wandered into their house. "Why would you drive on your own?"

"I don't know. I thought I was okay. I felt okay even after taking that cocaine. I thought I was well enough that I could drive home. It wasn't far away from the party, only ten minutes. I could drive for ten minutes. I wasn't even going on the highway. Just a back road to my house. I never even saw the other car; everything was dark ahead. I didn't even realize I hit them until the crash!" By now, his voice cracked as the memories flooded back. "It was the worst thing I ever did. I never wanted to hurt anyone. I wasn't trying to hurt anyone. I was a stupid kid making stupid mistakes."

"Mistakes?" Radha gnashed her teeth. "A mistake is pouring salt into your coffee instead of sugar. It's spelling a word incorrectly. It's covering your hot dog with ketchup before biting it and realizing you covered it in barbeque sauce. It's not killing someone!"

"No, it's not. It's a crime, and I paid for my crimes, okay? I spent nights cursing myself out, wanting to die, wishing I could take it all back! At the trial, things did work in my favor. I didn't do anything dirty. Everyone saw me as I saw myself: a pathetic, sorry kid who screwed up in the worst way possible. Even the victims grew to forgive me though it took a while. I did the time, Radha. I have stayed clean since. Isn't that enough?"

Radha took in his words but couldn't see him in the same way. He told the truth now. He was clean, and he hadn't hurt anyone since. Yet the more she went back to it, the angrier she grew. "You're at least alive to clean yourself up and move on. Your victims can't do that as easily. One can't do that at all. You expect me to feel sorry for you after that?"

"No, I don't want you to feel sorry. I'm the one who's sorry for not disclosing that part of my life. I never had to in the past. Most people understood that what I did was stupid and reckless. I explained it so many times. They agree that I've cleaned up my act. I've vowed never to do drugs or drink or get reckless behind a wheel again. I know it's a lot for you to take in, but…"

"Andrew, that's enough!" She cut him off. "No more, okay? We can't have any kinds of dates, big or small. There's a reason I can't, but I'm not ready to tell you. If you knew… well, you'd never believe it."

"Maybe if you told me what it was, I might. You know my secret now." He no longer tried to touch her. "It can't be just that bothering you. You exploded on me when you were perfectly fine earlier. What is this about? Yes, I hide my dark past from you. I'm sorry about that. I should have spoken when I had the chance. It's just that…I didn't want you to think less of me."

"It's a little too late for that now."

"Look, Radha. I was wrong for all of that. I messed up. I paid for it. Now, I want to make it up to you. I'll do one last thing for you. You don't have to talk to me, but let me try something. Ask me anything. Say the word and I'll do it."

By now, her heart dissolved into dust. He wasn't turning away, so she finally put everything down. Turning around, she kept her eyes away from him. "You said you'll do anything for me?"

"That's right. You name it."

She swallowed as she moved her gaze to the ground. "Then forget about me. We're done."

CHAPTER 20

Radha spent her free time ignoring Andrew's texts by applying for more teaching jobs. The community center opened more positions for the upcoming quarter. The moment she saw something brand new, she shot her resume off in their direction. This time, she didn't hold onto hope. She sent the resumes with no excitement. Without anyone giving her a little push, she only submitted them to give her something to do.

Maybe if I get a job... She eyed the unfinished art in the corner. After the last few seascapes, she couldn't bother herself to pick up that brush again. She didn't want to paint anything different. The inspiration ran out once more. With a crumbling house and Andrew gone, she desired nothing. Covering up the artwork, she closed her drawer of art supplies with no intention of using them.

Upon reading the articles, she found herself most confused by them. They all said the same thing; it was a terrible accident. Andrew got only a year and a half of jail time plus plenty of community service. For her, that didn't match up with the crime. What judge could look at manslaughter and think a year and half was a fitting punishment? The only logical explanation was the judge knew Andrew's family. He did them all a favor. Maybe it helped him in the end, but not the victims. A big accident like this wasn't bringing the victim back.

Despite her anger, Andrew still tried to get a hold of her. He texted her often, asking if she was apologizing for whatever he'd done wrong, and wanting to see her again. She didn't answer him, yet she didn't block him either. A part of her hoped that he'd repent for that crime. He'd pay for manslaughter with more than a year and half of his life. Other criminals got away with worse, and they died in the house. Why let him live? The articles talked about the families of the victims learning to forgive and move on. Some opted to help Andrew with his problems. They didn't see him as a murderer, but someone who needed to clean himself up. Live for those who couldn't live. They were kinder than she could be.

What is wrong with me? It should be the end. I shouldn't think about him anymore. She stared down at her phone screen with all the notifications. Every single one came from him. He went through explaining the same things in the articles. The families helped him out. They got him out of the dark spot in his life, which was why he stayed clean. They even helped pay for college, so he'd get his degree. One of the victim's fathers also got him his first job, which Andrew did with ease. She believed every word of it. Those families helped bring him onto his feet. Since then, he stayed away from drugs. Everything was back to normal.

Except it's not. Sitting on her bed, she tossed the phone aside and lay down. Above her, the ceiling covered in cracks, she waited for the fan to crash down. No wonder her mother complained so much. She was old with nothing to show for it. She didn't go on fancy trips, send her kids to the best schools, become a master at anything, or do something that changed lives. Boring. That word described her best.

A knock on the door didn't get her to sit up, though she left the door unlocked. "Come in!"

Lata pushed the door open to show her brand-new trophy. "Hey, I thought you might like this. Upper Deck sent it to you for winning the last contest."

Radha didn't bother checking it out. Another trophy for another worthless contest. "That's nice."

Lata sat down by her side. "You miss him, huh?"

"No, Lata. I'm lying in bed doing nothing because I'm a completely worthless human being." Radha rubbed her forehead. "You can stick a fork in me. I'm done. Finished. Over."

"Oh, that's not true." Lata picked up Radha's left arm and started to massage it. "You are suffering a major heartache. You thought you found the perfect man, and he turned out to be a killer. Okay, he was young when this happened. It was an accident, but it doesn't change the obvious fact. You know why the house wants to eat him. You let him go for that. It's for the best."

"But it's not what I want, Lata. I know all the facts. I'm struggling with them. I just..." Radha sat up and grabbed her phone. To her relief and slight annoyance, her sister Rupa sent a bunch of photos where her family traveled to Greece. Of course, Rupa timed this at the worst moment. She reminded Radha once again that her life was a thousand times better. That's why she could afford to travel to the sunny shores of Greece and sip wine in France. Radha only dreamt of those places, never getting close to them.

Lata glanced at the phone screen, admiring the crystal-clear shores of Greece. "Oh, that's beautiful."

"Yeah, my sister gets all the beautiful stuff. I'm trapped in a house that eats people." Radha flipped through all the photos of the beach, wondering if Andrew went to Greece. Was this before or after he left jail? Teeth clenched, she tossed the phone down on the mattress, letting it bounce up. "Oh, what am I going to do, Lata?! I'm crazy about this man!

I'm upset over what he did, yet my heart is saying go back to him. Forgive him. We can move on together. I don't want things to end like this."

"Then don't end things like this. Tell him that you still want to see you. You just can't invite him to the house."

"He'll want to come, though. He's asked me before. I can't keep lying and telling him that we're renovating it. That worked back in the day. Not now." Radha shook her head. "This is the best thing for him."

"Is it the best thing for you?" Lata picked up Radha's phone, swiping through the pictures. Pictures of the sea, giant pillars of stone, statues, and vineyards passed by. "Think about it. You and Andrew could have all this too. You don't need to push him away to keep him safe. Meet up with him somewhere else. Go to his house. Go on a trip."

"A trip?!" Radha took her phone back. "The most excitement we can handle is football night at the Upper Deck! You want me to leave the country with this man?"

"I said nothing about leaving the country. A trip can be something like a night in the next town." Lata pointed to the picture of a hotel room. "You can stay in a place like this and just enjoy each other's company. My late husband and I went on multiple, short trips. Getting away from the craziness of the world. It healed us quicker than being apart from each other."

Radha pulled her knees up to her chest, wrapping her arms around them. "You had a far better marriage than most people, Lata. You and your husband belonged together. It's no surprise that you don't date for long. You can't get over him. It's like that with me and Andrew."

Lata inched closer. "I think you should at least talk to him once. Tell him that it's not his fault."

"What do I do after that? I'll still want him."

"Well, you can make up an excuse. You can say that you're moving away forever. You got a really good job offer out of the country. Or you could say that something happened to your mother. She's really ill and you can't afford to date now!"

Radha shook her head. "He'd never buy either of those excuses. He knows how strong my mother is; she won't cave in easily to a disease. He's also heard me go on and on about how awful the job market is. He won't believe me if I get a job outside of the country, seeing I can't getone here."

Before Lata replied, a pile of dust landed on her shoulder. Gazing up, the crack widened now, inching closer to the ceiling fan. The house craved something. Their meat wasn't going to satisfy it for long. Sooner or later, they needed another party to keep their walls up. Radha stared at her phone, not getting a message from Andrew now. He understood. She couldn't talk to him right now. Her issues were in the way.

Not only my issues. Our issues. Next to her, the vase dropped three more petals. The flowers weren't dead yet, but it wouldn't take long for those stems to turn completely bare. Her throat tightened over losing the house. These souls weren't enough. Some lousy criminals wouldn't keep the roof over their heads. The house only wanted to eat Andrew for some reason. It wouldn't heal until it had him. So, now it came down to keep Andrew safe from it. If letting him go saved his life, then she'd let him go.

Someone else knocked on her door as she lifted her head. Veena entered with a plate of cheesecake. "I thought you might be hungry. This cheesecake's got your name all over it. Chocolate and peanut butter, your favorite."

Radha forced herself to smile. "Thanks, but I'm not hungry. I can't get excited about cheesecake these days. Not even my favorite kind."

"I know, but I was hoping it would give you some joy." Veena placed the plate on her nightstand, noting the newly fallen petals. "The house is hungry, huh? Don't worry, I'll feed it in a second." She stared at Radha and Lata, knowing that this went beyond food and the house. "You're still upset with yourself, huh?"

"Can you blame her? Andrew's still a nice guy. Yes, he committed a horrible crime years ago, but he's grown from that." Lata kicked some dust off the ground. "Unless he's still hurting people, I can't imagine why the house wants him."

"Probably for that reason: he did his time and, he paid for it. He wanted to move on, be a better man. I get that way of thinking." Veena joined them. "The house learned about him before we did. It still enjoys eating scumbags. It found one before we did. We just didn't look hard enough."

Radha leaned over, grabbed the plate, and cut into the cheesecake. "Well, I know if I were the house, I'd trade eating souls for eating this cheesecake any day of the week. It's just as messy, but at least it wouldn't be illegal."

Veena laughed. "Well, humans probably don't taste like cheesecake. My home needs something else to whet its appetite."

"I get why it wants Andrew. Everything makes sense, so the smartest thing would be to let the house devour him." Radha took another bite, savoring the chocolate and peanut butter mixture. It didn't heal her heart, but it satisfied her hunger. "We were so close, Veena. He really was the one. I think...I wish..."

Lata handed her the phone. "Give him a call. Meet him somewhere else. Stand your ground, though. Let him know why you're angry. More than that, tell him why he can't see you again."

Radha took the phone and opened Andrew's latest message. **I know you don't want to talk to me. You have every right to be angry over what happened. However, if you change your mind, you know my number.**

She kept writing sentences and erasing them.How could she answer a message like that? His other messages were filled with "I'm sorry" and "What can I do for you?" The way he wrote them, he couldn't understand the severity of any of this. The house craving him made a lot of sense. He only appeared pure and clean, all while harboring a dark secret inside. Given that it took place forty years ago, he figured no one would dig into his background.

I'm sorry. Yes, I'm still upset over what happened. I'm still struggling with it, but you're not the only one keeping a secret. Can you meet me tomorrow at the park? I'll be waiting…if you can find me.

Veena read over her shoulder. "If you find me? You're going to make the poor man work?"

"Not work. If he cares about me, if he really wants to be with me, then he'll do anything, right? I won't be hiding clues or anything like that. Just waiting in the park, somewhere out there, so he can find me." She decided. "If he succeeds, then I'll try to tell him why we can't be together. I'll do whatever I can to leave the house out of it but…"

"You're overthinking this. Tell him the truth." Veena took her phone. "He hasn't answered yet."

"Well, you're not answering for me!" Radha attempted to grab it, but Veena held it away from her. "Oh, come on! You can't change my plans!"

"I'm not changing anything. I wanted to send a photo of you from last year in the Bahamas, but…"

"Absolutely not." Radha went for the phone again as Veena tossed it over to Lata. "Okay, that's not funny. Give me my phone!"

"Okay, let me see...I'll send you a picture of me in the Bahamas." Lata typed it out before handing it back. "That's what you wanted to do, right?"

Radha gaped at the latest message. Lata wrote all that word for word. Groaning, she covered her face and threw the phone aside. "Oh, I can't believe you told him that! Veena was just joking about it, Lata! What picture from the Bahamas would I send him anyway?!"

"Um...that picture of your sister in the Bahamas!" Lata decided. "She went there last time, didn't she?"

"He'd know that was her!" Radha groaned, grabbing her phone and texting another apology. "Here, let me fix this mess! The last thing he needs is you two butting in!"

"He may not need it, but you do." Veena pointed out. "Breakups aren't easy, Radha. Sometimes, you're grateful they happened because the relationship wouldn't work out. You can't save that type of relationship. On the other hand, there are some breakups that destroy you. Your heart breaks every second you're not with them. You have that second breakup. I bet he does too."

Radha took in all those words. Yes, her heart broke every minute she sat alone in this house. Nothing good came her way until Andrew. She stared at the phone, checking on his message. He replied quickly. **Don't worry about that. I figured one of your friends wrote it. I'm glad you said something.**

Lata read over her shoulder. "Oh, he's not angry!"

"Why would he be angry over that? You made the mistake, not me." She placed the phone on top of her chest. "He's willing to talk to me. He wants to explain stuff. Oh, God, nothing good comes out of explanations."

"An explanation is just their way of dragging things out."

Veena agreed. "This is how men play with us. They say a lot, and don't do much."

She swallowed. Playing with her. Maybe those were the men Veena dated. They played with hearts and tossed them around. Andrew wasn't that at all. He'd never mess with her. If he believed every word, he would come around and find her. He'd want the answer to why she broke up. She could make up all kinds of excuses for him. They went too fast. She wasn't as fun as Chantal used to be. She wasn't ready for a relationship. She didn't want to bring him home.

"So, what do you think he'll do?" Lata asked. "Do you think he'll show up?"

"I guess I won't find out until later." She decided. "I hope he does show up, though. For us, I want him to come over. I want to tell him as much as I can. If he's telling his truth, let me tell mine. We don't need secrets between us."

"And then you'll get back with him?"

Radha sucked in through her teeth. "No. Then I'll leave him because that's the only thing I can do. It was all too good to be true. I knew it wouldn't last."

"But..."

She held up her hand. "Don't try to stop me. We're over, Lata. You don't need to convince me to change my mind. For his safety, we're over."

"I wasn't planning to change your mind." Lata shook her head. "And I wasn't talking about his safety. There's something much bigger at stake here."

"Yeah, the house."

Lata shook her head again, which gave Radha the real answer. The house wasn't all they needed here. It was their whole lives at stake. Their family history, all their ancestors worked to get, the lifeblood of every generation ran through those walls. Their house wasn't an inanimate object; it was their family. This was what they did it all for. The family members, living and dead, survived only because of the house. Now here she was, keeping it from eating something it wanted.

Only one would remain standing in the end.

CHAPTER 21

Though she never got a reply from Andrew, Radha went to the park anyway. Her heart told her to go there despite how empty it would be. She figured that he wasn't going to answer right now. He needed his time to think about everything. Andrew worked throughout the day, but she knew when he checked his phone. So far, he hadn't gone through it.

Give him some time. He's still struggling over this. He didn't think anyone would find out. He's struggling to come up with words for me. But, no matter what he says, he can't change what happened. The truth is out.

Radha stared down at her phone as the minutes ticked away, wind picking up and blowing the leaves around her feet. Andrew never answered her previous text, though he never said no either. If he cared enough, if he wanted to be with her, he'd come over here. He'd look around every corner of the park for her. She sent him the address as well, so he didn't have an excuse of getting lost. Everyone could follow directions if they had GPS and their phone to guide them around. The only reason he couldn't come was if he didn't want to.

Or if he got hurt. Maybe he got stuck at work. It's not like I've been keeping tabs on him. Why should I? He paid for his crime. She played around with her phone as messages from her cousins poured in. Lata and Veena kept asking if he'd arrived, what they were doing, and if they spoke. Not that there was much to speak about. With nothing coming in, the message rang clear: he was done as well. He didn't believe he could win her back. A sane person would never go back to him.

"It's for the better." She told herself as she flipped through their old photos. Nights at Upper Deck. The museum. Their walks around downtown. The meals they shared and the laughter in their conversations. They weren't too long ago, yet each moment burned in her mind. She hated herself. She hated losing him. She couldn't go back once the house stopped craving him. Not even a party could bring some life back into her. Every future, every moment she dreamed, all disappeared in those seconds.

Her phone went off with a message from Veena. **You're wasting your time sitting there. Send him a message. Say you're sorry. Give him something to cling onto.**

"Cling onto? I don't want to cling onto him! Why should he cling onto me?" She repeated. They didn't have anything he could cling to besides their memories. Not that they made many of those. He'd get over her the moment a younger, more secure woman entered his life. He wouldn't want to spend the rest of his life with an unemployed artist. He didn't have to live in this old house.

The house. Oh God, if he did show up, how could she ever explain the house? He never questioned her about anyone who went missing. No doubt other people heard about it. She saw mentions online about some of them who went missing, but no one got answers. They'd never get them. The house and her family kept the truth buried deep in those walls.

Maybe I should have told him about the house. He wouldn't stay then. He'd have good reason to leave me. She checked her phone once again for messages from her siblings. Once again, endless vacation photos poured in with the little message of "Wish you were here!" to burn her more. She hesitated to snap back. She dealt with enough of their escapades, so she turned her phone off and pulled herself off the bench.

He's not coming. I should have known. Walking away, she kicked the dead leaves littered along her path. These leaves didn't sting as much as the ones at home. She weaved around them, making her own path back to the car. Andrew gave up on her. Either out of fear or sadness, he decided it was the end. Clenching her fists, she shoved her phone in her pocket and walked all the way back to the parking lot. By now, more people started hiking around, giving her polite hellos as they went their way. She smiled back and returned those hellos, praying they didn't keep talking with her.

You're all very nice, but I don't want to talk. Not with you. Hand to her chest, she rocked back and forth on her heels- The time passing didn't ease any of the pain. The lack of response burned harder. Was this worth it? How could she give up on him like this for a house? No, it was the right thing in the end. It was for all of them.

Her hands trembling, she sent a long text to Andrew. **Look, I know we broke up. I can't forget about what you've done. I can't stop thinking about your victims. Sure, they might forgive you, and they may move on. At the same time, you did something that ruined their lives. It ruined your life. You can't ever escape that, and I can't ever stop thinking about it. At the same time, I can't stop thinking about you. I want to hear more of your side of the story. Please send a message if you get this.**

That did it. She hit 'send' and waited only a few seconds before checking it. Nothing came in from him, but Veena sent her a message back. **You should head back. It's getting**

late.

They all sent her messages like this, yet Radha couldn't leave. She decided to find another bench to sit on and flipthrough all the old photos. Instead of the millions of pictures from her sisters, she focused on the ones taken in recent days. Someone always found her and Andrew in the strangest positions. They always took the worst picture of her, but Andrew…he always glowed. His face bright red and beaming, he always wrapped himself around her. She never smiled as widely, even though deep down, she thrilled over every minute with him. She laughed in private and enjoyed being around him. How could she let any of that go? Maybe it wasn't in a place like the Alps or the Italian coastline, but it was their time together. They had magical moments.

FEED ME.

Head jerking up, she glanced around the area. No one. The only new thing she noted was a few cracks in the bench that were there before. The house wasn't haunting over here. It didn't break anything outside of itself. The hunger pangs grew as its voice continued taunting her.

HE IS NOTHING TO YOU. LET ME EAT HIM.

"No!" She hissed at a dog walking by. The dog stared at her for a second before running off with its owner in tow. The owner never caught her glaring even as the house continued to haunt her from a distance. YOUR ANCESTORS WON'T BE PLEASED. LET ME FEED ON HIM. KEEP US ALL HAPPY.

Gazing down at the ground, she found several fresh cracks in the ground. They weren't there before, so she pressed down on one with her toe. It widened from the force. She jerked back and pulled her legs as the cracks made their way up the bench. They ran up to the back of the bench, along with the area she sat in. Eyes darting around, she held her breath as all the cracks grew wider and split the ground open. The entire time, she heard the house. It never stopped taunting her as it broke everything around.

FEED ME!

"Really?!" She grabbed the sides of the bench as those cracks reached her. "You're still going on about this? I'm confused on what to do, and you still want to eat him?"

The cracks shifted again. LET ME HAVE HIM.

"Didn't you hear me? I can't let you have him." If anyone heard her, they'd believe she lost it. In a way, she had lost every bit of sense inside of her. "I know it's crazy. I should feed him to you. After all, he's not that different from some of the other people we bring in. Yet…I don't know. I can't let you have him. Maybe it's all we've done. I shouldn't care about it, and I do." She covered her face. "I don't know how I feel anymore."

The rustling nearby reminded her she wasn't alone. Calming down, she leaned into the bench and tried to force the house's voice out. People walked away from her, not noticing her unusual posture. She hadn't run anywhere, yet sat like everything drained out of her. The house always bothered her the most for food. She didn't know why. She wasn't the main owner, yet it came to her. It wanted her attention over everyone else's.

"I don't get it. Veena, Lata, even Ma goes on dates too. They've had lots of boyfriends. You never crave them. When I get someone, that's the one you want. Andrew did a horrible thing. I'll admit that. Was it justice? I don't know. I don't agree with it, but I wasn't there to know how things went down. All I have is his word. Isn't that enough?"

HE GOT AWAY WITH MURDER. HE GOT OFF FREE.

"No!" She snapped as the leaves blew around her. "That's

not what happened! You don't know that! The jury made that decision, not him!"

HE MUST PAY. Below her, the cracks grew wider and shot up towards the parking lot. Gasping for air, Radha sat up on the bench as that continued to creak and come undone. A new message swirled in front of her. MAKE ME HAPPY. GIVE ME WHAT I WANT.

"STOP!"

The final cracks split the bench apart. Radha fell, rolled onto her feet, and ran from the scene. Fumbling around for her keys, she found them and shoved them into the car door. Under her feet, no more cracks formed. No cracks on the ground and none on the bench. The cracking stopped as soon as she opened the car door and got in. By now, nothing taunted her. No one came around as she revved up the engine. The house's voice now lingered in the distance though it didn't affect anything. She leaned back for a second, trying to drown it out with music and the air conditioning on full blast. Bit by bit, the previous incident faded out, though she couldn't remove the house's cries from her head. The moaning for meals. The begging. It starved for something good.

FEED ME.

It wasn't just the house crying out. Her ancestors cried for his soul. They hated her for being indecisive. They wouldn't agree to her taking time on letting this man go. Her grandparents would have gone after him the moment they learned about the crime. He would never be allowed in their lives. Hell, her great-grandfather would kill him for even getting close to her. She had no problem when it came to the creeps they brought to the house. Many of them committed crimes a long time ago. They weren't that different from Andrew.

At the same time, he is different. I believe what he's saying.

Hand on the wheel, she reached to back out as something stuck out. Her fingers pressed down on the wheel and found it. A tiny crack. This wasn't in her imagination. She gripped the wheel and backed out slowly, her heart shattering. The house continued to ring in her ear as she drove away, her hands always grazing the crack in the wheel.

Feed me.

I'm hungry.

Give me what I want.

Sucking her breath through her teeth, she hit the gas and sped down the road, leaving all the cracks at the park behind.

Chapter 22

Radha's spirits never lifted over the next few days. No new job interviews or postings came in. The ones she did get interviews for ended up closing early, or someone else got the position. The best position for her, an art teacher for a middle school, gave her an interview, yet changed it every few days. By the time they settled on a date, she found out they gave the position away to another candidate. After that mess, she stopped sending applications. With her mind shaking from the day at the park, she didn't want to add more heartache to her list.

No one knows what they want. Hell, I don't know what I really want. She folded her resume into her drawer, locking it up. She didn't want to look at it for a long time. Everyone told her she had the qualifications, yet it wasn't enough. Even the most qualified teacher couldn't get in. No wonder her mother gave up working years ago. Swati warned her that the workplace changed over time. No one cared about how much experience one day. It all mattered if she could be useful or not.

"You're too sharp." Swati warned her. "You're a smart woman. These guys…they want people they can manipulate. They want people who'll work for peanuts. That's not you. You deserve the best job working with the best people. You want something to satisfy you for the rest of your life."

All of it made sense, yet Radha's spirits sank over the thought of less qualified people getting jobs. She'd seen the state of art classes. Most could barely draw a straight line now, let alone anything else. None of it was the fault of the students, of course. They just didn't get the right art education. The art teachers also weren't at fault; they only knew so much. Without any drive on either end, the arts suffered.

Maybe I should pack it in too. I'm not getting far with anyone. Not in love, not in employment, nothing. Her eyes fell on her phone. By now, Andrew stopped sending her texts. He no longer asked what was wrong, nor did he want an explanation. He wouldn't get one. A part of her almost texted him back, wanting to meet again. They could still be friends, after all. Friends could see each other in different places. They could eat in restaurants, visit museums, watch movies, and enjoy themselves.

No, I can't! She shut the idea out. They went too far to be friends now. They couldn't hang out in the same way she hung out with Veena and Lata. Every second she spent with him, she'd crave him. She'd want to go the distance this time. *Get a grip, Radha! Yeah, you were in love, but you can't love a killer. Even if he paid for his crime, it's still...it's just not right! That's going against everything you stand for!*

The house shivered as she moved out of her room. Typical. It reminded her that it wanted something she wouldn't give it. It still got fed its usual meals, but nothing satisfied it. No matter how many times she tried to force Andrew out of her thoughts, he remained there. Sometimes, his name slipped out of her mouth, and cracks formed around her. The house didn't forget him either. The cracks formed that small sentence, revealing its impatience.**LET ME EAT HIM.**

"I'm not giving him to you." She told the cracked walls. "You'll get fed, but you can't have him. I know what he did.

I can't believe I trusted him either. I know I should let you have him, but...I don't know. I can't do it."

She paused at the sound of a car cutting off the engine, which had her straightening up. Veena and Lata wouldn't leave work early without a good reason and her mother was spending time with other seniors. She wasn't gonna come home before evening rolled around. They weren't expecting any visitors either. Could it be the mailman? She didn't order any packages so perhaps it came for Veena or Lata. Maybe Swati borrowed her credit card and ordered things she wasn't supposed to.

That's probably it. Ma is always looking for new ways to spend my money...the very little money I have. She closed the door behind her and walked down the long-cracked hallway to the front door. *Anyway, I'll return this thing and we'll never speak of it again.*

The doorbell never rang, but she still opened to expect a package on the ground. To her surprise, no one was there, and no package lay in front of her. Leaves rustled in the wind as she stepped out for a better look. The tire tracks in the dirt could come from anyone. With no car in sight, she wondered if it came from a distance. Then again, they hardly heard any cars driving by, being so far from a road.

Maybe I imagined it. Closing the door behind her, she opted to spend time in the garden. Unlike the house, that one still flourished with its bright petals and leaves growing. Dewdrops sprinkled over blades of grass she walked around the back. The fragrance of roses caught her first. How could their house smell beautiful yet look ready to collapse? She shuddered over the sight of the cracks all around it. It clung on, but without the right nutrition, collapsing was around the corner. She brushed her fingers against several new red roses, their velvety petals warming her. At least they remained beautiful and big. They gave her a little happiness now.

"I'm glad you're still growing." She leaned over to get a quick sniff. "You smell wonderful."

"They really do." A familiar voice piped up. Her body stiffened as it went on. "You never told me you had such a beautiful garden. I'd stay here forever if I could."

She jerked upwards to face him. Of course. He came. She never gave him the address, yet he came and waited for her amongst those red, white, and pink roses. The angel statues stared down at him, sweet and silent, while the demon statues glared from the back. Fitting. Not all those statues approved of his presence. Nearby, a few rosebuds sprang out from the bushes. They'd grow in time. With a little sun, water, and love, those roses bloomed with all the other flowers. They swayed towards him, inches from touching him.

She turned to face the house looking down on them. Its meal came to it, yet it couldn't consume a thing. Not until Radha let him inside where it could slowly suck his soul out. The house drained everyone it wanted. Even now, she noticed him trying to balance himself on one of the angel statues. His feet stumbled as he hung on, head spinning. It started. The house drained him from a distance. It sucked out his life force as the flowers bloomed. No wonder the garden appeared lush and green. He was here.

"How did…" She couldn't force the words out. He was here. He came all the way here, waiting in her garden. "What did…" She shook her head. "You shouldn't be here! Why?"

"I had to see you. I looked up your address, which wasn't hard. As soon as I drove up, I wanted to knock on the door, but couldn't. I waited in here." He stood up straight, still using the statue as a crutch. Coughing, he leaned over and breathed hard, clutching his chest. "Forgive me, Radha. I'm suddenly a little woozy. I think I didn't eat enough for lunch."

Radha's lump grew as she blocked him from the house. This dizziness didn't come from eating too little. It all came from one place, the same place craving him. The house started sucking on him even though he stood outside. "Look, I don't know what you want, but you need to leave. I thought I made it clear last time! I don't want to see you!"

"Just hear me out a little bit. You need the whole story." He tried to move towards her as she started backing up. "Radha, what are you doing? What are you hiding?"

"Nothing!" She pressed her hands against his chest, fingers gripping his shirt. "Look, Andrew, I don't want to see you, but you shouldn't be here. This house..."

"It's a fine house, Radha. I haven't seen anything like it before." He gazed at the demon statues in the corner. "Okay, they're a little terrifying, but I can live with that. There's nothing wrong with the house itself. You've got a beautiful garden. So many roses..." He leaned near one of the red rose bushes and went for a rose. "I've never seen any that...ow!"

"What happened?" Radha got her answer as soon as he held up his finger, blood running down the side. "You forgot they have thorns, huh?"

"No, I'm aware. I thought I could pluck it without touching them...I guess I wasn't so lucky." He put his finger in his mouth as Radha gaped at the bush. In seconds, the rosebuds bloomed, covering all the green in red. His blood. The garden tasted his blood. "I should have asked if I could touch it."

She pulled him away from the bush as it continued to grow without him noticing. Not a single green leaf remained visible. Nothing but red petals covering it. "Come here, let's sit down. I'll run inside and get a band-aid for you."

"Let me come with you!"

"No!" She motioned him to stay. "It's okay! I'll be quick, I promise. Just stay right here and don't grab any more roses!"

She ran off before he got another word in, skidding down the hallways and hitting the nearest bathroom where all their first-aid things were. She found a band-aid and ran back, praying he heeded this warning. He didn't care about her previous warning, but maybe he'd stay away from the other roses. Getting hurt might have been a blessing.

It tasted blood. God, the house got his blood! She ran back to the garden to find Andrew staring at another rosebush, this one white. His finger bled over the white petals, dripping down the leaves. The white buds burst open before him as each drop landed on them. Radha raced to his side and held up the finger, now caked in red.

"Oh God..." She cleaned it up before wrapping the band-aid around it. "That's a deep cut."

"It's okay. It woke me up a little bit. As I walked around, I became so sleepy." He stifled a yawn. "Don't worry, I didn't touch any other rose bushes."

"And you shouldn't!" She warned him. "Roses have thorns, Andrew! You may not always see them, but they're there!"

He leaned back, eyeing the stained white roses. "Yeah, I can see that. One thing I don't get. That was a bud just a few seconds ago. I remember seeing it, wondering how beautiful it would become when it bloomed. Yet it bloomed right in front of me. Flowers don't bloom that quickly. Yes, some bloom in certain circumstances, like in certain weather and time periods. They don't bloom when blood falls on them."

Radha gulped. "What makes you think it bloomed because of your blood?"

"I saw it, Radha. I saw the blood drop on the bud, and it burst open." He lifted her chin, getting her to eye level. "That's not the weirdest thing, though. It's not why I'm here."

"Then why'd you come?"

Andrew rolled his eyes. "Radha, please…you can't keep doing this to me. I sent you messages. You treat me like I don't exist. I apologize, and it's not enough. I don't know what I'm sorry for, but I'm sorry. I never meant to offend you. I never wanted to hurt you, not even unintentionally. All I want is an explanation. You tell me what I did, and I'll go back to where I came from. I promise."

"Andrew, I…" Radha inched away from him. "I never wanted to…I never thought we'd get this far. I did ignore you. I was angry at you for hiding that. I'm still angry about it. Yet, the more I dwell on it, the less angrier I get.

She froze. Around her, the rest of the rose bushes grew as Andrew wiped the sweat off his forehead. "Are you okay?"

"I'm fine. Just a little warm, that's it. Kind of funny though. It's not as hot, yet I'm sweating up a storm. My entire body…" He fanned himself. "God, I think I need to go inside! It's getting warm even though it's dark!"

"Uh…that may not be a good idea." She rubbed his back. "You should stay here for a little longer. Let the fresh air cool you."

"I'm trying to, but I'm faint. I can't see anything…" He turned towards the house with its stone walls slowly closing, all the cracks now gone. "I might feel better if I lie down in there."

"No!" She pushed him back on the bench, letting her hands fall on his lap. "You cannot go inside! In fact, you shouldn't even be here! They…" Her eyes fell on the blooming rose bushes. The cracks on the statues sealed up. Andrew's blood. The moment it landed on something, it healed every part. "Oh God."

"What's wrong?" Andrew grabbed her so she faced him. "You're avoiding me and staring at the house. What is it?

What did I do to you?"

"Nothing!" She threw her hands in the air. "I know I've been avoiding you, and I'm sorry about that. I broke up for a good reason, Andrew. It's not you. It was never you. It's me."

"You? You never did anything wrong." He rubbed his finger. "God, it's burning. I've been pricked by roses before, but this is…"

"It's not your typical rose." She finished off for him. "None of these bushes are typical rose bushes. Haven't you noticed that?!"

He turned to the bush behind him, bursting with pink roses. "What's wrong with them? All right, their thorns are sharp, but those are…"

"No, it's not that!" Radha jumped up from the bench, pacing back and forth. Those roses with their bright petals mocked her as she struggled to explain anything. He came into the garden and brought it back to life. If he stepped foot in the house, then she couldn't save him. "You're not the first person to bleed because of those roses. Didn't you notice something odd about them?"

Andrew stared at all the roses swaying in the light wind. He wiped up the sweat on his forehead before trying to get up. As soon as he stood, he went back down. "Oh, my head! I don't know what's wrong, Radha. I was fine when I came here and now…"

"It's sucking you dry." She realized as her hands crept up to her mouth. "It got a taste of you, and it wants more."

"What are you talking about?"

She pulled him onto his feet and started to lead him away from the garden. Next to her, all the angel statues started closing their cracks, their eyes locked on her. They hated her. She took their food away as he stumbled around, aching and vulnerable. The longer he lingered, the more they drained him. "You must leave! If you stay, you'll die!"

"Die?!" He stopped right then, grabbing her wrist. "Listen, Radha. I may not be feeling well, but I'm not dying. I'm sure once I sit down, relax, and talk about all this, I'll be better. Right now, it's like something is sucking away at me. Draining all my energy."

"The house." She finished off as she pulled him from the garden. "It's the house, Andrew. That's the reason I broke up with you! That's the reason I never brought you around here. You saw those rose bushes? They're the ones draining you. As soon as you pricked your finger, you fed them. You brought them back to life."

She walked towards the nearest rose bushes, bright red like blood. Carefully, she held it between her fingers so the thorns wouldn't graze her. A few days ago, only a tiny red bud popped out of it. She spent days going through the garden, wondering if the meat wasn't enough to help it bloom. Andrew's blood brought them all to life, even the ones that wilted. Even now, that rose bush blew towards him. He sat on the bench again, unable to move on. She caught him as he fell into the bench, clutching his chest.

"This isn't a heart attack. It can't be." He rubbed his chest. "The pain burns, but I'm not getting the signs of cardiac arrest. You keep talking about the house, though. What about it?"

"It means…" She took his handkerchief and started to wipe up the rest of the sweat. "This house is old. It's falling apart. You know how everyone needs stuff to keep them going? We must eat to gain energy. So does the house. It needs food."

"The house needs food?" He repeated. "Houses aren't living things, Radha."

"Normally, no, they don't need food. This house has its

secrets. And me…I've got my secrets too. There were things I never wanted you to know. I…" She sniffled as the wind froze around them. Cold air. The next step kicked in when the house craved food. "It wants you. The house wants to eat more of you."

Andrew got up at that moment, though he didn't turn towards the driveway. Instead, he tripped along the rocky path while she caught him from falling. "I'm having trouble walking, Radha. You keep saying the house is draining me, but how? I didn't go inside."

Radha steadied him against her body. "Just stepping in the garden was enough. Once you pricked your finger, it ate a piece of you. It got your blood, and the rose bloomed. You see this bush?" She pointed to a rose bush full of white roses. "They were just buds! Look at them now!"

Andrew gulped as he stumbled out of the garden. Radha led him towards his car, fishing in his pocket for his keys. "I'm…I'm…I'm so confused, Radha. You learn the truth about me, so you dump me. I get that. I should disappear from your life, but then I'm suddenly weak from standing in the garden. Maybe I'm ill. Maybe I caught something on my last trip and it's…"

"It's not that." She whispered. "It's nothing you got on a trip. It's nothing you got from eating or touching or breathing in. It's the house. That's the one draining you out. It does that with anyone it's craving."

"The house is craving me?" Andrew slowly took in all her words, yet nothing came together. "I still don't follow you, Radha. I'm not following any of this."

She nodded. "I'll explain everything once I get you out of here. This house will eat you alive."

"Me? But…"

"No more." She pushed him into the passenger side of

the car. "Let's go, okay? Let's get out of here before you pass out." Behind her, the house healed itself with all the energy it got out of Andrew's blood. Cracks sealed themselves as more flowers opened, their scent drawing her in. Not now, though. This was the moment to leave.

I hope the house got enough of him to stop craving him. She glanced behind her to find it there. It would still be there when she got back. It would bother her for more of Andrew's blood. She'd keep refusing despite her conflicted emotions. They'd go back and forth. Then either it would win or she would.

In either case, she'd end up as the loser.

CHAPTER 23

Andrew wasn't heavy by any means, but he dragged his feet across the dirt path, unable to steady himself against her. He apologized under his breath as she got towards his car sitting in the driveway. Taking the keys, she unlocked it and led him towards the passenger side.

"Steady now, steady..." She pressed her hand against his forehead. Hot. After the exhaustion, fevers kicked in. He'd get the chills and warmth burning against his body. Then he'd collapse and pass out. She had to get him out of the way before the passing out part happened. "Oh God, you are sick!"

"How can that be?" He whispered. "I wasn't sick before. I wouldn't visit you if I was sick. You weren't answering your calls, and I get why, but I had to explain some things. I came for that reason."

"I know. Here." She helped him steady himself against the car, leaning on it. Whipping out her phone, she kept one eye on him and the other on the phone screen. One by one, she found the others and sent them a quick message. "Hang in there, baby. I will get this fixed up."

"You need to..." He groaned as he leaned over. "I can't... what's going on with me?"

"Here, here!" She sent the message and grabbed him before he fell. Holding him up, she moved to the other side of the car. "Come on. I need you to get a nice place to sit. You'll be more comfortable in the car than you are out here. I'll turn the AC to full blast to cool you down."

"Cool down?" He fanned his face. "Yeah, that would be nice."

Her phone went off and she checked her messages. Sadly, none came from the others, just a bunch of coupons and reminders. She quickly sent another note giving them the exact place and time. They'd get everything from that.

Meet me in the parking lot of Umble Park at 7 PM. This is an emergency.

No need to put more than that. An emergency usually means something horrible happened within the house. They'd arrive exactly where she asked them to. Lata would pick up her mother from the senior center while Veena would drop the man she'd been seducing. The house meant everything. It held precedence over everything else. Now that Andrew lost blood to it and sat in that passenger seat, breathing heavily, she needed their help.

"You take it easy, okay?" She opened the passenger side to let him in. "Just rest for now. We're going out."

"We are? Where?"

"Somewhere that you can heal up." She wiped his face with his handkerchief. "You're sweating bullets here, honey. You won't get better until you get away from this place. I'll explain it all when you're more lucid.

Radha helped Andrew buckle his seatbelt and leaned him into the seat. His head hit the headrest as he closed his eyes. She patted him on the shoulders, squeezing them as the color raced back into his face. "Are you feeling better?"

"I think so. That…whatever that was…it's taken me out. I don't get it. I just came from the doctor's office, and he said I'm fine." Andrew rubbed his eyes. "I've been going out of town and heading to beaches, and I don't get ill. I'm always careful, yet over here…"

"It's not because of you." Radha backed his car out and started to drive away. "You sit back, okay? I'll take you to the park where you can get some fresh air."

"The park? That sounds nice." He leaned towards the car window, watching trees pass by, each one bright and covered in green foliage. "It's like spring here. Flowers in bloom, green trees, cool breezes. Your little bit of spring."

"Yeah, it feels like a little spring." She eased onto the road and headed towards the park. Although Andrew was taller, she didn't struggle with adjusting herself in his car. Everything was in the right place. She checked the lanes before changing them and cruising towards the way to the park. They still had an hour before it closed. All she needed was an hour to cool him down. Turning on the AC, she put it to the very highest setting and let that cool air blast into his face. Andrew gasped as it hit, opening and closing his mouth like a fish tossed out. He coughed as the car lurched forward when Radha hit the brakes. Tires squealed as the car halted, lurching them both forward with the impact. Andrew gasped as he braced himself.

"What…What's going on?!" He demanded. "Where are we?!" Radha, what…"

"I'm sorry, I'm sorry!" She apologized as his breathing returned to normal. She pointed to the stoplight before them as cars drove in front. "The light went red suddenly. I tried to ease it but…"

"It's fine. It happens." He lowered the AC down one notch. "It's the cool air. I rarely need to put it on full blast since it cools down so quickly. Anyway, I think I'm starting to get a little better. I'm not as warm. The pain's gone too. What was all that about?"

Radha turned the road towards Umble Park. "We're almost there. Is the pain going away?"

"Bit by bit. The strange pain in my stomach's gone." He rubbed his stomach to soothe it. "Yeah, that's good. My whole body isn't as warm."

"I'm glad to hear that." She found a parking spot and eased the car in. An empty bench stared right back at them, lightly dusted, and covered in wet spots and leaves. It was no bed, but he'd heal quicker sitting here than driving around. No one else was around, so she cut the engine and stepped out. "Hang on. I'll help you to that bench. You take in the cool air, okay? Breathe in and out."

She opened his side door, draped an arm over her shoulder, and hoisted him onto his feet. He'd done her a favor by taking off the seat belt, the only thing he had enough strength to do. He leaned into her, his cologne wafting over. That smell. It never came from the roses, only him. They took it in and started draining him out. Slowly, she stumbled towards the bench, his feet also moving along. By now, the strength returned to his legs and his feet planted onto the ground. He could walk with assistance and, as she sat him on the bench, he took his arms off her. Splaying them out on his sides, he began to breathe.

"Oh God…" He whispered. "I'm feeling a lot better now. Being outside is what I needed though I wish I was close to the beach. Something about salt water…"

"I'm sorry. I can't drive that far right now." She took her place next to him, hand on his forehead. The heat no longer radiated off him and his sweating ceased. The color filled up his cheeks as his eyes blinked. "I wish I had some water. I'll text one of the girls to bring some."

"No, it's all right. The pain's fading away." He stared down at the finger covered in a band-aid. "All this came from me accidentally pricking myself?"

"It's not just that." Radha stared down at the ground. "Look, Andrew. I didn't think we'd see each other again. A part of me never wanted to see you. Yes, I can't forget about what you did, but that's not the main reason I stayed away. I never asked you to come to my house for a reason. The moment you stepped on the property, that's when..."

"The garden." He murmured. "I still don't understand. You keep talking about it like it's alive. I mean...yes, I know plants are living creatures, but..."

Radha silenced him as her finger went over his lips. "Save your breath. You need to get all your strength back before I can explain anything. I asked the girls to come over here and help me out a bit. I can only carry you so far."

"You don't have to carry me anymore. I think my strength is returning now. My feet are moving and my heart..." He touched his chest, tracing from top to bottom. "It's not palpitating. It's back to normal rhythm. Oh God, that was...I really thought that was it for me. I saw my entire life flashing, thinking about what I would never get to do. I went back to that time. When I was a young man, at that party. I relived every second of it."

Leaves fell around them, a constant reminder that all good things ended soon. Even the brightest green leaf could fall when a strong breeze blew through it. Their garden. It became that breeze knocking him out. It knocked anyone out, no matter how healthy they claimed to be. Watching him breathe in and out, his chest heaving up and down. The house almost got him, ready to suck him out. He didn't fall through floors or dissolve into the wall. No, it wanted to drain his life out and build itself up.

Up ahead, a red Chevrolet rolled into the parking spot next to Andrew's car. In seconds, Veena jumped out with her hands carrying water. Andrew's eyes brightened as she approached them, handing him one of the bottles. "I came as soon as I heard! Here you go! Sip slowly and take deep breaths."

"Thank you." He popped the top off and started guzzling it down, drops splashing down his chin. When he pulled away, half of the water remained inside. "Oh God! That was wonderful! I never realized how parched my throat was, but...whoa!" He grabbed his forehead again. "My head...I shouldn't have moved so quickly."

Veena helped him down. "You need to sit still for a little bit. Let the spinning stop. The more you stand, the worse it'll get."

"Right, right." He leaned back on the bench, keeping his head up. "My mind is so full of questions. I should rest, but all I wanted to do was talk. I want to explain how things went wrong, but no one wants to hear me out. Yes, I can't justify my bad decisions. I may have been depressed, but it's no excuse to get high and get behind the wheel. It's no better than getting a DUI."

"You only spent a year and a half in jail for it. The law worked in your favor somehow. The rest of the world moved on from it, but the house heard of you and wanted you to pay." Veena snapped her fingers. "Radha was trying to protect you."

"Protect me from what?"

Radha caught Veena's eye, hoping she'd have a better answer. The house belonged to her. If anyone could calm people down, she could. Her eyes twitched a bit as she relaxed and uncrossed her legs. "Okay, this is going to sound strange. I never tell people about the house beyond what my husband told me. It was built ages ago hence why it's made of stone. My grandfather said the house will always stay standing as a result. However, there's more to the stone walls and the garden. It's got…it's unique. I think of it as a curse."

"Curse? Your house is cursed?" He rubbed his head. "I think I need something to drink. Whatever you tell me, it may be the weirdest thing I've heard."

"You don't know how right you are on that." Radha spotted Lata's white Toyota roll in, catching her and her mother behind the windshield. The late afternoon traffic caught them, but they parked next to Veena's car. Lata stepped out with an entire supply of medication while her mother got out, throwing her hands in there.

"I don't believe it!" Swati groaned. "You finally bring a guy in this house, and it almost takes him out! If that ain't bad enough, the guy killed someone! How could you do this, Radha?!"

"Radha did nothing wrong! I should have called! I should…" Andrew coughed. "Oh God, I shouldn't have shown up like that."

"No, you shouldn't." Radha stopped him. "I get why you came. You're here to repent for your sin. Maybe you wanted to beg for forgiveness. The thing is…I'd have listened if you asked to meet somewhere else. Anywhere else. The house is…well, the house is not an ordinary house. There's something deep in those walls that brings it to life."

"Brings it to life? The house is alive?"

"Well, let's slow down a bit." Veena cut in. "We must start from the beginning. I gave you a little bit of history, but there's more. My house was built years ago, but it wasn't always a house. There was something hidden deep inside. Something that my husband and I didn't find out until later. It's not a place that everyone can tolerate."

"I think I get that bit." He stared at his finger. "If I knew your roses had thorns…"

"It's not just the roses." Veena went on. "The entire house…there's something else in it. Legend has it that my great-grandparents sealed their souls in it. They were so grateful to the house for providing shelter that they vowed to take care of it. I guess when they made that vow, it came to life. And like all living things, it needs sustenance. So, every now and then, it needs to be fed. Like you feed a child, you have to feed it too."

Andrew's eyes glazed over, though every thought hit him. "Oh. That makes sense."

"It does?" Lata blinked. "Maybe you can explain it to me because I didn't get any of it."

"What a surprise." Swati rolled her eyes. "Look, Andrew. Let's get straight to it. The house wants you. It wants to drain your life. It gets hungry like anyone else, and it's craving something specific: you. It's the only reason Radha never brought you around. She wanted to protect you. Of course, that was before she realized you were a bloodthirsty killer."

"Ma!" Radha snapped. "That's not what I said. Although I cannot wrap my head around any of this, I didn't think you were bloodthirsty. Just…" She turned away from him. "I'm sorry. I can't look at you the same way. I saved you for some reason. Maybe it's our memories together. I couldn't stop thinking about them. You told me you got better, you redeemed yourself, and…I want to believe you. I want to think you're a good person."

"Then believe me. Believe every word." He tried catching Radha's gaze while she focused on the leaves falling. Funny how their house went into full bloom while leaves dropped all over the park. "Is it true you wanted to save me?"

"I didn't want to put your life in danger. You put yourself in enough hell when you were younger." The urge to gaze into those eyes ate away at her. As awful as the crime was, he wrapped himself around her heart. A house wanting to eat him. A house craving his life. The house found him evil enough to devour, yet she couldn't give him away. "Now you can see why we can't be together. Not now, not ever."

"Radha, I…"

"Don't!" She started to walk away. "Don't say anything else! Nothing you can do will change a thing. I'm not a good person, okay? You're not a good person, and I'm not one either. That makes us even."

"No, it doesn't! It doesn't fix anything at all! Radha, hold on! I didn't…"

Radha didn't stay to hear the rest. She jogged down the nearest trail far from the others. Andrew couldn't chase her right now. His strength wasn't fully back for him to walk, let alone run after her. She didn't want to stay any longer. Veena and Lata could give him the rest of the story if he wanted it. The house called to her now. She made her choice, and now she lived with it. The house won. Her family won. As always, it got what it wanted.

And she'd be stuck there for the rest of her life.

CHAPTER 24

Radha finished her walk after an hour when everyone else had gone back. As she came around, she didn't find anyone's car. Andrew's strength returned now. He was well enough to drive himself home. If he was smart, he'd hate her too. He'd stay away from her, move far from the house. Let him try and fit into another town. All the facts laid out before her, it should have been easy to drop him. They could forget each other.

I can't imagine he's happy about any of this. Her phone gave her no new messages, except her mother telling her they went to get dinner. If she wanted to come home, give them a call. Well, she didn't need them. She had all the rideshare apps and always had them drop her off right in front of the driveway. They often asked to drive inside, but she'd stop them. No need for the house to suck a poor Uber driver dry simply for doing their job.

As for Andrew, he hadn't called the police. Maybe it was him making up for hiding his secret. She wouldn't spend time with him. He wouldn't tell on her. Every moment before, every second she spent with him, all of it was too good. He was the perfect gentleman until the past few days. He did his time, short as it was, and he hadn't gotten in trouble since. Of course, it still marred him. Her good things never lasted long. They would never go on those trips now.

Never have another dinner together. Never get the future they wanted.

As she got closer to home, a horrible burning hole filled up her body. She wasn't alone. The others hadn't come yet the house cracked up again. Curious, she ran around the back and passed all the new rose bushes. Not again. It couldn't happen. As she skidded to a halt, the perfume scent of the flowers struck her. No. It couldn't be.

Oh, please, please… Around her, the trees shook off their flowers, and their petals blew around. The sweet smell. A brand-new spring. How could that be? He couldn't come here. He didn't need to.

"I thought you'd never show up." Her blood froze as she turned her heel to see him. The one that she loved and hated at the same time. "I thought that really was it."

Andrew stood in the garden again, his body swaying back and forth. One small breeze would knock him over. The garden's power started to drain him, yet he refused to get out of it. He didn't want to leave so she chose to make her way in, keeping her distance. He didn't get it. No matter how many times she warned him, he didn't run away. He still had that one death marring him, the reason the house now sucked him dry. His face paled and he coughed, yet he didn't leave.

"Why are you here?" She whispered. "I told you everything! In case you were wondering, no, you're not off the hook with me!"

"That's just it, Radha. I know what happened has ruined your image of me. I can't change the past. I want to. Believe me. I'm desperate to change it. It took me a long time to come to terms with it. I can never get that label off me, no matter what I do. The only thing I can try is move forward. That's what you want, right?"

Radha swallowed. "Even if I do forgive you, the house won't. My ancestors...they survived by taking out evildoers who got away from the law. They...they came to this house years ago. To survive, they fed the house with what it wanted. Right now, it wants you. It sees you as the next meal. It got a little bit from you in case you don't remember!"

"Oh, I remember everything, Radha! I've been thinking a lot about what you said. It makes sense. I should stay away. I let you down in the worst way imaginable. I hid the truth. I pretended to be a great person when I'm not." He began. "I should turn around right now, and never come back."

"Yes, you shouldn't come back. After what you did, you shouldn't be near me." Radha sank towards the garden, the toxic fragrance of the roses wrapping her up. "Yet you're not leaving."

"I'm not going to leave. Not until you hear me out." He stepped forward while she backed away. "You can keep hiding in that garden, Radha, but it can't keep me from talking. We both have our dark secrets. I accidentally killed a person. You have willingly dragged people into your house to kill them. It doesn't make us all that different. Ancestors or not, you were a part of this. You can't hide that, just like I can't hide from my past."

Radha backed into a rose bush, ignoring the thorns against her wrists. The bright pink petals brushed against her back, spraying their smell everywhere. "You're right. I'm hiding from the world too. I'm hiding these dark secrets for the sake of my family. The only difference is I didn't get high for my crime."

"Exactly. You weren't high. You were perfectly lucid, just like your cousins and your mother. Now, I'm not here to judge you or call you out on hypocrisy. I came here because I can't stop thinking about you. The good times, the bad ones…I can't stop thinking about the house either. I get why you want to keep it alive.

Andrew swallowed as the toxic scent fell on him. The headache settled in first before the rest of the body went out. Despite that, he stood between the red and white rose bushes, trying hard not to fall to his knees. They wobbled, but he clenched his fists and went on. "You don't understand. When I'm with you…it's another world. It's a new feeling. It's something I haven't had since I lost my wife. You…You and your friends…you brought something back inside of me. Reminded me what life was all about. Am I perfect? No. I will live with what I did for the rest of my life."

Radha closed her eyes as his hands went towards the white rosebush. He touched one of them, careful not to touch the thorns. "You're going to get hurt. The garden's starting to suck you dry."

"I don't care. Radha, being around you has been the greatest feeling I've had in years. You taught me to enjoy life again. I want more of those moments. I want to go to Upper Deck with you and your friends for trivia and bingo. I want to eat in more fancy restaurants with you and go to the museum and park. Go to more IMAX movies and check out insect houses and dinosaur exhibits. Maybe…maybe…" He coughed as the wind picked up, pushing him forward. "I should get inside!"

"No, you shouldn't! I've warned you so many times! It'll be worse if you go inside!" Radha held her arms out as he dropped into them, body burning up. "Not again! Oh, Andrew, why didn't you listen to me?! Why do you keep coming back?!"

"Because…because…" His words caught in his throat as he mouthed out the rest. No sound, yet Radha got the message simply from the shapes of his lips. *I love you.*

"You shouldn't." She slowly led him towards the front door as the house's walls cracked. The garden wasn't enough. He needed to experience the rest. She pushed him towards it as it caved in. Pieces fell off, nearly missing them. "You are…the house…"

Radha opened the door as it came off its hinges. In the other direction, she got screams of all kinds. High, low, excited, and terrified screams rolled out of the remains of the door. Andrew stumbled inside and turned towards the first room. His hand fell on the doorknob as more dirt dropped on his shoulders.

"Radha, I…" He jumped aside as the walls started to crumble. Turning around, he tried to get out. "Radha, I should go!"

Before they could go, another scream hit the air, and more statues collapsed. Every memory in this room, every guest they had, every party they threw…it came down now. Radha grabbed his hand, but he refused to come with her. "What are you doing?!"

"I need to see this! All of this!"

"No!"

Dust fell over them as the walls started falling apart. She pushed the door open to let him in, vases toppling over and mirrors cracking around. The statues, all of them, now crashed to the floor. Trying to turn Andrew away, she pushed him back at the door. He refused to nudge, instead stumbling down the hall as the rest of the statues fell.

"Andrew! Andrew, wait!" She pleaded as he gained strength to run down the halls. The floorboards creaked and broke apart as she chased him. "Andrew, don't do this! Please!"

"You have to know, Radha!" He coughed as dust flew around. The house crumbled, yet he made his way towards the kitchen. "You have to know what I'd do for you! How I feel! If being eaten by this house is the way to prove it, then…"

"You don't have to prove anything to me!" Radha jumped as a statue fell right in front of her, smashing into thousands of small pieces. Jumping over the mess, she caught up with Andrew as he pushed his way into the garden. The doors collapsed with glass shattering all around. "You never have to prove anything! I know about this already! I know how you feel about me! You don't have to be in this house!"

"Then what?!" He fell in the garden as petals floated by. Red, white, and pink danced around them as the rose bushes started wilting. "How is this…"

"You. It wants you." She reminded him, falling to his side. "I'm so…I believe everything you said. I enjoyed every single second with you. Everyone else likes you, too, even my mother! And she hates everyone I ever dated! Not you, though!"

"What can I do for you, Radha? How can I prove this? What else do you want?"

Radha pulled him up, her arms around his body. "You."

"I'm sorry?"

Her arms tightened as she moved in, embracing his shivering body. The chills kicked in now that the roses started draining him out. All those buds burst open around them. She cradled him as he coughed around her, the pollen floating around. They couldn't stay. Rocking him back and forth, she counted down every second the house ate away at them.

"Radha! Andrew!" Lata ran over to their side and tried to drag them further away. "Come on! The house…"

"I know, Lata! The house is crumbling! I can see it!" Radha pushed herself to move on. "Where's Ma?! Where's Veena?!"

"Here! I'm here!" Swati waved her hands, coughing around the dust. "My back's aching, my legs are in pain, but hell, I'm alive somehow. I made it out of that mess!"

"Oh God!" Veena wrapped her arms around Radha. "I'm so glad you're okay. I thought for sure the house…"

"I got out." Radha gazed at the rubble behind them. Everything was gone. They finally won against the house, and she made her choice. Next to her, Andrew curled up and waited for her answer. He brushed all the dirt off himself and sat up, strength returning. The color in his face filled up. He grabbed her to get steady, almost falling when his head spun.

"Oh!" He rubbed his forehead. "That was…God, that hurts. I never thought…I didn't expect it to. You warned me so many times."

"It's fine." She got close to him, letting his head rest on her shoulder. "I kept so much from you. I didn't know how to explain any of it. I wanted to keep you from that place, and I realize now there was something that mattered to me more than the house. I can always get another house. Maybe not today, maybe not as big as this one, but I'd get one. There's something I don't want to lose. That's the one thing I want."

"And what's that?" He pressed a kiss on her forehead.

"I want you." She whispered in his ear. "I wanted you from the moment you bumped into me. I was afraid."

"Afraid of all this?" He waved his hand in the air. "You thought…"

"I can't live with you when I live here. I didn't want to tell you." She shuddered over the countless parties, endless victims, and disappearances thanks to the house. "I didn't want…"

"Radha, relax." He rubbed her arms. "I get it."

"You do? Explain to me because I can't figure it out. I

can't understand why you want to be with me." She lowered her gaze. "We've done terrible things, all of us. Things you can never imagine. Besides that, I don't work, and I'm struggling to find anything exciting in my life. I mean, my siblings are always traveling and trying new things. Their kids get to experience something every day. Me? I don't have any experience."

"That's true." Swati agreed. "She's pretty dull compared to my other children."

"Thanks, Ma. I really wanted to hear that."

"I'm not done. Yeesh, give an old lady some time to put her thoughts together." Swati got between them, waving at the rubble before them. "Look, Andrew. We don't have much anymore. We don't know what will happen next. Out of all of us, Radha's been down on her luck the most. I've seen her every night, wasting away in her room, and it's painful. Not because she's boring, but because she has so much to give. She's smart and funny, and she can entertain you. The problem is she never gets a chance. She never gets to show anyone what she's capable of."

Radha couldn't reply after that. Her mother rarely mentioned her good traits to anyone. Andrew, however, lifted her chin so she'd finally look him in the eye. Her eyelid twitched as he pecked her cheek. "What…What was that for?"

"I don't care about what happened in the past. We both had our secrets. We should have been honest with each other. It's over now. You wanted to protect me despite all I did."

"We don't need to protect you anymore cause we have no house." Lata caught Veena and Swati glaring at her. "What? We don't have one. I don't know where we're going to live."

"Well, I'm willing to help you with that part." Andrew wrapped his arms around Radha. "If you want my help, that is. I know I've caused a lot of trouble. I've screwed up. I want another chance with all of you."

"We'll need it." Veena walked over to where the rubble rested and pushed some parts of the house aside. "God, I can't believe it. All these years, our family…we have to start all over again. Find a new place. Our grandparents wouldn't be pleased."

"We can do that." Radha faced Andrew, grabbing his hands. "Now, I have something to tell you. I want to keep doing all these things you mentioned. The dates, the talks, everything. I really do like you. No, I love you. I know I'm not Chantal, but…"

"And I don't need you to be Chantal." He lifted her chin. "You're Radha, and that's who I want. You're a great person in your own right, no matter what's happened here. I want to love you for the rest of my life. Build a future together one day…if that's what you want. What do you say?"

Radha couldn't say anything after. She threw her arms around him as they dissolved into a kiss. Off to the side, she heard excited whispers from Veena and Lata. Even her mother, normally grumbly, sat back in pride. As they pulled away, they got one more look at the rubble their home turned into. Bit by bit, the rest of it crumbled. All their ancestors built, everything they stood for, no longer existed.

Every tension on Radha's shoulder, every sad moment, all of it drifted off as the last tiny 'Feed me' faded into the sky. No more. The cries ended. Those pieces soon disappeared as her friends nudged her. The house died. With nothing to sustain it, the bits no longer stayed on earth. It continued to cry, the words fading out, as the dust blew off. One more sentence got through.

Feed me…

The last piece disappeared, taking the spirits and family history with it.

Epilogue

Radha rolled down the car window as the giant glass building came into view. Her heart skipped a beat as Andrew pulled into a parallel parking spot, easing his way into that narrow area. She held her breath as he adjusted the car, making sure it nestled between the lines.

"You know, you don't have to park this close. I can walk up to this place from that big parking garage a block away." She nodded towards the garage behind them. "Not to mention, you can only spend…" She read the sign on the side. "2 hours. Are you sure that'll be enough time?"

"These interviews usually don't take more than an hour. I'm sure you'll be fine. If anyone bugs me about it, I'll move." Andrew checked the back seat where Veena, Lata, and Swati were squeezed in. "How are you ladies doing there?"

"I'm barely breathing, but that's normal at my age." Swati grumbled, trying to push herself forward. "I think you need a bigger car."

"You know, you didn't have to come with me." Radha grabbed her bag. "I could have taken the bus over here. It stops a few feet from this place."

"Eh, the bus? It's nowhere as comfortable." Veena squirmed in her seat. "Yes, we're a little uncomfortable. It's a tight squeeze, but nothing I'm not used to."

Swati bit down on her lip. "If I wasn't squished between

you two, I'd say something about that."

"Oh, don't worry about that." Lata reached over and patted Radha's shoulder. "This is it for you! I know you'll get it!"

"I don't know. I want it but..." Radha closed her eyes. "Even when I failed, I still had a home to come back to. I could hide in my room and wallow in my sorrows. Or if I was up to it, I'd go in the kitchen and eat the pain away. Then I'd talk to the house and tell all my problems to it. Now, I don't have that."

No one could argue with her. Without the house, they all wandered around for a new place to live. Andrew's home was big enough to keep them for now, but it didn't have that same spark of life in it. She couldn't talk to these walls or get comfort from the furniture. It hurt to have no home, yet she got some relief deep down. She wasn't chained down by it. The family history, the darkness inside of it...it no longer held onto her. It let all of them go the moment it crumbled into pieces. With their new freedom, they had nothing left. Nowhere to turn to, nothing to do.

Veena straightened her skirt out, checking her makeup in the window reflection. "I am seeing a real estate agent today. He's got quite a few houses to check out, so we're going to see them all."

"Oh, you're finding a new place to live?" Lata asked.

"...Sure, I guess I can do that." Veena shrugged. "Anyway, it's tough, but we'll get through it. You won't have to worry about us for very long, Andrew."

"It's okay. I don't mind the company. I admit it's a lot to take in, but...we all had our secrets. We're gonna learn to live with them." He turned to Radha as she checked herself in the mirror. "I promise you that you look fine. We're ten minutes early, so if you want to walk around or hang out here..."

"No, I should go." Radha unbuckled her seatbelt and

grabbed everything before stepping out. Leaning into the open car window, she faced all the people in the car. Everyone important in her life now sat there, waiting for good news from her. "I don't know how I can thank you. You probably had to pull a lot of strings for this."

"Ah, not that many. I told my good friends about you, and they saw your work. They're impressed. Everything that happens now will be up to you." Andrew patted her on the hand. "But if you really want to thank me, how about dinner tonight at La Fortuna? I can make reservations."

"That sounds great. I've never been there before!" Swati exclaimed. "I just hope they something that I can chew over there."

Radha rolled her eyes. "I'm sure he's just talking about the two of us."

Andrew laughed as he kissed her hand. "I was, but I guess the five of us can do something after your interview. Just tell me how it goes, good or bad."

"Yeah, of course. Wish me luck everyone!"

"Good luck, Radha! I hope you get it!" Lata waved at her as she stepped back. "You can do this!"

"She's right, you've got this!" Veena added. "You look great! You'll win them over!"

"Just don't blink." Swati warned. "Blinking is a sign of nerves. Stare wide-eyed at them, and they'll see you as the perfect employee, one who isn't shaken by anything."

"Either that, or they'll think I'm dead inside." Radha fixed her shoes before heading towards the building, with everything in her arms. It was strange not to ask the house for any luck. The spirit that roamed in it didn't show up. It didn't make its presence known in any other building. Whatever lived in it moved away. It was done.

The past few weeks took its toll on everyone. Swati

spent days cooking in Andrew's house, creating all kinds of things, but her joy in the food vanished. Veena and Lata stuck to their jobs, doing their best to bring more money in. They saved enough to get another place. The houses they searched for didn't have charm in them. These weren't homes to spend the rest of their lives in. Whether it was bad luck or some spirit working against them, she couldn't tell. All she knew was it would take a while to get another home.

It's not there anymore. I guess I'll be okay eventually. She pushed her way through the glass revolving doors. The receptionist and cops in the front waited for her to fill up the visitor book. Inhaling, she wrote her name down, faced them, and smiled as she clutched her portfolio.

"Hi, I'm here for my eleven o'clock job interview."

As the receptionist took down more information, a familiar 'feed me' rolled through her mind. *Feed me. Feed me. Feed me.* Shadow falling over her, she whirled around to find no one else there. Yet the crack on the wall said otherwise. Curling up to the top, she expected words to form. The infamous FEED ME would pop out any second. The spirits of ancestors followed her around, waiting for her to mess up. Shaking the crack out of her head, she glanced again to find nothing. No words.

"You may have a seat over there." The receptionist pointed to a couple of chairs in the corner. "I'll inform them you're here."

"Thank you."

Radha took her place as the crack on this wall lingered in her mind. She couldn't get that out. Even if she got this job, it would follow her. After all, her ancestors always said that no matter where they went, they'd always have their home.

Whether they lived in it or not.

THE END

ACKNOWLEDGMENTS

About two years ago, I was sitting around and watching one of my favorite sitcoms, The Golden Girls. It's a comfort show for me and there's something just fun about watching four older women living in a house together, sharing their lives and going through all kinds of adventures. I had also been listening to a lot of Encanto to prepare for our family's upcoming trip to Disney World. Somehow, the two ideas melded together. Four women living in a house that was sentient. But instead of being a kind house, it had a darker side to it. Let it be a house that ate souls.

Thus, the book was born. It went through its changes but I'm happy to share it with everyone now. Of course, it couldn't have come to fruition without the help of some people out there.

First off, thank you to Apprentice House and Loyola University for helping shape this book into the best it can be. A big shout to everyone who will be in the 2026 catalogue as well. It's been great getting to know you and your work.

Thank you to Abby Hill for helping to get me on the right track with this book. A thank you to Kevin Atticks for making this a part of your 2026 catalogue.

Thank you also to Amiyah Cobb for helping design the book and Emily Gott for getting all my promotional things together.

Thank you to Rebecca Lawrence for giving me some good tips and ideas on how to make this book a little stronger. Thank you for introducing me to other horror books like House of Leaves. Another thank you to everyone else who has laid eyes on this book at various stages. You've been a great help to me.

Thank you to those who follow me on social media, be it for hearing about my upcoming projects or you just like looking at the dog pics I repost.

Thank you to my spouse and my son. I can't ever forget about you. Thank you for being there.

Thank you for reading. I cannot forget about you for taking your time to go through the pages. You make every bit of this worthwhile.

And finally, a big thank for you being a friend to Susan Harris, the creator of Golden Girls, for being a huge inspiration and helping me get through writing on those long nights. And another thank you to the late actresses Bea Arthur, Betty White, Rue McClanahan, and Estelle Getty for inspiration and the laughter.

About the Author

Cithara Susan Patra has been writing for a very long time, dabbling in all kinds of work over the years. Having a degree in Spanish and French (as well as one in Business Management), they've spent a lot of their normal life being very busy learning new things. They've written for multiple zines over the year as well as writing novels in between taking care of their rambunctious child and working for the health department in North Carolina. They've also written plenty of poetry and short stories over the years. When not writing, they are busy taking care of their family, trying to cook new meals, traveling to interesting places, or trying to perfect their French and Spanish speaking skills.

Current social media:
Bluesky: cspatra
Instragram: citharapatra
TikTok: cspatra

Apprentice House is the country's only campus-based, student-staffed book publishing company. Directed by professors and industry professionals, it is a nonprofit activity of the Communication Department at Loyola University Maryland.

Using state-of-the-art technology and an experiential learning model of education, Apprentice House publishes books in untraditional ways. This dual responsibility as publishers and educators creates an unprecedented collaborative environment among faculty and students, while teaching tomorrow's editors, designers, and marketers.

Eclectic and provocative, Apprentice House titles intend to entertain as well as spark dialogue on a variety of topics. Financial contributions to sustain the press's work are welcomed. Contributions are tax deductible to the fullest extent allowed by the IRS.

To learn more about Apprentice House books or to obtain submission guidelines, please visit www.apprenticehouse.com.

Apprentice House Press
Communication Department
Loyola University Maryland
4501 N. Charles Street
Baltimore, MD 21210
Ph: 410-617-5265
info@apprenticehouse.com • www.apprenticehouse.com

www.ingramcontent.com/pod-product-compliance
Lightning Source LLC
LaVergne TN
LVHW010603100826
845148LV00014B/2832
9781627206518